Red Tape Protector

KATHY KULIG

Red Tape Protector

Cover design by Wicked Smart Designs
Edited by Shannon Combs
Published by Burnt Stilettos Press
ISBN: 0-9903439-3-6
ISBN-13: 978-0-9903439-3-6

Burnt Stilettos
Press

To my readers, with my deepest thanks

For your dedication and support, I'm truly grateful

Prologue

Julia Flynn, White House Press Secretary, wondered how many lines she would cross, how many laws she'd break, when the next assignment for the FLC included devising a plot to murder a U.S. senator. Life without the possibility of parole. Wasn't that the expected sentence for first-degree murder? Even if the person murdered was evil and deserved it? Unfortunately, she doubted a sex tape would be enough to destroy this man's political career and unravel his network of notorious connections. Julia stood in her office while the members of the First Ladies' Club filed in and seated themselves for the private meeting. "Please close the door on your way out, Heather," she said to her secretary. "Hold all calls and no interruptions."

Heather acknowledged Julia's wishes and left. Her team of men and women of the secret White House organization looked up at her with eager anticipation. The FLC—a well-trained group of secret service and ex-CIA agents, ex-military personnel, lawyers and computer experts—were selected for the delicate and dangerous assignments the first lady handed down to them. Many had special skills that would not be listed on any resume. Jobs and policies the president couldn't accomplish or change by normal, legal channels were commissioned to the FLC. Of all the sex scandals and manipulating schemes the team had been involved in the past, this, by far, would be the most challenging.

"Thank you all for coming on short notice." Julia crossed her arms and leaned against her desk. "We have a new project and target. This one will be very difficult and extremely dangerous on many levels. We've made mistakes on previous missions, whether we were directly responsible or not. We lost one of our own." The members cast their gazes to the floor at the mention of Alana's assassination.

"We all miss Alana," Zoe said. The ex-CIA agent had been friends with Alana.

"What's the project about?" Jason, Zoe's husband, asked.

"A certain senator has his sights set on campaigning for the next presidential election. We can't let that happen. The FLC has to do everything, I mean everything, in its power to stop this man."

"I don't like the sound of this," Johnny Vargas said in his tough Bronx-boy accent. "That's not what we're about. We don't fix or manipulate elections."

Julia knew she'd get some resistance. "Most people say they hate politicians, but most believe the majority of those in office truly intend to do the best job they can, even if they fail.

This man, however, is the extremely rare outlier who is a crook, a sociopath and a murderer. Recently, we've uncovered information linking him to activity overseas. The details we cannot divulge yet.

"You saying you think this senator is a spy too?" Jason asked.

"In some capacity, but intel indicates it's much worse. Unfortunately, authorities haven't been able to prove anything. We believe he has manipulated his way through the ranks, murdered opponents and lovers. He's brilliant and evil. It will be very difficult to trick him into a sex scandal."

"Can we coax him into the Red Tape Room?" Melissa asked. She was their lead Domme who organized the sex tape scenarios.

"Very unlikely." Julia strolled back and forth in front of her desk. "It's going to take more than a sex scandal to bring this man down. The president believes he's a threat to national security. If he became president, it would be devastating nationally and internationally."

"Don't we have an assassin who could take him out?" Johnny asked, always the practical one.

"You can't just kill a senator," Zoe argued. "A sex scandal is the better option."

The members didn't know the identity of the assassin who worked among them. "It's not that easy." Julia stopped her pacing to stand in front of the group. "We will have help. The Eagle Guards, a private military group, and we're getting a new team member. She'll be trained in security specifically for this case. You'll meet her in a couple months."

Johnny laughed. "We're getting outside help, and you're training a new woman. A lot of new elements added to the mix of a dangerous assignment."

"They're well-trained," Julia argued.

"Does this woman know BDSM *and* self-defense? Is she a Domme or a submissive?" Johnny asked.

Julia glared at him. "She'll be our new female assassin."

Chapter 1

Alana MacKenna stared out the hospital window at the rain-soaked streets of Washington DC. In the height of rush hour, pedestrians clogged the intersections, crouched beneath their umbrellas. She longed to be among them, back to her job and normal life, but her life would never be normal again.

She touched the bandages on her face and arm. The nurses and doctors had said the plastic surgery incisions were healing nicely, but there was no mirror in her room to check, and they'd refused to give her one. They'd told her the dressings were coming off today. It was already dinnertime and the doctor hadn't shown. There was no reason for them to keep her any longer.

The door to her hospital room swung open and Julia Flynn, White House Press Secretary, marched in carrying a large tote bag. "Are you ready to get out of here?"

"Hell yes," Alana exclaimed. She exchanged glances with Jag, the security agent, who had been guarding her room. He closed the door behind Julia. Flirting with him over the last few weeks had brought little response. He either had a girlfriend, or took his job way too seriously. If Julia was right, she doubted she'd see him again. Too bad, because the guy was hot.

"I thought you might be going a little stir crazy in here." Julia crinkled her nose at the uneaten dinner on Alana's tray.

Alana grinned as best as she could. The skin around her mouth pulled against the gauze and tape, but thankfully all the stitches were out. "Are you serious? I can finally get back to work?" Beneath the first lady, Julia was next in charge of the secret White House security agency, the FLC—First Ladies' Club.

Julia strolled across the room and dropped the bag on the bed. She smoothed invisible creases on the neatly made blankets. "You won't be working in the same capacity as you were before."

"Why not? It's been months and no further assassination attempts. The threat is over, right?" Alana was sure of that now. Why weren't they? "I see the secret service isn't parked outside anymore."

"Just because you don't see the secret service outside doesn't mean they're not there. The threat will always be there if they find out you're alive."

Tugging on her hospital gown, Alana wondered if she was too disfigured to appeal as a sexual seductress in their sex scandals. Maybe that was why Mr. Hot Bodyguard hadn't shown any interest. "Have you seen the results of the surgery? Do I look that bad, Julia? Be honest. They still won't give me a mirror."

"No, I think the doctors did a wonderful job," Julia said.

"I'll get you a mirror. The bandages on your face will be coming off for good I hear."

"Thank you. They told me soon, but the doctor didn't come in today." Alana rolled her IV stand over to a chair and pointed to another chair for Julia. Her boss shook her head.

"I'll talk to the nurse."

"I'm more than ready to go home, return to work, and get my life back to semi-normal—as normal as that is," Alana said. "When can I get out of here?"

"You hardly touched your dinner." Julia glanced at Alana's tray of food.

Alana shrugged. "It's not so easy eating taped up like this."

"Hmmm. Maybe the nurse will help you remove them if the doctor doesn't come in. You should eat."

"The food isn't that great anyway." Alana sat in her over-sized hospital gown and glanced at Julia's black Manolos. Crossing her feet, Alana tried to hide the terry slipper socks that came in plastic bags for patients. How she missed her pretty shoes and dresses that she wore at the White House or the thigh-high boots and leather corsets for other activities, either for a targeted official during an FLC mission, or at the BDSM club during off hours. There was something utterly satisfying about using a sex tape scandal to take down powerfully destructive men.

Julia looked her usual glamorous self, as if she were on her way to a business meeting, wearing an immaculate navy suit and cream silk blouse. Her hair color appeared a deeper red than the last time she was here. A bolder color. Alana's red hair was natural. Running her fingers through her strands, she realized she hadn't brushed her hair all day. And she was wearing the same hospital gown from the night before. She needed a bath and change of clothes.

Alana straightened in the chair and tilted up her chin. "Before I became a lawyer, I worked a few years as a registered nurse in an emergency room. I know my stitches are out and my burns have healed enough that I could be released. There's no reason for me to have this IV. They're not giving me medication, antibiotics or any other treatment. I'm peeing like crazy. I'm not dehydrated." She held up her arm with the bandage. "When can I leave?"

Julia smiled and took a long breath. Then she stood and walked to the window and gazed out. "As early as tomorrow, but your new position will require extra training."

"Tomorrow? That's awesome." Alana's voice warmed. "What kind of training?" Was this where she was reprimanded for screwing up?

"You can come back to the FLC, but you'll be working in another position. It's a very important assignment and we need to send you away for a few months for the extensive training."

"A few months? What for? I won't be working in the Red Tape Room as a Domme or submissive?"

"Not anymore."

"Has the FLC stopped using sex scandals?" Alana whispered.

Julia shook her head. "No, we find they're an effective weapon. We want you on our security team."

Fortunately, Alana's courtroom background helped her to remain calm and not blurt out what she really thought. She wasn't cut out to be in security enforcement. A bodyguard. Not very glamorous. "You mean train for the secret service? This is what the first lady wants?"

"Not exactly the secret service. You'll be working mostly undercover for the FLC."

"What's my other option?"

"You have no other option." Each word she emphasized and Alana sensed there was more that Julia wasn't telling her. "It was your arrogant curiosity that nearly got you killed. If President Aleid had discovered your identity before the blackmail had been completed, he could've captured and tortured you for information. Instead he just tried to kill you for revenge."

"I know what I did was wrong. Zoe tried to warn me. I'm sorry," Alana shouted. When Julia glared at her she lowered her voice. "Aleid was a bastard and I couldn't resist seeing his face when he got the news. I could choose to leave the FLC and return to private practice. My parents might one day talk to me again." On the other hand, she doubted that. Years ago they'd discovered she was into the BDSM lifestyle, and they'd cut her out of their pristine life. Heaven forbid her parents' friends at the country club discovered their daughter liked her sex kinky. "They probably didn't visit me in the hospital because they don't approve of my lifestyle choices," Alana explained.

"Hmmm." Julia didn't offer any sympathy. It wasn't like Julia to do that anyway.

"How is everyone at the FLC? I wished they had come to see me." Alana stood, gripping the IV stand so hard it rattled. Over the last several weeks, she couldn't be sure if they were angry at her for screwing up and risking the exposure of the society or if they were denied a visit because of security issues.

"They're fine." Julia avoided eye contact.

Alana huffed. "Be honest, Julia. Does the team want me back or not? No one called or came to visit. They didn't even send a card."

Julia gave her a sympathetic nod. At least she made an

attempt to understand how Alana felt. "Their lack of contact is for your safety and theirs. I'm sure you can appreciate the situation. President Aleid's hit men might come after you again. Or they might threaten your family to find you."

Her friends from the FLC could've found a way to see her if they wanted. "Doesn't Aleid think I'm dead?"

"We're not sure. We've been watching the hospital and your apartment, and we think they may be suspicious that you weren't killed."

Alana covered her face with her hands. "Fine. I get it." She wondered if her ex-boyfriend, Liam, even knew about the bombing, and, if so, was he upset? "Is my family in danger?" Feeling the roughness of the bandages reminded that her recklessness had placed people she cared about in danger.

"We don't believe so. It wouldn't be wise to contact any family members or friends though."

"Yes, of course." It took Alana several moments until she could trust herself enough to speak. "Julia, what we do at the FLC is important to me. I didn't mind the risk of setting up brutal psychopaths to destroy them politically. But I was wrong to step over the line to watch the president take them down. I didn't think I was putting anyone in danger."

"No, you didn't think, that was the problem. Do you have any idea the scandal this would've caused had it become public?"

"Yes, I do now. It would discredit the White House."

"Nationally and internationally." Julia took a breath and closed her eyes. Alana wondered if she was doing one of her quick meditation routines. Julia was known for those metaphysical displays.

"It won't happen again, Julia. I was good at what I did. But I can't be a security guard."

"I'm sorry you feel that way. We won't have you preforming the sex scandals again. The first lady won't take that chance."

"What about letting me leave the FLC, give me a new identity. Before the FLC, I worked as a nurse and a lawyer, I could do either in a witness protection program."

Julia shook her head. "No deal. You work for us in security, or you're on your own and take your chances that Aleid's hit man is still out there. If you don't take this position and the training that goes along with it, we'll give you back your old life, your old name, your old apartment, no new identity."

"That's not fair. Why would you do that?"

"Because we need you. Finding someone to train for this position could take months. And then months more for the training. We don't have that much time."

"You're not going to force me into this job?" Alana was surprised they'd consider her after how badly she screwed up.

"You have forty-eight hours to decide."

"I don't need the forty-eight hours. I appreciate everything you've done and your concern, but I want my life back." Groaning, Alana marched over to the bedside table, opened a drawer and pulled out gauze, a roll of tape and tore off a couple pieces with her teeth, then yanked out the IV from her wrist, dropping the needle, bag and tubing into a biohazard container. Blood dripped from her wrist. Julia watched, but didn't move.

Alana dabbed at the IV site with gauze, held pressure on it for a moment then secured the bandage in place with the tape.

"I would like to continue at the FLC, Julia. But not as a security guard. Seriously, look at me. I exercise but I'm nowhere near the physical shape needed for that work."

"If we didn't think you could handle the position, the offer wouldn't have been made."

"I understand." As a professional, Alana knew that burning bridges at this level was a bad idea. She still wasn't doing this job.

"Once that time is up, you won't be able to ask for help. Even if Aleid's men come after you."

Alana closed her eyes. That stung. She was truly on her own. "What's in the bag?"

"Clothes and a few personal items, some cash."

Alana opened the bag and picked out the wallet among the clothes, pair of shoes, boots and a coat. There was about a hundred dollars in cash inside. She held up the wallet. "Where's my ID, driver's license, credit cards?"

Julia gave her a curt smile. "I'll stop by tomorrow with all that, the key to your apartment and a cell phone. After the two days all you IDs will become valid if you choose to leave us. But it will only be a matter of time before your enemies discover that Alana MacKenna is still alive."

Alana intended to have her identity change and to leave town before that happened. "What about my car?"

"It was sold, as were your personal items. You'll be reimbursed. We had to make it look good in case Aleid's men checked. We took over the rent on your apartment for now, and asked the landlord to keep the place furnished." Julia strolled to the door then spun around. The smile was gone, her expression severe, and Alana thought she looked scared. She was fingering the large amethyst crystal pendant she always wore.

"Good night, Julia. Thank you for the clothes."

"I'll see you in the morning."

She'd make a lousy security guard and if she failed, what were the consequences? She wasn't hanging around to find out. Her family had set her up with a trust fund and they thought she'd spent it all. She hadn't. It was sitting safe, in an unnamed account in the islands. The FLC may have closed out all her finances after her fake death, but they wouldn't have discovered that one. It would be enough for now.

Liam would help her. If not as a friend, then because he owed her. As his lawyer, she once had gotten him out of a jam. He'd return the favor if asked. His business dealt with international trade of motorcycle parts and accessories. He had a lot of connections, legal and not so legal. He knew people who could help her get a new identity and help her disappear.

Screw the forty-eight hours. Life threat or not, Alana would take her chances on the run. After she got to her apartment, she'd look for her hidden stash of money then find Liam. How long would it be until the FLC decided she was too much of a risk? She wasn't sure where she was going yet, but she was sure she was through with the FLC. Alana tossed the wallet into the tote bag. Considering her options, she knew what she had to do. Get the hell out of there and as far away from DC and the FLC as she could.

Chapter 2

The minute Julia left Alana's room Jag Denison knew it wasn't good news. "What's going on?" Jag asked. "Is she okay?"

Julia closed her eyes and took a breath. "Take a walk with me, Jag. We need to talk."

"I can't leave my post. Should we call the nurse?"

"She doesn't need the nurse." She waved him down the hall a few paces. "Just so she can't overhear."

"What's the problem?"

Julia crossed her arms and lowered her voice. "Keep a close eye on her tonight. I need to make arrangements with your boss. Since she won't agree to my offer, we need to be more convincing. I'll be in touch later with details. Make sure she doesn't leave. I'll be back in the morning."

"You think she'd try to run?" Lately, Jag had noticed Alana's cabin fever now that she was getting better. Who wouldn't want out of the hospital after being stuck here several weeks?

"Alana's upset. She might. She's always had a mind of her own. That's what nearly got her killed. We're letting her out, but for what we have planned, she'll need to be watched. If Aleid's men suspect she's still alive and try to go after her, maybe she'll change her mind."

Nick Barone, his partner, strode up to them, back from his break. "Everything okay with the princess?" He grinned, but his smile quickly faded after he noticed Jag's stern expression.

"Fill him in," Julia said. "Expect a late night. And maybe the next couple of days." She marched off toward the elevator, her heels echoing down the hall.

"That doesn't sound good," Nick said.

"The plans have been moved up. We're taking her out tomorrow." Jag repeated what Julia had told him about Alana refusing the offer. "Damn, I hate to think the hell she'll be in soon."

Nick patted his shoulder. "Careful, man, don't get hooked on her now. Bad idea."

"Yeah, I got that. It fucking sucks though." He'd always known their situation was impossible, but that never stopped him from wanting her.

"Guess I need to make some phone calls," Nick said. "It's going to be hell for all of us."

After fifteen minutes of buzzing the nurse, Alana gave up and swung open the door. Jag stood there alone, blocking her way. "Yes, ma'am?"

Alana looked up at fierce blue eyes and a deep-set brow. Jag usually worked nights with one other guard. "Where's your partner?" She glanced down the empty hallway. No patients or hospital personnel. Normally she heard carts rolling up and down the halls and voices of nurses, doctors and cleaning people at all hours of the night.

It was too quiet. Where was everyone? It was almost seven thirty and all the nurses should have returned from their breaks. The hackles rose on the back of her neck. After the car bomb and Zoe's abduction, she'd become overly paranoid. Would she ever be able to live without looking over her shoulder? Now that they were letting her go, she hated to sit around. If it wasn't for the stash of cash she had hidden in her apartment—and hoped was still there—she'd try to leave town tonight. She didn't need to waste Julia's time by waiting for the forty-eight hours. She'd made her decision.

She bit her lower lip and a rolling sensation swept the pit of her stomach. "I need to see my nurse. She's not answering the buzzer."

He frowned. "Are you in pain?" His tone changed. Softer. Was he concerned?

"No, I need a bath, and I want to remove the bandages."

One side of his mouth quirked into a grin. "Can't you take a bath by yourself?"

"I can, but I need supplies so I can change the dressings." She touched the gauze on her left arm. "And I want a bath. My room only has a shower. They've let me use one of the empty rooms down the hall." It was also closer to the back stairs. If they left her alone for a few minutes, she might have enough time to get away.

He frowned. "I'll send her as soon as she gets back from her rounds."

She stepped into the hall and he blocked her from going farther. "Honestly, I could ask someone at the desk myself. I just need a few things."

"It's against orders for you to leave your room." He pressed his lips together. He wasn't amused. "You work for the White House, Ms. MacKenna. You know what it means to follow orders."

"I do." She winced at that because not following orders was what had gotten her into trouble in the first place. Did he know? "But I have left my room when they've given me the luxury of a hot bath. Besides that, they're letting me leave tomorrow. I don't think I need a guard anymore."

"I haven't been given a change in orders," he argued.

Alana huffed. "I used to be a nurse and I know how to care for wounds. I could get the supplies myself from their supply shelves."

He shook his head. "It's for your safety. They don't want you to leave this room."

She studied him for a minute. "You're not like the other guards, the ones who work days. I don't know what it is. Are you secret service?" Alana raised her chin, trying a different approach, but it did little to help her confidence. Without heels, she was five-foot-ten and still looked short compared to this guy. He was muscular, but lean, like a cross between a weightlifter and marathon runner.

"How am I different?" He raised one eyebrow, perhaps amused by her observation.

"I don't know. The others are obvious secret service in their black suits and coiled earpieces. So cliché."

He glanced down at his outfit, the same as the others, then pointed to the same earpiece. "What's different?"

"You don't belong in the suit. You don't look comfortable. I imagine you in camouflage, combat boots and hoisting an enormously heavy automatic weapon like in one of those military thrillers."

He smiled and let out a grunt of a laugh. The man could smile. "You have good observational skills. I used to be in the military. But from what I hear, you could work on your sound judgment." He tapped a finger on the bandage on her arm.

"Funny," she said. "And who told you about me? What did they tell you?"

His pleasant manner suddenly froze to the original stone-set, unemotional state. "I'll ask for your nurse to come to your room. Wait inside." He pointed to the center of the room as a signal for her to move so he could close the door.

Alana planted her feet in the doorway. She wanted out of this place so badly she could taste it. It was Friday night and Liam would probably be at Paradise Underground. She doubted they'd let her in with the clothes Julia had left her. They required proper attire. And it was a little late to go shopping for fetish wear. She didn't have much cash on her either. "I'll wait here. I'm bored, the walls are closing in. Why don't you tell me what your real name is and where you're from? Is Jag a nickname?" She glanced down the hall, looking for Beth, her nurse, or another nurse or aide. No one was in sight.

"Jagger Denison. I'm from North Carolina." Dark amusement glimmered in his steel-blue eyes.

At the club, she could read men, knew if they were dominant or submissive, could tell if they were experienced or virgins to the lifestyle. She could also tell if they were lying. This guy she couldn't read. No emotion. Was he this cold in bed too? "You prefer Jag?" She smiled.

He nodded. Power and authority radiated through him. His gaze swept her room, scanning for what? Hidden dangers? Then he returned his focus back to her.

She checked the time. Seven-thirty. It was going to be a long night. "I'll start my bath. If you like, you're welcome to watch." She hoped she could embarrass him into giving her a few minutes alone. A few minutes were all she needed.

An eyebrow rose. "She won't be long. You're not her only patient."

I bet I'm the only one with twenty-four-hour guards.

He spoke into his radio to a partner somewhere. "Ask Ms. MacKenna's nurse to stop by her room when she has a free moment." He listened to his coiled earbud while studying her. "Your nurse is attending another patient right now. She won't be long."

Alana leaned against the doorframe. "Thanks. I'm sorry. I'm going a bit crazy in here." That part was true.

"It's for your own safety."

She shrugged a half-hearted apology. "What do you know about me?"

He stared down at her and took a deep breath before speaking. "A high-profile individual made an attempt on your life. If they find out you're still alive, they'll try again."

"So if I become someone else, I'll be safe."

"That might be the only way."

She held up her bandaged arm. "This gave me a new outlook on life. I don't want people dying because of me. And I don't want to die because of a careless mistake."

"It's not as bad as you think," he said. "There are always alternatives."

"I agree." She was working on those. A few minutes later, Beth, Alana's nurse, came by with extra towels, soap and a clean hospital gown. The thirty-something nurse always had a pleasant smile. She had large brown eyes and dark-brown hair cut in a short style that highlighted her cheekbones and the slight bump on her nose. The strap around her neck holding her ID badge had sparkly pink ribbons and sayings for Breast Cancer Awareness Month. Beth Terrell had an athletic build and wore expensive running sneakers. She bragged to Alana when they first met how she lived five miles from the hospital and ran to work every day no matter the weather, and showered in the nurses' locker room.

"My, aren't we in a hurry for our evening bath," Beth said cheerfully.

"Thanks, Beth. I need a good soak after my meeting with my boss."

The nurse smiled. "It's a little chilly this evening. I'll see if I can dig up a nice terrycloth robe. How's that?"

"Terrific." Alana faked her enthusiasm. She glanced at Jag and caught a twitch of a smile.

"Doctor says we can remove the bandages on your face for good."

Clasping her hands together, Alana nodded. "I'm ready." But she'd remove them herself, without doctors and nurses and bodyguards to gawk at her. What if the scars were awful? This bathroom had a mirror, hers didn't. It seemed odd that she didn't have one in her bathroom. Beth explained it had a crack prior to her admission and maintenance had removed it, but they hadn't yet replaced it. Alana assumed the stubborn security guards wouldn't let maintenance in for the repair.

"I'm sure you are." Beth laid out soaps and towels. "Call if you need anything. Don't worry if your bandages get a little wet. Buzz me when you're finished, and I'll be in to remove them and change the dressings on your arm." She dropped packages of gauze, tape and supplies on the counter before she left.

"Thank you." Alana really did like her nurse. The woman

had a heart of gold and worked way too many hours. After Beth left, Alana turned to Jag. "So, are you going to watch me bathe or listen from outside?" She added a sultry note in those last words and was rewarded by a slight tinge to his cheeks. Finally, a show of emotion. Sign of life, the man was human. "Sorry, I know I'm being a bitch." The lack of sex did that.

His gaze lowered and she studied those unreadable eyes as she anticipated his answer. "Take your bath, Alana. I can't watch over you if I'm watching you."

"Ha, good point. Too bad." She had to stay calm if she was going to manage to sneak out tonight.

"I'll be right outside if you need anything." He closed the door.

She doubted she'd get the opportunity to slip down the back stairs now. Embarrassing the man didn't work either. She'd have to find another way. She filled the tub and arranged the soaps and shampoo, then slipped into the water. She let the soapy water ease over her breasts. The silky warmth eased some of the tension and turned her on, knowing Jag was just outside. She couldn't help fantasizing about the guy. He was wicked hot and had been guarding her for weeks. His thorough attention and quiet sense of control intrigued her and would be good traits if he was a Dom. If he was in the lifestyle. She considered asking him a few times, but the right moment hadn't come up. An image of him wielding a leather flogger fit him. That thought hardened her clit. He didn't seem to be the type to be submissive, then again, she knew powerful, kick-ass men who had the courage and strength to relinquish control to a Domme. With Jag, she suspected he leaned toward the dominant side.

Forget about the hot stud. She had to plan out every step for her new life, starting with meeting Liam. Every detail had to be worked out like one of their perfectly executed missions at the FLC. She also needed back-up plans. What if Liam wouldn't help her, or if he had moved?

A knock at the door jolted her. "Alana?" Beth asked. "May I come in? I have your robe."

"Sure."

Beth walked in and dropped the folded robe on the sink counter by the gauze and supplies. After giving the room a quick once-over as if looking for something, she handed Alana a tiny cup with two tablets and a cup of water. "Doctor stopped by and checked your chart. You have a slight fever."

"What's this?"

"Antibiotics. Low dose. Just a precaution. If the fever isn't better by morning he's ordered blood cultures."

Alana felt her forehead. "Funny, I don't feel like I have a fever." She hoped they wouldn't change their mind about her leaving in the morning. Another reason for her to go tonight.

"Low grade. Probably nothing. I'll check it again in a few hours. Would you like me to bring you some tea after your bath?"

"That sounds nice."

Beth pointed to the pills and waited until Alana took them. "Drink all the water so you don't get dehydrated." She turned to leave. "Call if you need anything."

"Thank you, Beth. You can leave the door open a bit. It's stuffy in here."

After Beth left, she heard her and Jag whispering in the next room, but couldn't hear what they were saying. Then it got quiet again. "Are you out there, Jag?"

"Yes." His voice was rough and sexy, and tugged something deep inside her. The man made her ache in ways she hadn't in a long time. She rested her forehead against her knees. The hollowness in her chest widened. Another time, in another world, maybe they would have had a chance. Now was the worst time to get the hots for a guy like Jag.

The other guards had been professional, alert and stoic, and made her feel safe. Everything about Jag was methodical with a heightened sense of awareness like a predator. Every movement was slow, graceful, perfectly organized.

"What do you do when you're not guarding White House employees?" she asked.

"I keep busy with other projects."

She groaned. "Not work. Fun. What do you like to do for fun?"

"Work out, run."

"That doesn't sound very fun. What about relaxing things. Do you have a hobby, like to travel, have a stamp collection?"

He chuckled. "No stamps. Although I play chess. More of an outdoors guy. I like to fish."

"Finally." She sighed. She poured more hot water into the bath and slid down into the water, allowing the tension to ease from her body. "Where is your favorite place to fish, Jag?"

"Cape Hatteras. My family has a place there. And my brother and I share a boat."

She closed her eyes and imagined walking on the beach with him and could almost drift off to sleep. "Sounds wonderful. Wish I was on the beach now and this nightmare was over."

"You'll survive. You're tougher than you think," Jag said.

"Did they ever tell you who tried to kill me, or why?" she called out to him. As images of the bombing drifted into her mind, she shoved them away.

He didn't answer.

"Come on," she pressed. "You were hired to protect me.

You know someone tried to kill me. They must've told you more." After several weeks stuck in this place she really wanted to have someone to talk to about the bombing. But couldn't unless he was cleared and already knew.

He paused for a moment. "You work for the White House. You were involved in negotiations of a top-secret project, something went wrong and your enemy blew up your car."

"Is that all?" She always wondered how many of the secret service knew about the FLC. Soaping up a wash cloth, she slowly washed herself from the top down. It was impossible to wash herself and not think of him pleasuring her. She gasped as she slid the cloth between her legs and pressed.

"You're not to have visitors because everyone believes you didn't survive the bombing. It's for your safety and national security that it stays that way."

She winced at his words. Maybe he did know the whole story.

With the scented shampoo, she washed her hair twice. The day of the explosion, she had tied her hair up in a twist. Normally, she left it long. Lucky she did, or it might have burned off. Most people thought her red hair wasn't natural, but it was thanks to her Irish heritage, and it was one feature she was proud of.

Grabbing two towels, she wrapped her hair in one, then stood to get out of the tub. The room spun a bit and she had to grab the sink for support. Maybe she did have a fever. She dried off, then gently peeled the bandage off her face, but avoided the mirror. Not yet, but she would look soon. Her fingers tightened around the spigots as she adjusted the temperature of the water. She washed at the sink with the sterile soap and pads the nurse gave her. The wounds stung and itched but they were healing. New pink skin was growing on her arm. She wondered if she'd have large scars.

She then replaced the bandages on her arm and set out supplies to attend the surgical wound on her face. Beth would be impressed with her technique. Now would be a good time to check her appearance in the mirror. If the results were bad, she'd rather be alone. She'd stalled long enough.

After removing the towel from her head, she combed out her hair, then carefully removed the gauze dressing on her face. This was the first time she'd taken off the bandages herself. Even though Julia and Beth had insisted the scars were healing well, Alana was afraid to look.

Gripping the sink, she looked up into the mirror and gazed into her reflection.

An image of a different person looked back. She gasped, her chest too tight to inhale a breath. She stared, trying to comprehend the nightmare before her. It wasn't her. She didn't recognized herself. Same red hair, but not her face. Oh my God. What had they done to her?

Alana screamed.

Chapter 3

Alana's scream ripped right through Jag. "Alana? What's wrong?" He yelled. How could she be in trouble inside a bathroom? When she didn't respond, he barged in.

Naked and shaking, she stood in front of the sink, staring at the mirror, her fingers stroking her cheeks, nose and mouth. "Oh, no, no, no, no." She breathed in and out in short, gasping gulps. "No, no, no, no."

She didn't even look up when he entered. He closed the door for privacy in case anyone came into her room. Unfolding her robe, he draped it over her shoulders. Shaking and with a faraway stare, she didn't acknowledge him. He suspected she was in a bit of a shock. He wrapped his arms around her from her back and pulled her against him. Her breathing slowed to a more normal rate.

"What did they do to my face?" she mumbled, then

shrieked. "They changed my face. I look awful."

Jag couldn't figure out what she was talking about. The burns were minor, hardly noticeable now. Fine lines from the surgery incisions remained. They were healing well and would be practically invisible in time. Why was she so upset?

"It looks like it's healing well. I can hardly notice any scars." A knock at the door made them both jump.

"Jag? Everything okay? I heard a scream and saw you go in."

"Fine, Nick. She had a scare." Jag opened the door a bit to show his partner.

"A scare in the bathroom? What's scary in a bathroom?" Nick frowned. "Need a nurse or something?"

"No, I don't think so. She'll be fine."

Nick raised one eyebrow and Jag returned the look with a deathly stare. "Fine, I'll be out in the hall if you need anything."

Alana hadn't taken her gaze off her image in the mirror.

"What is it?" he asked.

"Haven't you seen pictures of me before the accident?" She glared at his reflection.

"No, I haven't."

"Then you can't see. They altered my face." Her voice cracked. "My nose is slimmer and smaller, my cheek bones more prominent, my lips thinner. I loved my full lips. This is awful, just awful. I want my face back. Why would they do this? I didn't think the accident was that bad." She shook so violently now her teeth chattered.

Some things he couldn't tell her yet. He hadn't realized they'd planned to alter her appearance with surgery. "Want me to get your nurse to help you dress?" Why they'd done the changes made perfect sense to him. Surgically altering her looks was drastic, but would insure she'd never be identified by someone she knew. It would work well for her new assignment too, safer for everyone considered.

She gripped the cold porcelain sink as tears streamed down her face. "My fault. My fault. I did this. I did this," she mumbled on the edge of hysteria as she continued staring at the mirror.

Tightening his grip on her shoulders, he turned her around. "It's all right." Gently he guided her arms into the terry robe, resisting the urge to take in the sight of her full breasts and curvy hips, not to mention more intimate places.

He secured the robe with the belt. Holding onto his upper arms, Alana stared at him without seeing him. Her tears had stopped, but her eyes looked glassy and unfocused. Eventually, she'd come out of this. He needed to stay close and give her time for her mind to work through it.

Finally, she gazed into his eyes. "What man would want me like this?" She rested her forehead against his chest.

"I don't know what you looked like before, but I think you're beautiful now."

She turned away and covered her face.

"Don't," he said.

"What?"

"Try to hide your injury. I have a few. Consider them a badge of honor."

She laughed with an edge. "There's no honor in this injury. I earned it through my own stupidity." She bowed her head.

"Was anyone else injured?"

She shook her head.

"Then it was a valuable lesson. Get over it and move on."

Her body slumped as if she lacked the strength to

continue standing.

Gripping her shoulders, he turned her around, then lifted her chin. "You're a beautiful woman, Alana. Scars will heal in time."

"No wonder the FLC doesn't me back at my old job? What man would find me attractive looking like this?"

He squeezed her shoulders and she leaned against him. Her warmth felt enticing. It had been a test of his willpower not giving in to her flirtations over the last few weeks. As her guard, it was not the time or place, not yet anyway. "You'll find another job if that happens, and men will look past the scars."

She touched his hand. "You don't understand my job. It requires that I be attractive to men. Even the security guards could be asked to step in to a sex tape if necessary."

"Ah, but you are attractive." He stroked her hair and fought his own arousal. How easily he could slip into his Master role, to care and protect. He sensed her pain and vulnerability and wanted to comfort her. He understood his mission and knew through experience that new trainees adapt easier if they were willing. Alana was not going to be very willing. That could be a problem.

Her hands stroked over him, his arms, chest, down his stomach and to his hips where she tightened her grip and rocked her pelvis against his cock. Now he was hard, and fucking horny. He should stop now, but she felt damn good. Her hand brushed over his bulge and his breath caught. "Hey, hey. Probably not a good plan."

She untied her robe. "You said my face was beautiful. What about the rest of me?"

This time he took a long look. He hadn't anticipated anything like this. The bodyguard in him was telling him to leave now, but the man in him wasn't moving a damn inch. He could spend hours with this one, taking her places she never knew her body could experience. "You should get back to your room."

"Soon." She took his hand and placed it on her breast. "Tomorrow I'm going away for training. Tonight I want you." She slipped her hand inside his pants and squeezed his cock. "Can you deny you want it too?"

He groaned. Julia had told him to keep an eye on her and don't let her leave. He doubted this was what Julia had in mind. "What I want and what I was hired to do are two different things."

She dropped her robe to the floor. "We're adults here. And after tomorrow, we might not get another chance."

He laughed low in his throat. "For a submissive you're very demanding and cocky. Did you behave like this toward your targets?"

She arched an eyebrow and leaned back. "What do you know about my targets?"

"Since your accident, the first lady has hired additional security for her secret society, the First Ladies' Club. I know you worked as a submissive to manipulate dangerous, foreign political figures. I've also seen the Red Tape Room."

"Julia should've told me. I take on the role that's needed. Usually submissive, occasionally a Domme. In my personal life I prefer my submissive side. The cocky, demanding attitude comes from my past life as a lawyer."

"Might explain a few things." He rolled her nipples between his fingers and applied enough pressure to make her jerk. "I prefer my submissives compliant and honest. And to trust me. I don't know if you can do that."

She nodded, smiling. "You are in the lifestyle. I had a feeling, or maybe I had hoped you were." Her hands stopped fondling his cock, but he didn't want her to stop. "You wonder if I could be compliant." Slowly, she slid down his body and knelt on the floor, her head resting at his feet.

Oh God. Between breaths his heart broke, mended and soared. He couldn't speak or move. What had she done to him with such a bold gesture when she hadn't known him for long?

Crouching to her level, he cupped her chin and slipped an arm around her back to lift her to her feet. "You made your point." He brought his lips down on hers, gently at first, then checked to see if she was all right.

"That's good. Don't stop now."

He didn't want to hurt her. He kissed her harder and fought the urge to take her there on the bathroom floor. When he drew back from this kiss, she was gasping and shoving his hand down to touch her breasts. "Submissive, huh?" he teased.

"Horny. Don't make me tie you up," she teased back.

"If anyone is going to be doing any tying, it will be me," he said in a gravelly voice. "I'll have to see how well you handle commands first."

"I can do that."

"Then kiss my neck, right here." He pointed to a spot just below his ear.

She gave him a quick kiss.

"That was nice, now give me a better one."

This one she did much slower and used her tongue and scrapped her teeth over his skin, lighting his body on fire. "Good. Much better. That's a start. Do you like the feel of leather stinging your skin? A flogger, a crop, a belt?"

"Yes," she whispered.

"Let's see how much." He eased his hand between her legs. Fingering her slick feminine folds, he brushed passed her swollen clit and shoved a finger deep inside her channel. She was wet and ready for him to take her much farther. "I thought you would like that."

Heat and lust surged through him. Swinging her around, he pressed her against the wall, arms captured over her head with one hand while his other stroked her pussy. "When we have more time…"

"Yes."

His fingers pinched her clit and she groaned. "Shhh. No sound."

She nodded. When his finger thrust inside her channel, she arched her back and moaned softly. Her juices flowed over his fingers as he picked up the rhythm. "I'm going to come if you keep that up."

"Good." He thrust a little deeper and she quivered. Damn, she was close.

"I don't suppose you have any condoms on you? I'd really love to feel your cock inside me."

He let out a long breath and kissed her, but didn't stop fucking her with is hand. "No, I don't."

"Crap." She struggled beneath his grip. "Let me pleasure you too."

He shook his head. "It's about you this time." He didn't let up. Her vaginal walls clenched around his finger and he knew she was coming. Gasping, she bit her lower lip to keep from crying out. He took her mouth, hard and deep as he plunged in and out her cunt until she was completely spent. Resting her forehead against his, she laughed softly.

"That was amazing. If you release me, I can return the favor."

"Another time. I need to take you back to your room."

"How late is your shift tonight?" she asked as she slipped on underwear and her hospital gown, then the terry robe.

"Until morning."

She didn't respond.

"Why?"

"I have to give Julia an answer to her offer in the morning."

After she gathered her things, he led her out to the hall and back to her room. Nick had been waiting there and gave him a curious look. Had he figured out what went on in the bathroom? He didn't give a fuck. It wasn't any of his business. Jag turned to Nick and held his posture erect and formal, sending an unspoken message to not give him any shit. "I'll stay by her room for now, you can hang by the nurses' station."

"Right. How am I not surprised?" Nick said as he strolled off down the hall.

"What time is it?" Alana asked.

"Just after nine-thirty. Why?"

She shrugged. "There must be a pharmacy nearby. You could go out and pick up condoms. Tell your partner I have a craving for peanut M & Ms or something. We have all night."

He smiled. "I think you're very persuasive, Ms. MacKenna. I'll send Nick to watch your room while I take a run."

She groaned. "That's not necessary. I'll lock my door until you get back if you like. It won't take you long."

He studied her. "Not a good idea."

She rolled her eyes. "Really. How long have I been here? No one has made an attempt on my life. Right?"

"Right."

"They would've tried by now."

He nodded. "Keep it locked until I get back."

Alana waved him on, hoping she didn't sound too anxious. "Go make your run. You'll be back in five." She closed and locked the door, knowing he'd wait to hear the lock catch. The moment she heard his footsteps retreat down the hall, she quickly put on her shoes, jeans and sweater and stuffed her wallet into the pocket of her jacket.

It tore her up inside having to deceive the guy. Manipulation was her expertise. He didn't deserve it. At another time and place, she could easily see them together. But her life was a disaster right now. The FLC surgically restructured her face without her permission, planned for her to work at a job she has no skills or interest in, and a madman may still be after her. She was through with the FLC as of tonight.

Opening the door, she peeked out and saw Jag as he got onto the elevator. It wouldn't give her much time, but enough.

This was it, no turning back. Liam would help her once she explained what happened. Her landlord might let her into her apartment to gather her cash and things if she could convince him who she was. She glanced down the hallway again. No sign of Jag, Nick or anyone else. She shot out of her room toward the back stairs. The stairwell was dimly lit. Alana bolted down the first flight, skipping steps two at a time. She didn't dare look over her shoulder or she feared she'd trip and break her neck. A whimper rushed out with each gasping breath. Although her muscles ached and head pounded, slightly woozy from whatever meds they had given her, she wasn't about to slow down. As she ran past the door to the fourth level, the door swung open and someone grabbed her and slammed her against the wall.

"Where the hell are you going?" Jag asked through clenched teeth.

Her heart stopped and she couldn't breathe. A moment later, Nick leapt from the upper set of stairs, taking four or five steps at a time.

"You were right. She was going to make a run for it," Nick said, shaking his head. "Not smart."

"What's the point of keeping me here?" she snapped at him. "Julia gave me forty-eight hours. I'm making it easy. I've made an early decision."

Shoving past him, she took one step down, but he lifted her off her feet and held her against the wall. "You seemed to like the rough stuff before, or were you just playing me like you do your targets?"

"You didn't seem to mind either way," Alana argued. Was he angry that he thought she had sex only to gain his trust and trick him, or angry because she tried to escape? "I can't stay here. I know I screwed up. Just looking in the mirror for the rest of my life will remind me. How can I work for…" She stopped, glancing at Nick. She didn't know if he also knew about the First Ladies' Club.

"You can go back to her floor," Jag said to Nick. "We'll be up in a second. She's not going anywhere, are you Alana?"

"No," she answered, feeling defeated. Jag eased his hold on her. If not tonight, then tomorrow. The adrenalin rush mush have exhausted her. She couldn't keep her eyes open.

"Don't tell anyone you tried to run," Nick warned. He marched back upstairs, leaving Alana and Jag alone.

Something in Nick's tone frightened her. "Why did he say that?"

"Julia has her reasons for making you wait out those two days." Jag took a deep breath and let it out in a frustrated huff.

"Julia always has her reasons, doesn't mean they make sense."

"Why?" Jag asked after Nick was gone.

"Why am I leaving? Or why did I seduce you?"

"Obviously the sex was a means to an end. You used it to distract me. At least you think you did. You're good at your *job*, that's why I had a hunch."

She winced at the way he emphasized job. "I don't know if I can do what you do. What if I screwed up? They just don't fire people. After everything I learned today, I wanted to get as far away from the hospital and the FLC as possible." The members of the FLC knew there was an assassin among them. One of their own was killed when she tried to reveal the existence of the organization to the media.

"You can learn. I can teach you. Others will too."

She shook her head. "It's not in my nature to do survival training, fighting and such. I hated camping and don't care to shoot guns or want to learn how to fight with my feet and pound bricks with my head. Those martial arts guys are crazy."

"Explain that to Julia in the morning. Maybe she'll come up with another option like witness protection."

Her heart swelled. He did care and wanted to help. "No. She told me no witness protection. If I don't agree to their terms, I'm on my own and risk knocking heads with Aleid's hit men." She'd have had the same risk if she had been successful in leaving tonight. "Maybe after I lay low for a while, things will get back to normal. Aleid's men will be convinced I'm gone and give up.

"Will you tell them that I tried to run?" Alana asked Jag.

"Not as long as you don't try it again."

She sighed. "Okay." She reached up and kissed him on the cheek but he didn't show the warmth he had earlier. "And I wasn't faking the sex before or using it to manipulate you. You're hot and I'm not sorry it happened. Although, I did get a little carried away. I guess I was upset and not thinking clearly."

"Who were you going to meet when you left?"

"Don't ask me that."

"Whoever it was, it's a good thing you didn't make contact."

"Why?" A chill filled her body.

He didn't answer and she didn't press him.

She walked upstairs to her floor, feeling foolish. Again her arrogance had gotten her into trouble. She may have graduated with two degrees in the top five percent of her class, but Julia was right, she lacked in common-sense skills. What made her think she could outwit two secret service guys, if they were SS?

"I guess you never made it to the pharmacy," Alana said as she walked to her room, staggering a bit down the hall. Jag grabbed her arm to steady her. "No condoms or M & Ms?"

Jag didn't answer.

"Lighten up, Jag. I was just making a joke." She pushed open the door to her room and Beth stood there with her hands behind her. Nick stood beside her. "What's up, Beth?"

A chill shivered up her back. Beth's usual sweet demeanor was replaced by a stern scrutiny. "Change of plans." She held up a syringe.

"No, don't, please." Alana glanced at Jag, pleading. The expression on his face held a flicker of regret. For a man who never showed emotion, that scared her. Nick took one arm and Jag the other, holding her in place while Beth administered the drug. "Why are you doing this?"

"Apparently the sleeping pills didn't work," Beth said. "Julia wants you to stay the night. Julia always gets her way."

In a matter of seconds, the room spun and her muscles relaxed. Jag scooped her up in his arms and she tried to force her eyes to stay open as he carried her to the bed. "Bastard," she murmured.

"Don't worry. I'll see you in the morning."

Vaguely, she felt her T-shirt and jeans slide off her body, replaced by a hospital gown. As she was laid onto the bed, blankets were drawn over her and she drifted off to sleep as if she were floating on a calm lake...

Chapter 4

After Julia left the hospital, she drove back to the White House and marched straight to the entrance of the Red Tape Room. "Open up, Mr. Vargas."

Johnny Vargas, one of the secret service agents and FLC members, straightened and stepped aside. "What if they're training, ma'am?"

Julia glared at him. Only Johnny could get away with arguing with her. "It's not on my schedule. And I still need to go in. It's urgent."

Johnny hesitated a second. Only two people were allowed to open that door when it was locked, Julia and the first lady. "Yes ma'am. I heard they received a new box of equipment. Thought they might be testing things out." He smothered a grin. His tough Bronx accent equally matched the well-honed set of muscles that no crisply pressed business suit could hide.

The guy acted like a thug, but he had a heart of gold, overly protective of women. He had three younger sisters.

"Good. We're going to need new supplies. We have a number of presentations planned over the next several months."

Johnny punched the keypad and unlocked the door.

"Who's in there?" Julia asked.

"Zoe and Melissa, Jason and Tyler."

He led her into a small vestibule. The next door leading into the Red Tape Room was closed. "Would you like me to check to make sure they're not—"

"No, thank you, Johnny. I have an assignment for Zoe and Jason. This can't wait." Without knocking, she opened the door and marched into the Red Tape Room, the underground BDSM dungeon in the White House.

Johnny left, closing the door behind him. Jason and Tyler were hunched over a spanking bench turned upside down and working with a pair of wrenches on the frame. "I think that should do it," Jason said. "It just needed tightening."

Zoe and Melissa stood at a long table, unwrapping items from several large boxes. "Nice selection," Melissa said. "Flavored oils and three new vibrators."

"How are the new supplies? Finding everything you need?" Julia asked Zoe and Melissa.

"Very nice, Julia. The outfits are gorgeous." Zoe pointed to a rack of fetish wear mostly red and black leather or lace corsets, skirts and dresses." Then she held up a new flogger. "The leather on this one is so soft. We're packing up some of the older or worn items."

"Good." Julia answered a bit too quickly.

"Something wrong?" Zoe asked.

"I need to talk to you and Jason right away."

Zoe studied her boss for a moment. As an ex-CIA agent, Zoe was good at reading people, no matter how hard Julia tried to hide it. Jason was ex-CIA too. Some of the members in the FLC had military training, others had their expertise in multiple languages. "Do you want us to come to your office?" Zoe placed the flogger on the table.

"No, it would be better if I spoke here." Julia addressed Melissa and Tyler. "Would you wait outside?" Julia noticed the worried look on Melissa's face. They'd all been working for the White House and especially the secret First Ladies' Club long enough to know that not all missions could be revealed to each member.

"Of course," Melissa said. "I have work at my desk. We can do this later unless we have an urgent presentation, then call me. I'm available to help in any way you need me."

"Same here, Julia," Tyler said.

"At this stage, there is nothing you need to do. But thank you." Julia waited until the two left, then pointed to the bondage bed for Zoe and Jason to sit. The bed always reminded Julia of a medieval torture device.

"Is everything okay?" Zoe sat with her back stiff and her focus on Julia.

"We have an issue that needs your immediate attention. You'll need to leave DC tonight. Both of you."

"Do we have a new target?"

"In a way, you do, and this will be an off-site mission. And one that will be difficult to accomplish."

Julia closed her eyes and took a long breath. "You'll be going to a military training facility run by a consulting security agency."

"What agency?" Jason asked.

"The Eagle Guards."

"They're good. A tough bunch," Jason said. "Why are we using them?"

"We're training a new security agent and needed something outside secret service, and the FLC."

Jason leaned forward, resting his arms on his legs, waiting for Julia to give them more. Or maybe they wouldn't get more intel until they reached this facility.

"We plan to utilize the Eagle Guards on future projects, especially those that take us outside the White House or the US," Julia added. "I'll fill everyone in on this later."

"We need more security?" Zoe asked. "Do we have a large project coming up?"

"Yes, we're getting another security agent, a female. And we need two FLC members with your training in on this one."

"Don't the Eagle Guards have enough people to train this woman? Or am I guessing there's something more…" Jason said.

Julia nodded. "Yes, this is a special case." She hesitated again and grasped her amethyst pendant. The energy stone would be of little help to ease the anxiety in this situation.

"All right, Julia. What aren't you telling us?"

Julia glared at them. "The woman you're going to train is Alana."

"What? Alana's dead." Zoe leapt off the bed with her arms stiffly at her sides. Jason grabbed her and pulled her back down.

"No, she's not," Julia said. "I'm sorry we had to tell you—"

"Why the hell were we told—" Zoe shouted, tears filling her eyes.

"Calm down," Jason ordered. "It's obvious. To protect her. Is she okay?"

"She was injured. She had some burns. I must warn you, we did surgery to alter her appearance. She wasn't too happy about her new position and wants to go back to her life. She wants to leave the FLC."

"She can't do that. If President Aleid's men discover she's still alive, won't they try to kill her again?" Zoe asked.

"Most likely," Julia agreed. "We believe Aleid's hit men have been watching the hospital and her apartment since the accident. We intend to prove that to ourselves and to Alana in the next two days. Once we do, she'll see she has only one choice—join our security team with a new identity."

Zoe punched the bed. "You're risking her life to prove a point?"

"We're proving a point to save her life," Julia countered. "She'll be under constant surveillance."

"It's risky, but I think it could work." Jason patted Zoe's hand.

"If Aleid's men don't kill her, they could abduct her, torture her for information on the next line up of FLC targets, then kill her. She knows too much. About the FLC, how we run it, who's in it…" Julia said.

Zoe rubbed her forehead. "I see the situation. What do you want us to do?"

"Be part of the team to watch her, then work with her at the facility. She'll be given a new identity, and you'll notice she looks different."

"What will we be doing at this facility?" Zoe asked.

"Help her with her training. Convince her to stick to this program. It's rigorous and parts she may not be receptive too," Julia said. "Her handler has orders to take care of the problem if Alana doesn't adjust to her new role."

Zoe knew what taking care of the problem meant. And

she knew Alana too well. She wasn't one to follow rules. They couldn't risk having Alana out on her own. She'd pissed off some really bad people. Alana's life depended on her success in the program.

"If she fails, it'll have to be dealt with permanently. She doesn't get another chance. There's one more thing."

"That is…?" Zoe asked.

Julia hesitated for moment. "She doesn't know everyone, all her friends and family believe she's dead."

⊱⊰

The next morning Julia and Jag escorted Alana to her old apartment. Alana practically skipped up her one flight of stairs. Entering her place gave her mixed feelings. The familiar furniture and environment was comforting, but memories of the car explosion came flooding back. She'd parked on a side street that day, because she'd found a good spot and was going back out in a couple hours. That choice may have saved her life and done less damage than if she'd parked in the garage and the explosion had been confined.

"Most of your personal belongs have been moved out, except the furniture," Julia explained. "We expected to move you to a new place. Arrangements for your things can be made later."

Now she had her life back and anxiety weighed on her chest, making every breath an effort. Once she met with Liam and made arrangements with a new identity, got her funds from her account in the islands, she'd move far away from DC and begin a new life.

"Thank you, Julia," she said. "I appreciate everything you and the FLC has done for me. I'm very sorry for all the trouble. I won't be here long."

"You have forty-eight hours," Julia reminded. "Stay

around long enough to think things through. You've been through a lot. The FLC still has a place for you."

"Thank you. I'll give you the forty-eight hours." *Unless Liam has a better plan.* Alana looked at Jag and her heart clenched. She was going to miss him. After all the weeks in the hospital, she hadn't realized how much she had grown attached to him. Now she couldn't say what she wanted to with Julia there. There was so much she wanted to say to him.

Jag nodded as if he understood what she was thinking. "Watch yourself and be careful. You might still have a price on your head."

Alana waved him off. "I doubt it. After all this time?" Both Julia and Jag didn't answer and that scared her. "Thanks for watching over me." She swallowed, trying to clear the lump in her throat.

"There's a little bit of food in the refrigerator." Julia handed Alana a cell phone. "My number's in the contact list if you need anything. I'll be back at this time in two days."

Alana nodded. She exchanged glances with Jag as he and Julia left and her heart broke. She doubted she'd ever see him again. Bad timing for them. In another life perhaps.

After they left, she marched over to the built-in bookcase and wiggled out the bottom strip of trim. Her hiding place for cash. Reaching inside, she retrieved the envelope where she had stashed several hundred dollars. Not a ton of cash, but a small emergency fund. She doubted she'd be around to see Julia in two days. For security sake, she divided the cash in her purse, wallet and stuffed the rest in her jeans pockets, then grabbed her coat and apartment key. She was going shopping.

It was about a half mile to the small mall, far from high-end boutiques, which was fine as she was looking for a few basics. As she walked, she glanced over her shoulder and noticed a black van slow down as it passed. The hairs on the back of her neck stood out and she looked around for an escape route if she needed to run. The van continued on and made a turn down the block.

Cars and pedestrians clogged the morning streets. She doubted anyone was after her. Just paranoia, or it could be Julia's people watching her or even trying to scare her into coming back. Still she remembered Jag's warning and kept an eye out for the van. When she noticed it coming up the street again, she ducked into a coffee shop and waited for it to pass before leaving. This time she jogged down the sidewalk and tried to blend into a crowd of people. She made her way to the parking lot of the mall.

She entered the superstore, grabbed a cart, and headed to the women's section. Rolling up and down the clothing isles, she tossed in T-shirts, sweaters, a pair of jeans and leggings, PJs and a few changes of underwear. She scrunched her nose at the dull selection. No pretty lacy or silk bras and panties, no corsets for her visits to Paradise Underground, no fashionable couture. Basic survival clothes. She threw in a pair of sneakers and socks, then headed to the luggage section. There she found a duffle—not too bulky—to lug all her stuff. Her last trip was to the pharmacy section to pick up travel-size toiletries. One last item she picked up as she left.

She yanked the tag off the baseball cap and stuffed her long, red hair under it. She hated hats, but if she was being followed, this might help. The van didn't appear and she slipped into a laundromat next door to her apartment building. She knew they had a payphone because she'd used it a number of times after she'd put her cell phone through the washing machine and she didn't own a landline phone. She didn't want to call Liam with the cell they had given her in case it was monitored.

"Hello, Liam? This is Alana. Please don't hang up. We need to talk. I need your help."

The other end of the phone was silent. Alana wondered if he had hung up. "Alana is dead. Who the hell is this? What do you want?" Liam spat out in an angry tone.

"Who told you I was dead?"

"It was all over the news."

"Of course. It's not true. They were protecting me. I need to see you right away."

"Really?" He still wasn't convinced. "You might sound like her, but you're not, and I don't fucking care to find out what you're up to."

"Can you meet me? Please? I'll explain it all then."

"No. Whoever you are, I'm hanging up now."

"No, don't, please wait." She took a breath and thought a second. "I kept you out of jail when I represented you. If it hadn't been for some fancy paper work and filing, and calling in a few favors, you're little import/export business inconsistencies could've gotten you six to ten."

"That was client confidentiality. What did Alana tell you?" he shouted.

"I was the one who helped you. Now I need a favor. Just meet me at the Fried Fog Coffee Shop. You know where. I'll be waiting at our usual table. We used to go there a couple times a week."

"Alana and I did," he agreed. "Fine, one hour."

She disconnected the call and rested her head against the phone. *Thank God.*

When she got back to her apartment, she dropped onto her sofa. This would work out now. How would he react when he realized it was her? They'd parted as a couple last summer, and even though it was an amicable split, he had his moods. She didn't believe he'd have any reason not to help her get the necessary identification documents so she could start a new life. She leaned her head against the back cushions and closed her eyes. They had been at Paradise Underground the night he had broken up with her.

Perhaps there had been love between them, but not that undeniable chemistry, intoxicating love that draws two people together. During the time they were involved, she was never convinced Liam was the right Master for her. He had satisfied the physical cravings, her masochistic desires, and had a way of taking the edge off a stressful day, but in the back of her mind, there was something missing, an emptiness she couldn't explain. On that night, he had ended their relationship and she remembered it clearly.

In a private BDSM room, he'd taken off her blindfold and ordered her to remove her clothes, then sit silently on a chair. A simple task to get the scene started. She was a lawyer, after all, not some mousy secretary, and not always the compliant submissive. Tonight she wasn't being compliant. After removing her clothes, she stood by the chair instead of sitting.

He gave her a little smack on her thigh. "Are we going to start like this tonight?"

"No, Sir." She smiled inside, enjoying the sting from the slap, then sat and focused on her knees. She'd behave now. Apparently satisfied, he finished setting up. She liked to test his mood so she could prepare herself for what to expect during that scene. This private room had all the usual dungeon furnishings, a spanking bench, St. Andrew's Cross, a restraint bed, and this one even had a cage. All the rooms had eyehooks secured to the ceiling, walls and floor. Masters could get quite creative with their submissives. Liam was friends with the owner and could reserve the room on weekdays for free.

In nearby rooms, the sensual beat of music, moans and screams echoed through the walls. It was turning her on. Alana sighed, anxious to get on with the session.

Her hand slid between her legs and touched her swollen and sensitive clit. Quickly, she yanked her hand back. He'd know and would punish her severely this time. He wouldn't allow her to come and wouldn't fuck her if she attempted to pleasure herself while she waited.

When he finished arranging his toys, he stood over her and held a hand out to her. "Please stand now." Chill bumps rose from her scalp to her toes. Her nipples tightened. With his first grunt of approval, her pussy clenched. "Nice," he said. "You look beautiful tonight."

He walked around her, no contact yet, and she so wanted him. "Have you obeyed my instructions, sweet?"

"Yes, Sir."

"I see you wore low heels, good. Did you touch yourself while I prepared? I know how impatient you get."

She hesitated.

"Ah. You did disobey me. What did you do?"

Alana's stomach plummeted as she stared at the floor. "Sir, I started to touch myself. I forgot, but quickly stopped."

He smacked her hard on her bottom. He reached around and pinched a nipple hard enough for her to feel the sharp pain. Then he raised her chin. "Forgetting isn't an excuse."

"I know. I'm trying, really I am."

He took a deep breath and walked across the room. She had disappointed him again. Maybe she wasn't meant to be a submissive. Maybe it was her attitude, or maybe they weren't meant to be together. She couldn't decide. Instead of feeling joy and wanting to please him, all she felt was concern that she would do something wrong, that she shouldn't be with him. A few moments ago she was turned-on by the sounds of the others in nearby rooms, not anymore.

Liam pressed his lips to hers. A gentle kiss that slowly turned intense and seductive as his tongue slipped inside to tease her mouth. But the kiss fell flat, cold and unemotional. Alana moaned, hoping to sound more passionate than she felt. She wouldn't slip her arms around him. He hadn't given her permission yet.

He broke the kiss, gazing at her with dark, dangerous eyes. Her pulse raced as she waited for his next move. "This won't do, Alana."

"I don't understand." What did she do wrong? He hadn't given her a task or order, had he?

He walked across the room and grabbed her clothes that were neatly folded on a chair and brought them back to her. "Get dressed. We're done. I'm sorry."

Slowly, Alana stood and slipped her clothes on her chilled body. "Are we going to your apartment instead?"

"No." He crossed his arms over his chest. "We're just not making a connection. No one's fault."

Standing there, she saw grief etched in his eyes, a rush of conflicting emotions tore at her heart. Arguing wouldn't help the situation.. He was right. She was relieved yet saddened, and at the same time, not at all surprised. The love between them wasn't enough, no spark remained, and it was fading into indifference. And that was the saddest part of all. "No harm done, Liam. It's best that we're honest with each other."

"I agree."

She kissed him on the cheek. "I'll get dressed and call a cab."

"I can drive you home."

"No." Her voice was a little sharp. "I'll call a cab."

The honk of a horn outside her apartment brought her back to the hard reality of the situation. She'd spent a couple years in this place, but it didn't feel like home anymore. As much as she loved DC, she couldn't stay. She hadn't even decided where to go yet. Texas, Colorado, Arizona, or California? Maybe she'd get on a bus and decide on the way.

The walk to the coffee shop wouldn't take her more than fifteen minutes. She got up and looked out her window. No black van, but there was a uniform cleaning truck parked in front of the apartment. No reason it should look suspicious except there were a couple people sitting in it. She couldn't make out what they looked like. The sooner she got out of DC, the better.

Checking her watch, she decided to head out early, but left through a side entrance of the building and took a back road, then cut across to the main street. She walked so fast, she was practically running. If the meeting went well, maybe she could convince Liam to take her to a bar for lunch. She could go for a beer. Two blocks away, the lime-green lights on the Fried Fog Coffee Shop sign appeared and her body relaxed a little. The owners were a couple from Cape Cod who said they got the name from when they lived on the cape. The fog would roll in so thick off the ocean, Cape Codders would say you could fry it up with your fried clams. A twinge of sadness tugged at her heart. The small shop held many memories and she'd miss the place. She even had a few good memories of Liam there.

She barely heard the squeal of tires behind her. Then footsteps of heavy boots slapped the sidewalks. Another vehicle slammed on its breaks. Alana turned toward the traffic to see if there had been a close call of an accident. She hadn't heard a crunch.

The next moment she heard shouts and gunshots. The piercing cracks rang through the noise of the traffic and people. Chaos instantly broke out. Cars raced down the street, and people screamed and scattered in every direction. Alana crouched, not sure which way to run. Then a cloth bag was slipped over her head. She tried to scream, but her voice was muffled. As she struggled to get away, strong arms wrapped around her, then another shot fired close by and she was released.

Tugging on the bag over her head, Alana ran blindly hoping she wouldn't run into traffic. Then someone lifted her off the ground and flung her inside the truck. Scrambling to fight her way out, she heard the door to the truck slam shut before she could get up. It sped away.

Someone yanked at the hood and she punched and kicked him. Finally, the cloth slipped off her head. She was face-to-face with Jag.

"What the hell is going on?" Alana asked.

"Both hit men were killed," the driver said. "The other team is there now."

Alana noticed the driver was Nick.

"Glad to see you're okay, Alana," Beth said, giving her hand a squeeze.

"Sorry for the rough stuff," Nick added. "We were afraid something like this might happen."

"Leaving your Jeep here, Jag, or do you want to follow us up?" Beth asked.

"Todd's driving it up. He met with Julia about an upcoming project, but he'll be working with us for now."

"So Aleid still thinks I'm alive?" Alana asked, changing the subject. She didn't remember a guard named Todd who had watched over her, but he must have connections with their group.

"We believe he suspects," Jag said. "We don't know what he knows now since his men failed to pick you up. And they're dead now."

Alana scanned her surroundings. A black van. She'd heard gunfire but never saw anything with the hood over her head, including the dead bodies. "This wasn't an elaborate scheme to fake a kidnapping and scare me into accepting Julia's offer? Beth did say Julia always gets her way."

"No, it was real." Jag pulled out his Sig Sauer pistol and released the magazine, showing her the ammunition. Not blanks. "Julia guessed Aleid's men would make a move the moment any woman closely fitting your description moved into your apartment."

"We took care of these two," Beth said. "There's a good chance he'll send more. You'll have to be prepare."

Alana clenched her jaw and said, "I can never go back to being Alana can I?"

Jag shook his head.

"What now? Where are we going?" Alana asked.

"Where do you think?" Jag leaned back in his seat and pulled a cap over his eyes. "Get some rest. You have a long ride ahead."

Chapter 5

The sound of birds woke Alana, but she was still too groggy to open her eyes. Bacon smells wafted into her room, reminding her that she hadn't eaten dinner the previous night. Her stomach growled. Opening her eyes, she took in the strange surroundings and a jolt of fear shook her.

They'd practically abducted her. But the alternative would've been much worse. They'd stopped along the way for food and had been driving for ten hours, heading north. She wasn't quite sure where they were. They could be in Canada for all she knew. She'd fallen asleep after the last rest stop for food and didn't remember arriving. How had she gotten into her room? Damn. Had someone drugged her drink? What was it with these people? Could she blame them? She had tried leaving on her own once, then had tried meeting up with Liam after they'd told her not to contact any friends or family. They were going to make her do things their way whether she liked it or not. Her plan could've worked, maybe. If Aleid's men hadn't stepped in.

Wood paneling covered the walls. The ceiling had rough beams, even the floor was hardwood. The bedframe was made out of smoothed logs and to her horror her wrists and ankles were strapped in spread-eagle fashion. Definitely, making sure she was doing it their way this time. This looked like a log cabin. Shades covered the window, so she couldn't see outside. She tugged on her bindings, attempting to get free. The restraints were the padded ones hospitals used for combative patients and nearly impossible to unbuckle. She wasn't going anywhere at the moment.

A creepy feeling made the hairs on the back of her neck rise. She was being watched. On the wall across from her bed was a deer head with a huge antler rack. What possessed people to hang animal heads on the wall as artwork?

Heavy footsteps approached from outside her room. The door swung open and Jag stood there with a tray of food. He didn't seem surprised or pleased that she was awake.

"You'll need to eat. You have a busy day." He placed the tray on the bedside table and gazed down at her. A blanket partly covered her and she was wearing the T-shirt she had on last night, minus the jeans. They were folded neatly on a chair by the dresser. Her shoes were on the floor.

"How long was I out?"

"How are you feeling?"

"Bastard, untie me." She tugged on her restraints.

He unfastened her wrists, then her ankles. "We didn't want you taking off again. Or wandering around the camp or getting lost in the mountains."

"We? Who's we?"

"It'll be explained later. Eat now then get dressed. Meet us in the common room downstairs." He opened her dresser and pulled out an army-green T-shirt, sweatpants and a hoodie sweatshirt. "There's underwear in the top drawer. You have a pair of boots and athletic shoes in the closet, wear the athletic shoes. You'll need them for later, after the meeting."

"Where are my clothes, my suits and heels? If I'm going to a meeting, I should be wearing something more appropriate." She couldn't help but add a little smartass to her words. Jag glared at her. Sitting up on the edge of the bed, she pressed a hand to her forehead as her head swam a bit. She tried ignoring it. As long as they were letting her get back to work, she'd present herself as a professional. The secret service wore suits. "Who'll be at this meeting?"

"You won't need your business clothes while you're here," he said. "Everything will be explained at the meeting."

She stood too quickly and the room tilted. Arms flailing, she reached out toward the wall in front of her for balance and missed. Jag's hands gripped her shoulders, steadying her. Closing her eyes, she tried to calm her breath and tamp down the panic rising in her chest. Since the car bomb, her life had flipped upside down and she couldn't gain any control. She'd liked her small apartment in DC, liked her challenging job with the FLC and her occasional visits to Paradise Underground. One indiscretion took it all away. She shoved back from him. "Who drugged my drink? And why? Where is this place?"

He puffed out a breath. "I was following orders. We felt it was necessary because you weren't being cooperative, tried running away and contacting friends."

Guilty as charged. Not trusting her legs to keep her upright, she sat back down. "My head and muscles ache."

He frowned. "You're still feeling the effects of the drug?"

She rubbed her temples as if that would help clear her mind. Everything was foggy. Thinking back, images of the previous few nights flashed through her mind. She saw her changed face in a mirror, remembered sex with Jag—or almost sex—then her conversation with Liam and the hood shoved over her head, the gunshots. "You and Nick rescued me." She wondered if Liam had heard the commotion and gunshots. It wasn't far from the coffee shop.

He nodded. "Who's Liam?

"A friend."

"Does he know you're alive?" He studied her for a while. "You were going to meet him."

Would they harm Liam? She couldn't put him in danger. "He said he heard Alana was killed on the news. I'm sure he thought I was trying to scam him. He didn't believe it was me calling."

"Why see him?"

If she didn't tell him they would research the guy and figure it out eventually. "He has connections. I represented him as his lawyer once. I planned to get a new identity and leave town."

Jag raised his eyebrows as if impressed. "What else? Think. What details do you remember of this trip?"

She could only recall a few shadowy images during the journey. "Very little, a few small towns, a deserted road through the mountains and a number of cabins. Someone carried me to my room. After that, nothing."

"Learn to be hyperaware of your surroundings and remember details. If you were to get drugged, you can better assess your situation and the dangers." He nodded. "Good that you remembered some."

"I remember enough that I'm not sure if I can trust you."

She wondered if he thought she meant the hot-and-heavy naked stuff in the bathroom. Despite her predicament, her nipples tightened and her sex throbbed. Damn him. She definitely hated him for making her feel aroused right now.

"We drugged you because you were unpredictable. And the situation required it."

She picked up the restraints and tossed them on the bed. "I guess these could come in handy if you have something kinky planned for later." The smartass attitude should be expected considering what she'd been though. He stared at her, not taking the bait to get into an argument.

A shiver skittered up her body at the thought of submitting to him. She couldn't help it. As a submissive she craved being bound and submitting to a powerful man like Jag. The joy of relinquishing control at the hands of a skilled and caring Dom, and allowing him to awaken her body to explore beyond her sexual limits thrilled her.

Amusement flickered in his eyes. His fingers stroked the side of her cheek, down her neck and across her collarbone. She closed her eyes. "Yes, I do believe you'd enjoy that."

He laughed low in his throat.

She would enjoy an intense session with Jag under different circumstances. "I need to pee."

He took her hand and helped her up. "Bathroom is in there." He pointed to a door. "Don't try to crawl out the window. We'll find you. By the way, besides the plastic surgery, you have a GPS chip imbedded in your skull. Julia doesn't know you tried to contact your friend. Scenes like the near abduction one you just had draws media attention. The FLC loathes media attention. If Julia believes you're a risk of exposing the FLC, they won't give a second thought to eliminating you. We've been told you must complete this training successfully—"

"Or I get sent to a nowhere town to work at a convenient store?" She grinned. She'd be damned if she'd let this guy get to her.

"The orders are to put a bullet in your head."

Alana glared at him and he didn't flinch. There was something in his face that said he wouldn't hesitate a second. That chilled her more. Could he follow through on his order?

She marched into the bathroom and closed the door. After she peed, she leaned against the sink and gazed into the mirror. Not only didn't she look like herself, she looked like hell. What kind of nightmare did she wake up in? She splashed cold water on her face to keep back the tears. She really fucked up royally. She found a brush on the sink and fixed her hair.

The knock at the door made her jump. "Alana, come out and eat. They're waiting for you."

"You haven't told me who?" She opened the door.

"Part of the team who will be training you."

She sat on the bed and stared at the tray of food. "This is a lot. I usually have coffee, yogurt and fruit." There was a plate of scrambled eggs, bacon, two pancakes, mixed fruit and juice.

"Eat as much as you can," he said. "You'll burn off the calories."

She took a bite. "Where am I?"

"That's what I expected your first question to be. Assessing your situation like where you are, what the dangers are, and other things will become automatic. You're at a private training facility in the Vermont mountains. Years ago this was a hunting lodge with separate cabins, but it's been abandoned for over twenty years. You're also about forty miles from the nearest town worth mentioning, so even if you didn't have that tracker on you, you'd have a long hike into town."

"You're serious about killing me if I don't make it, or if I try to run away?"

"Very serious. You will make it. I took clothes out for you and put them on the dresser. Eat, get dressed, don't bother showering. You'll be getting dirty. Come downstairs in ten minutes. There's a watch on your dresser. Put it on. You'll need it for a stopwatch and to keep track of your schedule." He started to leave then turned back to look at her.

Alana hadn't moved off the bed. She'd stopped eating, barely touching her food. How could she eat? Her guess was that watch had another means to track her too. She was a prisoner.

He came back to the bed, sat beside her and took her hand. "You'll be okay. You wouldn't be here if they didn't think you could make it. That's why you're here. We're going to teach you." He squeezed her hand. "I'm here to help you."

The sincerity in his voice rang true and she wanted to believe him. She stood and walked to the dresser, looking at the items he had told her to wear. Her new identity. "But I'm still a captive here."

He came up behind her, his fingers squeezed her shoulders. He sighed and turned her around. Keeping her arms pinned to her sides, she gazed up at him as conflicting emotions slammed into her. Defiant and angry one moment, she then struggled with admitting her fears and collapsing against his chest.

His eyes turned dark and sultry as he drew her closer. "Oh, hell," he murmured then bent to take her mouth in a bruising kiss. The steeled reserve unleased. Arms wrapped around her, then his hands slid down to her ass and slipped down her panties. He pressed her body against his hard cock.

They both moaned as the kiss deepened and grew more

aggressive. She too, grabbed his ass, then dared to grasp his shaft, stroking its hardness with the heel of her hand. He groaned, lifted her T-shirt to bare her breasts, and moved lower to suck a nipple. The intensity of sensations ignited her nerves in a straight line to her clit. God, she was wet and didn't want him to stop, wanted more.

Jag caressed her breasts while he sucked each nipple until they were both red, erect and sore. He ran his hand over her stomach in a torturously slow trail to her pussy. Teasing her clit, he separated her slick folds and shoved a finger inside her channel. "Yes," Alana groaned.

"You like that?" he asked with a gravelly tone.

"Yes, Sir."

"Good." He didn't even question her answer, calling him Sir. It was a reflex.

"Am I right about calling you Sir? You did say at the hospital that you were in the lifestyle." Normally, she discussed this before she had sex with a new partner, but their situation was far from normal.

"Yes. I've been a Dom for ten years."

"I thought our fooling around at the hospital was a one-time thing," she said.

He shook his head. "One night with you will never be enough, Alana."

"Then you like the idea of me being your captive." She put her arms behind her back, jutting out her breasts, teasing him, baiting him.

"If you're going to accept a role as my submissive here, it happens only when we're alone, and I say when. Outside, you're a trainee under my command and those working with the Eagle Guards Security Team. The others can't know."

"It might make this program more tolerable."

"Then place your hands on the dresser and spread your legs wider. We'll use red, yellow, green as safewords."

She did as asked and her body tensed. Her nerves fired up in response to his first order. Of all the fantasies she'd ever had as a submissive, a captive scenario most turned her on. This was a bizarre place to play it out.

His hands slid over her back and shoulders. "You are tense. Alana, in here I can bring you great pleasure if you follow my instructions. You like the idea of being my captive?"

"Yes, Sir."

"Good. Out there you will not treat me any differently than the other trainers. Can you do that?" His hand smoothed over her ass, his fingertips gliding between the cheeks.

"Yes, Sir. I'll treat you as I will the others."

"Good girl. If I see our scene play here is affecting your field training in any way, I will end it immediately. Do you understand?" He plunged his finger in and out of her pussy and rubbed her clit with the tips of his fingers from his other hand.

She gasped. "I understand, Sir. I will do my best to please you on the field and as your submissive." She rocked her hips into his plunging finger in rhythm to his strokes. He was playing her perfectly.

"Keep your eyes on me in the mirror, sub. Go with it."

"Yes, Sir." Her heart soared. A little longer and she'd come.

A knock at the door shattered her. He pulled away from her, adjusted her T-shirt, while she tugged up her panties. He made her sit on the bed and slid the table of food in front of her. "Start eating," he ordered quietly. Then he opened the door. "Hey, Beth."

Beth looked inside the room. "What's taking so long?

Everyone is waiting."

"She's still a little groggy."

"Hi, Alana." Beth waved, smiling. Instead of her nurse's uniform she was wearing a green T-shirt, sweats and sneakers. The same clothes Jag had left out for Alana. "Need help getting dressed?"

"Hi, Beth. No, I'm fine. I'll be right down, thanks."

Beth nodded. "All right. Don't take too long. The director is getting antsy." She left and Jag closed the door then walked over to the window and opened the shade. He crossed his arms and stared outside. It occurred to her that she hadn't looked out yet. She got up and stood beside him, following his gaze. Sunlight filtered through dense hardwood and pine trees surrounding a dozen cabins, some larger than others, a few Jeeps and trucks and a dirt road that disappeared into the forest. Large mountains rose beyond the trees far in the distance. No sign of buildings or houses or roads other than the ones below. "Nothing like DC."

"Not even close."

She glanced up at him and was stunned by the intensity of emotion in his eyes.

"What is it? What's wrong?" She placed a hand on his chest, her heart breaking, not knowing what was troubling him.

"This. Us. It's going to be a long, several months. It may be a bad idea for us to pursue this."

"Perhaps. But then some things are inevitable. Like me being here?" She made a smirk.

"Inevitable?" Jag asked. "I'd call it luck that you're not in a body bag. Hitting a key fob several yards away from your car that sets off the car bomb early. That's luck. The FLC has decided to invest a lot of time and money into you, when it would've been easier and less risky to put you in a body bag. I call that luck too. So don't push it, or it's inevitable that luck of yours will run out."

Her eyebrows rose. "I get the point"

"Learn to control that cockiness, or your time here will be short-lived. I think you understand what that means."

"Yes, I do." The attitude final drained.

"Maybe I can teach you a little about control and obedience. It might help curb that edge about you." His gaze wandered over her, making her pussy throb and breasts swell. How did the man do that with just a look?

"I'll consider that." Her mind couldn't wrap around what he was suggesting.

"I'll meet you downstairs," he said.

"All right. Promise me something."

"If I can," he said.

"If I'm screwing up and they're considering abruptly ending my training, you'll warn me so I can at least try to fix it."

He nodded, knowing what she meant.

"Eat, quickly. And eat it all. You'll need the energy."

"Why?"

He smiled. "You'll see."

ⅎ℞

Damn, she was gorgeous, and Jag knew in a few moments he would've had her coming. Hopefully, as her training got underway, his burning need to control her, sink deep inside her, would subside. He had a job to do and their lives depended on it. Normally, he wouldn't consider having a sexual relationship with a trainee—completely against policy—but in Alana's case, she might be more cooperative with some D/s training. The consequences of her not cooperating were bad for all involved. He had to admit, he was doing it because he was excited by the idea of her.

Vulnerable and tough at the same time, she'd been thrust into an impossible situation and untrained to handle it. It was amazing she had survived this long considering the stress. The woman had him hooked the moment he had seen her in the hospital room several weeks ago. With any luck, his team would help her through it. Whether or not she approved of what they had in mind, was another matter. From now on, her life would never be the same.

He rubbed his forehead. What had he been thinking, practically fucking her at the hospital and again the day she arrived at the facility? Yes, he wanted to take this hot sub deep into subspace. Under his control, she might experience new depths within herself, but he also knew how lousy he was with relationships, and his timing was piss poor. A little BDSM interaction, if worked discreetly into their horrific schedule, was fine, but an involved relationship wouldn't cut it.

His job took him on international assignments for months at a time and he could never discuss with lovers where he was going, what he was doing or when he'd be back. He couldn't call or email or allow them to do the same. Not a good set up for a long-term relationship. He was assigned as Alana's protector, trainer and handler, not as her lover. He marched down the stairs, promising he'd keep his cock in his pants for both their sakes.

"What's taking so long?" Greg Adams, the director asked.

"She's still feeling the effects of the drugs," Beth answered. "It may take several hours or a day for her full recovery. We gave her a large dose."

Greg shot Beth a look. His question was to Jag, not Beth. "Beth is the medical expert." Jag headed off Greg's retort. "She seems to be steadier now and she's finishing breakfast.

Had some vertigo when she first got up."

Greg mashed his lips together and scratched his gray beard. At forty-five, the ex-military and ex-CIA member was in better physical and mental shape than most men fifteen years younger. "Then after her introduction to the program, she'll have her hour session of martial arts, and only a 5K run instead of a 10K. Weapons training after that, a shower then meditation with Li. Before dinner she'll meet with the barber and work out something about her appearance and in the evening she'll have three hours of foreign languages. Beth can check her after the 5K. If she still doesn't look well, she can skip weapons training until tomorrow and rest for an hour. We'll hold off on the hand-to-hand combat and knife training until tomorrow. Any questions?"

"Can we tell her exactly where she is and why she's here?" Zoe Summers asked. She and Jason Merritt, both ex-CIA agents and members of the FLC were also friends with Alana. They had also recently been married.

Greg considered their request for a moment. "She's been told she's being trained in security for the FLC, that's all. Focus on her skills. Her first test will be to make a guess as to where this facility is located."

Zoe nodded. "Julia said Alana understands added security is necessary after the last projects."

"Do not give her further details except her identity," Greg warned. "She'll be briefed about her upcoming missions at the end of the program."

Jag took the chair next to Jason. If she didn't have what it took to survive the training, she wouldn't live very long once she left the facility. Even with a 24/7 bodyguard.

"Come join us, Ms. MacKenna," Gregg called out to Alana who stood at the top of the open stairs. She descended cautiously. When she focused on Zoe, she squealed and ran down the rest of the way.

"Zoe, Jason. Thank, God." Alana rushed across the room to her friend and gave her a hug. "It's such a relief to see you both. I can't wait to get back to work"

"We're glad that you're okay too," Zoe said, hugging her back.

"Want some coffee?" Nick held up a pot from a side table.

"No, I'm good. Thanks, Nick."

After Alana greeted the members of the team, she focused her attention on the moose head over the large stone fireplace. "Was that shot in this area?"

"Not while we've been here," Greg said. "Probably when the hunters used this place."

She turned to other trophies on another wall. "That's a huge black bear."

Nick laughed. "The wildlife in the area is the least of your worry."

"I'm not worried," she argued. "I'm making an observation. We'd have to be pretty far north for bear that size or moose."

Greg nodded his approval. "Good. We're located in the Great North Woods of a region that stretches across four states—upstate New York, Vermont, New Hampshire and Maine. It also enters Quebec. This area is very remote and rural, considered an unofficial region and has no official population. It has a small airport that is also off the grid. There's twenty-six million acres of forestland so I wouldn't try running away again."

Alana had expressive eyes. Wide, like a trapped animal, and her hands gripped in tight fists. Jag groaned inwardly. She had so much to learn. "I'll be your handler," he spoke in an authoritative tone.

"What's that supposed to mean?" she asked. The attitude she'd lose quickly enough. He had to admire her boldness.

Greg got in her face. "Your handler will be on your ass 24/7 to make sure you stick to the program. Listen to what he and the trainers say. Follow orders without question. Your life may depend on it. Understand?"

"Yes." She backed down a little but maintained eye contact.

"Your schedule is posted. You won't be late for any session."

"I understand." The room grew quiet and everyone stared at her. Alana waited for Greg to speak, instead he poured himself a cup of coffee.

"Tell her, Zoe," Gregg said. "Get it over with, then take her to the shack for her first lesson."

Zoe glanced at Jason and back at Alana. "I have some upsetting news."

Alana grabbed Zoe's arms. "What is it? Is everyone in the FLC all right?"

Zoe nodded. "Let's go to the shack for your martial arts class. I'll explain on the way."

Jag expected Alana to argue, but by the seriousness in Zoe's voice, Alana conceded. She glanced at everyone in the room, perhaps expecting to hear a comforting word. Beth was the only one who smiled.

"It's for the best, Alana," Beth said. The woman was a good agent, but not always the most tactful or compassionate.

Jag didn't envy Zoe's job right now.

Chapter 6

Stomach quivering with nerves, Alana walked beside Zoe. At least she had two people she completely trusted, Zoe and Jason. She realized she had a few doubts about Jag after he abducted her, although she believed he felt he was doing what was best for her.

"Just tell me the bad news, Zoe, and get it over with."

Zoe handed her an insulated jacket. "Put it on. The shack is a couple-hundred-yards walk. You'll freeze."

"What the hell is going on? Why is the FLC going to all this trouble? Don't they have enough security with the secret service?" The cold air cut into her skin. Alana slipped on the jacket and zipped it. "Brrr, it's cold. Just give it to me straight what Greg is talking about."

Zoe stopped walking and grabbed Alana's arm. "You've been brought here to train you like a military boot camp to learn about weapons, survival skills, martial arts, computer and foreign languages and a number of other things. When they're finished, you'll start working in security."

"I got that from what Jag told me. What aren't you telling me?"

"Your job description will change quite a bit and they may have you do other things. That will be explained later."

"Are you trying to tell me I'm fired from the FLC?" Alana groaned.

"Not exactly."

Alana snorted. "Just say it."

"All right." Zoe took a long breath and let it out. "The first lady decided that the missions within the FLC have become more and more dangerous, so all members, especially the women, must take special training. Yours will be more extensive though."

"Okay, considering the maniacs we've had to deal with, self-defense, martial arts, some weapons training are good ideas. I've shot guns a number of times at my grandfather's place. He and my dad were hunters. That won't be hard. Will the others be coming here too?"

There was a long silence. "No, only you. That's the training shack." She point to a large log cabin hidden beneath a stand of hemlock trees. Dried leaves from fall crunched under their feet, and the air smelled crisp like snow. A few smaller cabins were scattered around, and beyond an open grassy field was a lake. "What are the other cabins used for?"

"Supplies mostly. It's about a forty-five minute drive into town."

"Are you sure we didn't fly to the Outback?"

Zoe grew quiet again as she stopped walking.

"This doesn't sound all that upsetting. I can understand

why the first lady is doing this and I appreciate everyone's help."

Zoe nodded, her eyes glistened with tears. "This isn't going to be an easy program. Most everyone on this team has been in the military, or like Jason and I, trained in the CIA. Trust me that there are going to be things you don't think you can do, but it will be necessary."

Whatever this news was that Zoe wasn't telling her, it couldn't be good and Alana didn't want to hear it right now. She'd been through hell the last several weeks. How much more did they expect her to take? She marched into the shack. The building looked like a small gym with weights, workout equipment and large padded mats on the floor.

"Funny, Jag said not to trust anyone." Alana picked up two eight-pound weights and started doing bicep curls.

"You have to be very aware of your surroundings from now on," Zoe said. "Observe everything with a sharp, objective eye."

"You had this same training?"

"Similar." Zoe strolled into the room, turning away from Alana.

Setting the weights back on their shelf, Alana stood there, hands on hips. Something didn't feel right. "What am I missing here? You look upset. And that's scaring me. Don't bullshit me."

"Okay." Zoe crossed her arms and faced Alana, then placed a hand on Alana's shoulder. "Except for the first lady, Julia, Jason, and those on this team, everyone has been told you didn't survive the explosion."

"What?"

"The first lady decided you'd be safer if your assassins thought you were dead. This is why you're going through this program, in case they discover you're not. And it appears they did, or at least suspected."

"Wait. The members of the FLC think I'm dead? What about my family and friends?"

"They all belief you were killed. They were notified."

It made sense. Liam said he'd heard she had been killed on the news. Alana dropped to the floor onto her hands and knees. Her head and shoulders sagged.

"It's all my fault. I know I don't get along with my family, but I never meant for them to suffer."

The bomb. Alana had a mini flashback. Being cocky and stupid was what got her here. President Turi Aleid from Chad was a bastard. Not only had she wanted to take part in the scandal that would eventually take him down, she'd wanted to see the man fall. See his face when the president showed him the video and gave him the ultimatum—sign the treaty or all his enemies would get a copy, enabling them to destroy his credibility and political career and posh lifestyle. Political blackmail. This was how an evil leader falls, not with bombs, wars or sanctions, but with a simple sex tape. It was amazing how the enormous egos of powerful men could be their greatest weakness.

But when Aleid had charged out of the Oval Office that day, there had been a lot of confusion. Aleid had left through a different door and ran straight into Alana. He had recognized her immediately, spotted her ID badge and later tracked her down. He had known who she was and where she lived.

Again her cocky attitude had nearly gotten her into trouble. She had left her apartment early that day, unwilling to wait for an SS escort. They'd been watching her place and escorting her to and from work as a precaution. Alana had a very secure building. She had thought the FLC was overreacting. As she had strode across the parking lot, she had pressed her key fob to unlock her vehicle several car-lengths away. The explosion had knocked her to the ground. A security guard had held her down until police and an ambulance arrived.

She hadn't remembered much except red and blue flashing lights, sirens and smoke. She had awoken in the hospital with Beth checking her vitals. She'd been out a couple days and had a bandage around her head, face and arms.

"I should've died," Alana said, trying to push the nightmare of that day out of her head.

Zoe came over and put her arm across Alana's shoulder. "You can't predict what evil men will do."

Alana bit back angry tears. "No, you can't. But I really fucked up. Now I know what people feel like when their house burns down and they lose everything."

Zoe gave her a sad grin.

"What next?" Alana asked. Her words were cold and stiff. She hated being sharp with Zoe. Considering what she'd been through over the last twenty-four hours, she had little patience left.

"Do the best you can at training. You'll be given a new name, identity and appearance. This is why you have the barber on schedule today and why they did the plastic surgery. As of right now you are no longer Alana MacKenna. You will never speak that name again and no one will refer to you by that name."

"What's the new name?"

Jason walked into the shack with an Asian gentleman wearing a dogi and army jacket. He wasn't a large or tall man, but he had a presence and moved with power and grace. She guessed this man could mortally wound a man much larger and more intimidating. Kind eyes glimmered with intelligence far beyond the knowledge of an average man.

Zoe stood abruptly and tugged on Alana to do the same. By Zoe's formal stance, Alana assumed this man held some authority in her training. Now was the time to offer a good impression. Jason made the introduction. "This is Shen Li. He'll be giving instructions and also doing your meditation classes."

Shen Li stepped up to Alana and bowed slightly. "Ms. Carla Hillman, my pleasure. Are you ready to begin your first class?" His voice was soft, but authoritative.

"I'm sorry, sir, I'm Alana Mac—"

Zoe cleared her throat. Alana glanced over to her friend who gave her a warning look.

"Of course, Mr. Li," she said, sensing a tremor in her voice. She tried to smile, but gave up, knowing it would look forced. "I'm Carla Hillman. It's a pleasure to meet you. I look forward to working with you."

Carla heard Zoe let out a breath. "Hello, Mr. Li. We're ready for our first lesson."

After two hours of weight training and practicing the basic stances, kicks, blocks and punches, Carla was sore and exhausted. Mr. Li bowed to Carla and Zoe. "Lesson for today is over. I will see you, Carla, for meditation this afternoon. Do not be late."

Carla and Zoe bowed in return and thanked him. "I'll see you for the afternoon lesson."

After Mr. Li left, Carla and Zoe plopped down in a chair and Zoe handed her a sports supplement drink. "Why do security guards need meditation?" Carla laughed. She understood the importance of focus for martial arts training but formal meditation?

"Meditation has numerous benefits for soldiers and security agents. Heightened sensitivity and concentration, remaining calm in high stress situations, learning to control your emotions and facial expressions. With proper training, you can lie effectively, slow your pulse, breathing and lower blood pressure, beat a lie detector and many other things."

"I hadn't thought of that." She sipped her drink. "I could go for some coffee."

"Drink it all, and drink some water," Zoe ordered. "Jag will be here soon for your run."

"God, a run now? I don't think I could manage a walk around the compound." She leaned her head against the wall and closed her eyes. When she heard the door to the cabin open, she ignored it. Something was tossed into her lap.

She opened her eyes to see a heavy hoodie sweatshirt, a hat and gloves. "Put them on," Jag said. "It'll be easier to run in than your coat. Let's go so we can stay on schedule and be back in time for lunch. Greg is giving you a break. We're only doing a 5K instead of a 10K."

"A 5K!" Carla moaned.

"Don't let Greg hear you complain or he'll triple it."

Carla stood and put on the insulated sweatshirt. "Are you coming?" she asked Zoe.

"No, we're setting up the rifle range for after lunch. Have fun."

Jag helped Carla adjust her backpack outside the main lodge. "Why don't they have to run?"

"They're in better shape and will do runs with us when you can pick up your pace."

"And why do we need the pack? We're not going to be gone that long."

"You need to get used to carrying the weight. Your pack

has typical survival gear—food, water, poncho, clothing, sleeping bag, tools, rope, first aid kit, lighters, knife, weapon and ammo and other items. You'll learn how to pack it and always have it ready."

"It's heavy. How am I going to run in this?"

"If you were stuck somewhere without it, you'd be sorry," he noted. "Let's get going. You don't want to miss lunch. We're on a schedule."

Jag led her out onto the path and kept her at an easy pace to start. The brisk air burned his face, but he'd warm up quickly. He scanned the woods as in all directions. With the leaves down, he could see pretty far. There wouldn't be much cover for this exercise.

"It is beautiful up here, even though it's cold. It looks like it could snow." She puffed out her words, but she didn't seem winded yet.

"Always be aware of your surroundings, Carla." It would take a while getting used to calling her the new name. "Keep an eye out for movement, glance behind you occasionally. Don't make excess noise and avoid breaking branches. If there's a sign of danger, get off the path or take cover immediately. If you're being pursued or suspect you might be, avoid roads and trails, use your orienteering skills. We'll teach you that."

"What danger is out here?"

"From now on, you need to expect it. Become paranoid. Use your senses, smell, hearing, sight and your instinct. If the birds or animals suddenly take off in a certain direction other than the one you're in, maybe something spooked them. What could that be?"

"There goes my idea of a romantic stroll in the woods."

She teased, but he wondered if there was a hint of truth in it. The chemistry was there. He wasn't sure if either of them could resist the heat between them. If Greg realized there was something he might remove Jag as her handler and he didn't want that.

They had run barely ten minutes before Carla started breathing heavily, her shoulders drooped. "Can you slow down? I haven't done a run like this before. I always did light jogs on the treadmill at the gym."

"The first kilometer or two is the hardest, hang in there. Breathe in through your nose and out through your mouth."

Right now, running beside him, he couldn't take his eyes off her. She looked hot in the pair of sweats.

"Anything else I should watch for?" she asked between gasps of breath.

"Movement, color, shapes, smells, sounds, lack of animal sounds like birds or insects. Rocks and tree roots so you don't trip. Use all your senses. Be aware of your surroundings until it becomes instinct."

A cold breeze howled through the evergreen branches. It was a restless, haunting sound. The overcast sky was a silver gray and blocked the sun. Squirrels and chipmunks scurried over the dried leaves. He liked the peaceful silence up there. Peaceful, could be misleading. He'd learned that the hard way on several missions, watched men die. He would not let that happen again to his team or to Carla. She may hate him by the end of the program, but she would be prepared. Losing her respect and friendship was a risk he'd take if it would save her life. She had no idea what she was in for. What ripped him up inside was that he wasn't convinced he could protect her once she left.

Peering through the trees in all directions, he couldn't see much other than outlines of more mountains in the distance. No houses, buildings or farms. The trail climbed up a steep hill and halfway up, Carla begged Jag to slow to a walk. "I can't run, honest. I have to walk this hill."

He gave in. Wheezing in and out, she tried catching her breath. "Short break, but keep moving."

"Thanks. I could think of a more fun way to get exercise," she teased between her pants.

Jag stopped and glared at her. "We have to be careful that the others don't find out about us during your training or Greg is likely to assign you to another handler."

"Sorry. Just kidding."

He grabbed her arms and shoved her back up against a large maple tree. "We're alone up here though." Her gloved hands were pinned against the rough bark as Jag's mouth came down on hers hard.

"Oh, God," Carla said between breaths.

He kissed her again, plunging his tongue deep in an intoxicating long exploration of her mouth. He moaned and leaned back to look at her. "Keep your hands against the tree." An order. She easily complied.

"Yes, Sir."

He unzipped her hoodie and yanked up her shirt and bra top and admired her breasts. The cold air chilled her skin and nipples. His thumbs rubbed them roughly, and she arched her back begging for more. "Hmmm. I bet you're wet."

"Yes."

He slipped his hand down her sweats and tapped her clit to make it plump. Then he slid between her folds and moaned. "Yes, you are very." He shoved a finger inside her channel and Carla cried out.

"Jag." She gave a sweet sigh and rested her head back

against the tree.

"What did you call me?"

"I mean Sir. That's so wonderful."

"Better. But we don't have a lot of time for this. You have a schedule." He pulled his hand out of her pants and she groaned. Unable to resist, he sucked on each nipple until she gasped and begged for him to stop and take her. "I have a task for you." He pulled out a chain with nipple clamps.

"Now?" she asked.

"No, wear them at dinner. Not too tight. You'll have to wear a sweatshirt so they can't be seen. Remove them after the meal." He handed her the clamps.

"Okay." She stuffed them inside her pants pocket.

He then turned and ran up the trail. "Try to keep up. We don't have far to go. We're almost home."

Thinking about tightening the nipple clamps and how raw and sensitive she'd be instantly aroused her. She did have a high threshold of pain and if her Dom gradually worked her up to it, she could come with the stroke of a flogger between her legs.

Nipple clamps and flogger. Oh, Lord, she was getting hot. Jag slowed his pace and took her hand. "Okay, we'll take it easy on this last stretch so you can cool down."

"Good. I was about at my limit." Watching his tight ass as they jogged down the hill made her realize that focusing with him around would probably be her biggest challenge in this program. Her lungs and chest burned. She decided she hated running.

After about a mile, he checked his watch and stopped. "We're making good time. Let's stop so you can catch your breath and sprint the last stretch."

She leaned against a large tree and gulped in gallons of air. "That sounds like fun," she said with a sarcastic tone.

Tree bark splintered on a branch a few feet away with a *thud, thud*. An instant later, Carla heard the sound of high-powered rifle shots.

"Down." Jag whispered, shoving her flat at the base of the tree. "Oh my God. Who's out there? Have those guys found me?"

He pulled his gun out of his pack and loaded the clip. "Keep your ass down."

"I'll get my radio out of my pack." She lowered her voice to a whisper, but couldn't hide the hysteria in her tone. As she pressed her body into the dirt, she fought the urge to scream and run. "We have to warn the others."

"They heard the shot. I'll call them as soon as we have cover. Crawl on the ground but keep your head and ass down, use your legs like a bullfrog to move you. Watch me."

She was clumsy at first, but she caught on pretty quickly, except for the noise of kicking leaves and the humming. "Carla are you singing?" he whispered.

"Huh? Oh, I didn't realize. It's nothing."

"Don't hum and move quieter."

More shots were fired, a different gun. It sounded like a bigger one, but from the same direction. Carla covered her head and froze. "There are a couple of them. Can we hide somewhere?" she whispered.

"That's my plan."

She crawled behind him to a copse of mountain laurel, a dense tangle of underbrush that continued up the rest of the hill. They wouldn't be able to find them in there. Jag pulled out his handheld radio and pressed to call.

"Base camp, shots fired. Coming from the east side of the

facility."

"Jag, this is Jason. It must be our team at the firing range practicing."

"Then someone is practicing on us. We're on the north trail, several hundred yards above the range. Two shots just missed us by a couple feet."

"Jesus. I'll let them know. Maybe they thought you returned or a gun misfired? I'll check it out."

"Should we head back?" Carla asked.

"No, we wait until we hear confirmation from Jason."

His radio sounded again. "Jag?"

"Go ahead, Jason,"

"They were target practicing. They thought you were on the south trail, not the north one."

Jag swore. "Okay, we're coming back. Tell them to point their fucking guns at the fucking targets, not the fucking woods, goddammit."

"Copy that." Jason signed off.

"Do they usually shoot in the woods like that?" Carla asked.

"No, not unless we have a field exercise planned." He helped her stand. "Let's get back. We're running late now, and I want to clean up before lunch and give hell to the idiot with the gun."

"Can we walk back?" she asked. "I'm wiped out."

"No." He grabbed her arm so tightly it hurt. "You have to push yourself beyond what you think you can accomplish. They aren't going to waste time with someone who is slacking."

She pulled her arm out of his grip. "I understand this is important. I'll do my best."

He shook his head, his face firm and unyielding. "No, you

don't get it. This isn't pass-fail, Carla. There is only pass and consider the passing score to be ninety-eight."

She was unnerved by his attitude. Something within his tone of voice held an element that went well beyond the military regimentation. What if she didn't meet their standards? What if she did?

Chapter 7

When they got back to the lodge, the team was in the mess hut. "We're way behind schedule. Take a quick shower, change into the camouflage and boots and meet in the mess. You only have a few minutes to eat lunch before you have your session with Mr. Li."

She sighed. She would've loved to have indulged in a hot bath. "I'll be down in ten or less. I'm starved."

Ascending the stairs to her room took much effort. With each step, she had to force her muscles to move. She hoped she could stay awake during Mr. Li's meditation. *Right after lunch?* She was likely to fall asleep.

The mess hut had a rustic look with light pine paneling and thick tables and chairs, straight out of the seventies. She grabbed a tray and the cook handed her a healthy helping of stew, rolls, a slice of apple cake, milk and water. She grabbed an apple and handed back the apple cake. The extra calories, she didn't need. The cook looked insulted. "Watching my weight," she explained.

He laughed. "Right."

She sat down next to Zoe. "Better eat quick," Zoe said. She was already finished with her lunch. Greg walked by her table and glared down at her. "Your next session is in five minutes. How do you expect to be on time when you don't wear your watch? Always be prepared." He made a disgusted mashing of his mouth and walked away.

Glancing at her wrist, Carla realized she'd left her watch in her room. She'd taken it off to shower. She took large spoonfuls of the stew and drank most of the milk. But her stomach felt nauseated.

"I heard about the shots," Zoe said.

"Scared the crap out of me. Do you know who was shooting at us?"

Zoe nodded. "Beth." Beth was sitting next to Jag, hunched over a cup of coffee looking grief-stricken. "She was trying out new scopes on the rifles and focusing them at a various distances. She said she thought she heard Greg say you and Jag took the south trail, not the north. Greg's not too happy with her right now."

"We were lucky she didn't hit us." She ate a little more stew but lost her appetite. "What time is it?"

"One-oh-five."

"Crap. I'm late." Carla jumped up. "See you later at the firing range?"

"Yes, better make a run for it. Mr. Li doesn't like it if you're late."

❧☙

Carla walked into the small cabin used for yoga, exercising

and Mr. Li's meditation classes. The sounds of New Age music played softly in the background and the scent of eucalyptus and sage incense reminded her of a luxury spa. Yep, she was going to take a power nap during Mr. Li's meditation. The lights were low and it was taking her a minute for her eyes to adjust from being outside.

"Hello, Mr. Li. I'm sorry I'm a few minutes late. We got back late from—" A hand grabbed her wrist and a foot or shoulder hit her in her solar plexus. The wind was knocked out of her. While she gasped for breath, her feet left the floor and she spun around in the air and landed hard on her back.

She didn't move. She waited for the room to stop spinning and the silver motes from drifting across her vision.

"Good afternoon, Ms. Hillman. Don't be late for my class again."

She still didn't move. She was assessing the damage and hoped she didn't break anything. "Mr. Li, I will be on time from now on."

"Get up, Ms. Hillman."

Slowly, Carla got to her feet and the moment she did, Mr. Li's foot stabbed between her ankles and made a swift movement. She went down again. At least this time she didn't do a flip in the air.

"Not fast enough," he said. "Get up."

She jumped to her feet and stood at attention.

"Better. Now sit and relax. We'll get started. We have a lot to cover before I take you through a guided meditation."

Carla sat facing Mr. Li with her legs crossed, back of hands resting on her knees, mirroring his position and focusing her attention on him. She didn't need to be body slammed on the mat again for not following directions.

"There are many benefits of meditation, especially for

those who are training in military or security-type careers. It can enhance performance, concentration, build resilience and help with stress. Meditation helps to increase body awareness and alertness vital in combat situations."

She found that interesting even though she wasn't training to become a soldier, but she thought it better not to argue with Mr. Li. She had enough bruises for one day. Instead, she nodded.

"Now close your eyes and focus on your breathing. Taking a deep breath in…and out. And draw the air down into your abdomen. Keep breathing in through your nose, out through your mouth slowly. Calm your mind and allow the thoughts to drift away."

Sitting there listening to her instructor, she finally relaxed. Probably the first time since the explosion in DC.

"Imagine the earth's energy drawing up from the floor and entering your feet, healing any negative energy and pushing it out of your body. The joints of your toes and ankles expand and loosen so the chi energy from the earth can enter and energize you."

She focused on his words and tried to imagine as he said. Her feet felt tingly or numb from sitting.

"Continue the flow of energy up to your knees and allow the energy to enter the joints of your knees and then your hips, releasing any negative energy before moving upward up along your spine."

When his guided meditation reached her spine, she sat a little straighter and tried relaxing her muscles, which were stiff from the earlier run. She was so out of shape. She couldn't keep up during the run, felt like a klutz during the martial arts exercises and she was late to her meditation class. She had to find something she was good at. Jag hinted that the team and the FLC wouldn't tolerate her failing this program. What would they do to her? Kill her? They could, she knew that. Another member of the FLC had been assassinated a while ago when they discovered she'd planned to reveal the secret organization to the public. If they felt Carla was a threat, they could eliminate her too. She had to prove to them she was too valuable to lose.

"Ms. Hillman! You're losing focus."

She jumped out of her daydream. "Sorry, Mr. Li." *Please don't fall asleep*. She had to do something right today. And this was easy.

"Center. Let's continue. Draw the earth's energy throughout your body and out of the top of your head. Have that fountain of energy curve back down into the floor and back up through your feet, making a circle of energy. Keep the flow going."

She could see it and did feel more centered, if that was what he meant by centered.

"Then imagine another source of energy from the universe above you, entering at the top of your head and flowing down through you, filling every space and exiting out of your feet into the earth. Once it reaches the earth it too will curve upward and flow back into the top of your head so you have two fountains of energy flowing in different directions."

His voice drifted off and her body was floating on a calm sea. The sun was warm on her face and the air fresh. Every muscle in her body released any tension. She didn't know where she was, but she welcomed the peace and wanted to stay for a—

Something kicked her foot. A fish? Something kicked her harder. She blinked and opened her eyes. "Wake up, Ms. Hillman."

She opened her eyes wide when she realized she'd fallen asleep. "I'm so sorry, Mr. Li. I must have drifted off during the meditation."

"That happens sometimes when you first begin. Keep practicing this meditation like I showed you and you'll go into a deep relaxation without falling asleep."

"Thank you. I enjoyed that."

"You may go. I believe it's time for your training at the rifle range."

Checking her wrist, she groaned and realized she'd never went back for her watch after her shower. She stood up and bowed to Mr. Li. "Thank you."

ॐ

She raced back to her room and grabbed her watch, then passed Jag on the way to the rifle range. Her ankle was a little sore from how Mr. Li body slammed her to the mat. Jag notice the limp. "That from our run, or Mr. Li?"

"Mr. Li."

He chuckled. "I told you he doesn't like it when we're late."

"I got that now."

"Zoe and Jason will work with you at the range. It takes time to learn all the weapons. Don't expect to be an expert on the first day. It'll take weeks. I'll stop by later."

"Thanks. That takes some weight off."

He walked her to the range, then left. Zoe stood at a high bench, shooting a pistol at a target across the field. Jason handed Carla a pair of safety glasses and ear protectors. "Zoe will start you off today. Jag or Greg will come by later for the heavier stuff."

After Zoe finished her round, she checked that the gun was unloaded and placed it on the table. She stepped away from the table and took off her glasses and ear protectors. "Hi, Carla, how'd your session go with Li?" She frowned. "You look upset. What's wrong?"

Carla glanced around to make sure no one was close by to hear her. "Zoe. I'm scared to death. I'm failing miserably, and I still have computer skills and foreign languages to learn. I'm not cut out for this."

Zoe gave her a sympathetic smile. "I'm sure you're exaggerating. It's your first day. Give it time."

"No, really. I'm awful. I couldn't keep up during my five-mile run."

"Jag said you only did 5K."

Carla groaned. "Then it's worse. I'm so out of shape I couldn't do the five miles. I couldn't do the moves during the martial arts class, I was late for Mr. Li's meditation class, and I fell asleep. Jag says if I don't ace this program, they won't have any use for me. He's hinted I'll end up in a body bag like what happened to Celia Aldridge."

Zoe put an arm around Carla's shoulder. "That was different. Celia had planned to expose the FLC to two major newspapers. Your situation was a mistake, not intentional. You're valuable and the FLC wouldn't go to this much trouble to eliminate you. This isn't the mob."

Carla let out a long breath but she didn't feel completely at ease. "I still need to do great at something. Can you help me?"

"You'll get better at all of this. You can't expect to run a marathon in only one day or become a black belt in a week. Have you shot a gun before?"

"Yes, lots of times. My dad and grandfather were hunters. At my grandfather's property in upstate New York I learned how to shoot a variety of guns."

"Good, then you're ahead of the game. We'll start small and work our way up. Put on your protective gear and let's get started."

After a few hours, Jag and Greg arrived. Carla had an M-16A2 assault rifle and she'd been shooting at a paper target three-hundred meters out. Her shoulder ached from the recoil from the various rifles, but this was one lesson she enjoyed. Maybe she was taking out her frustrations.

"How's she doing?" Greg asked when he approached the range. Carla cringed at his stern expression and tone. She guessed he suspected she had done lousy at this too.

"She's doing great," Zoe said.

Carla wanted to hug her friend for the support. Jag had his usual calm demeanor. She had no idea if he was pleased or not. More than anything she wanted him to be proud of her. If that was possible.

"Show me," Greg ordered, nodding toward the M-16. "Take a few rounds at the three-hundred-meter target. He and Jag put on ear protectors. Carla donned her protective gear and picked up the rifle. She aimed and noticed the wind hadn't changed from earlier so she wouldn't have to make angle corrections. She took six shots and placed the gun down.

Without a word, Greg picked up the field glasses and checked her targets. His eyebrows rose. "Now the five-hundred target."

She took another six shots and Greg checked again. This time she saw a slight twitch of a smile. "Have you shot guns before, Carla?"

"Yes, sir. At my grandfather's farm. They were hunters and collectors and we would target shoot as kids."

He nodded. "Has she tried the M-24 or the Minimi yet?"

Zoe had showed her the various weapons and allowed her

to shoot each one. The Minimi was a M-249 Squad Automatic Weapon or SAW used as a sniper weapon and so was the M-24.

"She's taken shots with all of the weapons, but she needs more practice. There's a lot she has to learn."

"No problem," Greg said as he examined the weapons. "There's a great deal to learn. I want Carla to double her sessions each day at the range. You're doing well, Carla. Keep it up."

"Thank you," Carla said. A compliment from Greg meant a lot. She doubted he was generous with praise.

Fortunately, she had time to run back and get her watch, so he wouldn't yell at her for being late for her next meeting on the schedule, which was a haircut. She didn't want to think about that. She doubted there would be a highly skilled hair stylist here. They were going to butcher her hair.

Greg picked up the Minimi, loaded it and placed it on the table. "Here, Carla. Try this one. It's loaded and ready to be fired. Zoe can show you how to load it later. I want to see how you shoot. Pick the target at a thousand meters."

"I've not tried one that far yet."

"That's okay. I'm not grading you." He demonstrated the safe operation and components of the gun, then handed it to her. "Give it a try, but take your time."

She leaned on the bench and took an estimate for wind-speed angle correction and peered through the scope. Taking a breath, she held it, then let it out and squeezed. The shot fired and echoed through the range. Anxiously, she waited for Greg's word as he looked through the binoculars.

"Try again. You were slightly off to the left. Small correction." His tone was even and professional, not accusatory.

Carla took another shot and she could see through the scope that she hit within the target.

Greg whistled. "Nice. Another twenty minutes practice and you're done for the day."

Checking her watch, Carla noticed her appointment was in five. "Greg, my appointment with the barber is in five minutes."

Greg smiled. "I'll tell Todd you're going to be a few minutes late."

Chapter 8

In a small room in the main lodge, Todd Jacobs, the barber, stood at a sink, squirting creams into a bowl. He looked to be about Greg's age, early forties, had a military cut and wore camouflage and combat boots. He was tall and lean, not as muscle-bound as the other men on the team, but strong like a marathon runner. He had kind eyes and chocolate-brown skin. Large hands held a bowl where he mixed her hair-color solution. His rolled-up shirt sleeves revealed large, taut muscles.

His demeanor fit more with someone who handled a M-24 sniper weapon, not a hairdryer. This was not going to be a good cut. "Todd? I'm Carla."

Pointing to a chair, he smiled. "Have a seat, Carla, I'm ready for you."

"Please tell me you're not going to give me a buzz cut."

Todd laughed. He had a nice, hardy laugh. Finally, someone with a sense of humor in this place. "No, it'll be shorter and we're changing the color. No more red. I understand we need to go for a new look." The *new* was emphasized and she got the meaning.

"But I love my red hair." She didn't explain she already had a new look that started with the plastic surgery. Had he noticed the healing scars?

"Don't worry. You'll have a stylish cut. I was trained in New York City and I give more than military cuts. We're going to make you a brunette. I chose a color to complement your green eyes."

"Why brown? Why not blonde? Just asking. Not too short. I like it long."

"The color was chosen for security. As a brunette you'll blend in when you go overseas in the Middle East. Same for the cut."

"Overseas? No one said I was going overseas."

Todd shrugged. "In your job, anything is possible."

"It seems strange that they would have a barber on this security team."

He laughed. "I am a regular member of the Eagle Guards. I don't just cut hair." He didn't sound offended. "We couldn't exactly bring in a barber from outside to this top secret facility. And I've used my talents during a few rescue missions."

This time Carla was curious. "How does that work? A makeover during a military rescue?"

His expression turned grim. "A few years ago, we were hired by a private construction business in Cairo to safely escort the CEO, his wife and son out of the country. They were friends of the Egyptian president and when he was forcibly removed from office and replaced by a military leader, the CEO decided it was time for him and his family to leave. Since friends and associates were considered potential threats to the new regime, the new ruler executed many of them in the streets. We decided the CEO and his family needed disguises and new identities. I did a damn good job in changing their appearances. They passed through several check points and safely crossed the border."

Before Todd started, he turned her back to the mirror on the wall. That made her nervous. Todd chopped off the length of her hair then applied the color. She was used to paying two to three hundred dollars at a stylist in DC for a trim and deep condition. After he washed out the color, he moved on to the final cut. Carla felt her body tighten.

Strands of her hair drifted to the floor with each snip of the scissors. When he took an electric razor to the back of her neck, she had to bite back tears. *Control your emotions*, Jag had said. Todd was following orders.

While he snipped, he talked about his six-year-old son and wife who lived a few hours away. Carla barely registered his words. All she could think of was watching the bits of her identity tumbling in shreds onto the floor.

She swallowed the lump in her throat before attempting to speak. "Sounds like you miss your family."

He let out a breath. "I do. But I enjoy my work too. It's important."

"How long have you and the team been working together?"

"About five years."

She tried not to cringe with each snip of the scissor. "What did you all do before?"

"We're all from various military branches, except for Mr. Li."

"And what did he do?"

Todd laughed. "No one knows for sure. We think NSA. I wouldn't ask him though."

"That's probably a good plan," she agreed.

After he finished the blow-drying, he spun her around in the chair to face the mirror. "All done. What do you think?"

Carla gasped. It was short. Really short and she hated it. What she hated the most was that she didn't recognize herself at all. All traces of Alana were now gone. Tears welled up in her eyes.

She was truly dead.

Strong hands squeezed her arms. "Hey, hey, I know it's a big change. Give it time, hon. It's necessary and it'll grow on you."

She dragged herself out of the chair. "It's not that. It's a nice cut. I can't... It's been a long day. It'll take time to get used to the change, like you said. Thank you, Todd."

Carla ran back to her room, hoping she wouldn't meet anyone along the way. She closed her door and let the tears fall. Hide her emotions? She was doing a lousy job at that as the sobs shook her body. She didn't know who she was or what she was becoming.

A knock at the door jolted her. Crap, couldn't she get five minutes of misery to herself? "Yes," she called out weakly.

"Open up, it's Jag."

Jag wasn't sure what rattled him more, seeing her red eyes from crying or the big change in her appearance. He hardly recognized her. But her hair and color looked good. "Wow, it's different."

That set her off. She burst into tears. *Crap.* He walked in and closed the door.

"I hate it. They took everything from me and now the one feature I loved most, my hair."

"I think it looks sassy."

She shot him a steely look. "Not helping."

He drew her into his arms. "There are reasons for all of this. I'm here to help you."

"I know. I'm trying."

"At the rifle range you looked pleased with yourself," he said. He meant it as a compliment and hoped she took it that way.

"I am. I finally managed to find something I could do well. Even Greg seemed impressed, I think."

"He was. This is a training facility. Which means you train. Don't be hard on yourself, but don't make excuses. One thing you do need to learn is to guard your emotions and your responses."

"You mean not lose my temper?"

He grunted. "Much more than that. You're eyes are very expressive. As a Dom, that would be very helpful to me in our sessions, but if you're in a hostile situation, your expressions could give you away. Panicking or staying cool could determine whether you live or die."

"I think I understand why everyone here has a cold attitude, steely eyed stare all the time. How do you learn to do that?"

"Control and awareness. I'll help you with that. Tonight, after your language classes, I want you to meet me in that small storage hut at the end of the compound." He pointed out her window to a building that looked more like a rundown shack. "It's not used much. I'll begin teaching you how to control your emotions under stress."

"What are you going to do?"

"You'll see. Be there at nine-fifteen sharp. My punishments are severe if you're late."

She smiled, finally, then stiffened, looked up at him and frowned. "What happens when I'm finished with this program?"

"You can't go back to the FLC as Alana. When you do go back, no one but Zoe, Jason, Julia and the first lady will know who you are."

"Don't they trust the other members of the FLC?" she asked.

"You should trust no one. The fewer people who know, the less risk of your enemy finding out."

She pulled away from him and sat down on the bed, crossing her arms over her chest. "Todd said my hair color and cut were selected because I would blend in if I had missions overseas or the Middle East. No one said anything about me working overseas. I thought I'd be working inside…the White House."

"I know about the Red Tape Room. We've been called in on standby for added security on occasion. We assisted during Zoe's abduction. We had our contacts and team set up to retrieve her if needed. Some of your assignments could take you overseas."

"Julia said I'd be working security now. I figured it was because my scars would not be appealing to a target for a sex scandal."

Jag sat next to her. "No, it has nothing to do with your injuries."

"I still think there is something you and the others aren't telling me."

Jag gazed out the window. It was dark. Nighttime came early this far north in the middle of winter. The weather report called for snow. He hoped they had their supplies in. "Carla, you've had one day here. Training is scheduled for a reason to prepare you physically and mentally. Any mission they may have planned for you will be given to you when you're ready for it and no sooner."

She let out a frustrated huff. "I just like to know things ahead of time so I can prepare."

"During a mission, shit happens, Murphy's Law applies, and you can't always be prepared. So you have to expect the unexpected and deal with it without hesitation. Your life could depend on it."

She nodded, but he didn't know if she truly agreed, or was tired of arguing.

"Dinner is at six. That's in ten minutes."

"Okay. I'll be there."

"And after your language classes?"

She didn't answer right away.

"Don't think too far ahead," he warned. "You won't be sent on any missions unless you're fully trained and prepared."

She sighed. "Okay. After my class, I'll meet you at the storage shed."

☙❧

In the mess hall, Beth and Zoe sat with her during dinner. Carla barely contributed to the conversation. Her mind and body were exhausted. How was she going to concentrate or remember anything at her language classes? Jag kept glancing at her from a couple tables away. Didn't he say they were supposed to be discreet? She gave him a polite smile and finished eating the bland chicken dinner. She'd excused herself early so she could shower and change before her classes. Then she'd go to meet with Jag.

A jolt of reality slammed into her. She'd forgotten! Her

hand slipped inside her pocket and felt the chain of the nipple clamps. She had forgotten to put on the clamps as he had instructed. That's why he was looking at her, to get acknowledgement that she'd completed his task. Maybe he'd forgotten too?

While he was talking with Nick and Todd, Carla got up from the table, cleared her tray of food and ran upstairs to her room.

෫ාඥ

Walking across the compound, Carla felt her boots crunch on the frozen ground. The temperature dropped during the afternoon and the air chilled her throat with each breath. How were they going to run in this weather? And what if it snowed? If her assassins didn't discover she was still alive, this program would surely kill her in a few weeks.

At nine-fifteen she entered the storage shed. The glow of a lantern flickered through the small one-room building. On one side, a fire burned in a potbelly stove, warming the shack to a comfortable temperature, almost too warm. Boxes and crates were stacked along the walls and in the center of the room. "Jag?"

"Over here," he called out from the other side of a tall stack of wooden crates that came well over Carla's head. In a pair of jeans and a tight T-shirt, he stood next to an open duffle bag that appeared to have a variety of bondage supplies—ropes, a flogger, a vibrator and bottle of what she assumed was lube and also a towel. What was stuffed farther inside, she couldn't tell.

"Do you always carry that stuff with you?"

He grinned. "I keep it in the back of my Jeep." He lead her behind the wall of crates and she gasped. A set of pulleys, ropes and chains were hung from hooks in the ceiling in an elaborate BDSM restraining device.

"Wow. How long did it take you to do all this and how do you hide it?"

"Most of it has been here. It's used to haul the heavy boxes around. I just improvised a bit and brought my own toys." He pointed to the duffle bag.

"I think I'll like this kind of training the best." She walked up to him and waited for his first command.

"You remember you safewords from before? Red, yellow and green?"

"Yes, Sir."

"Good, then first of all, you're wearing way too many clothes for this session. Take everything off to your underwear, then stand with your legs apart and your hands clasped behind your back. There's a chair for you to put your things."

Carla's body instantly heated with his command and her pussy throbbed. How quickly she responded to him. She relaxed. Maybe he did forget about dinner. The clamps were in her jacket pocket. "No pretty lacy undies, I'm afraid," she said, not able to look at him for the moment.

"You're still beautiful, although I do prefer the lacy undies. Did you complete my task at dinner?"

Crap. She groaned to herself. "I completely forgot."

"Where are they?"

"In my jacket pocket."

"Get them. Then kiss me right here, a simple task." He touched his cheek. "There will be a mild punishment for not following instructions."

Her bare toes curled against the hardwood floor. The anticipation of what would come made her impatient and horny. She handed him the nipple clamps, then kissed him where he had pointed. Her body shivered, but she wasn't cold.

"Are you warm enough?" His hands rubbed her arms.

"Yes, Sir. It's quite nice in here." Glancing around the shack, she tried to imagine they were at a dungeon like Paradise Underground, not at a secret military compound.

He snorted. "Not the ideal place, but we have to be discreet. Not sure how Greg would feel about your handler being intimately involved with you."

"It's fine."

He pulled her into his arms and kissed her slow and deeply, making her knees wobble. She soaked in the warmth and strength of his body, welcoming the security of it. But how secure and safe was she?

Lifting her chin, he focused on her face. "I see worry in your eyes. I need to know what's going through your mind before we go any further."

She shook her head, unable to put into words all that she was feeling.

His fingers gently stroked her cheek. "Carla, I understand you're concerned about the program. You're doing fine. We'll work through any difficulties. You can trust me."

"I thought you said to trust no one."

He took a deep breath and let it out. "Always expect the unexpected. In any operation, there are potential threats or traitors. But you can trust me out there and in here. That I promise. My job is to help you and protect you, and I'll do everything in my power to do that."

She relaxed. "Okay. I trust you. But trust works both ways. You have to trust me too."

"How do you mean?"

"I nearly betrayed the FLC before, and I know I tried sneaking out on you before at the hospital. It won't happen again. I wouldn't betray the Eagle Guards or you."

"I believe you. Don't give me a reason to break that trust."

Her mind was still tumbling over a few unsettling things about the program, but she didn't know if now was the time to bring it up.

"What else?" he said. "You have more concerns."

She studied his face. "My gut tells me they have something in mind for me other than the FLC."

He didn't answer right away, not denying or agreeing. "As far as I know you're being trained for the FLC security team. For anything beyond that, nothing is set in stone. When you're in this line of work, you won't know until you're ready to know. Does that make sense?"

"I suppose." She let it drop for now.

"I have to follow orders as do you. Some information I'm not allowed to share."

"That I do understand."

"Good. Now we put that out of our minds." He smiled. "We don't have much time and I want to make the best of it." He hooked his fingers in her bra straps and slid them down over her shoulders, exposing her breasts.

"How much time?"

"You let me worry about that." His gaze ran up and down her body, and his thumbs rubbed over her nipples. They tightened from his touch and she lifted them, wanting more of his caresses. "You have an amazing body."

"Thank you, Sir. I'd like to lose a few pounds."

He laughed. "I disagree, but you will during this program. Now remove your bra and panties, but do it slowly."

She resisted the frenzied urge to rip the thin strips of clothing standing between her and Jag. The fierce need in his eyes told her that he too struggled with restrained passions.

She continued with her deliberate striptease and dropped the undergarments on the floor.

"Step over to the restraints."

She glanced at the door.

"The only words that should leave your mouth are, 'Yes, Sir,' or your safewords or pleasure words. I take care of everything else. The door is secure. Don't make me ask twice."

She smiled and her body ignited with his firmness. She did feel self-conscious, but also turned-on. The idea of someone giving her commands designed to please her was such a joy compared to all the commands she'd received all day. "With pleasure, Sir."

She walked to the center of the space where the pulleys and ropes hung. Methodically, he tied her wrists and extended her arms over her head, then tied ropes around her ankles and spread her legs wide. Anyone could walk into the shack if he hadn't locked the door, and she didn't remember him locking it. She felt exposed and vulnerable. Her cheeks flushed and her pussy was wet.

"How do you feel? The ropes aren't too tight?"

"No, Sir. They're fine." She glanced at the door.

"Don't look at that door again, or I'll have to give you a severe punishment. Eyes on me."

"Yes, Sir."

His hand explored her body from her shoulders, cupping her breasts, over her abdomen and hips, then her ass, thighs and calves. When he slid his hand back up, he stroked her pussy and tapped her clit.

Carla jumped from the intense stimulation. "Ah, sensitive and aroused already. Nice." He removed his clothes and she couldn't take her eyes off how amazing he looked. Muscular and toned arms and legs, broad chest, and the tightest ass. His cock was hard and fully aroused. Seeing him in the lantern light made her insides all shivery. "I don't want you to look anywhere but at me."

She grinned. "That won't be hard, Sir."

He smacked her behind. "Cute." From his duffle bag, he retrieved a flogger. He made a few swings and snapped the air, all the while watching her expression.

She loved the flogger. To her it was like an intense massage that awakened all her nerve endings and at the same time relaxed the tension out of her muscles.

"You're smiling. I assume you like this?"

"Yes, Sir."

"Good." He smacked her on her ass with the thongs. The sting radiated through her, followed by warmth. He continued with light hits and harder hits and her body swayed to the rhythm. After a time, he struck her breasts then between her legs.

She moaned and her body quivered from the smoldering pain and searing pleasure. God, he was good. All the worry drained from her. No longer was she restrained, but floating. Every inch of her body tingled and her cunt clenched, aching to be filled by his cock. "Sir?"

"You okay?"

"Oh, yes, Sir."

He put down the flogger. Carla sighed in relief then sucked in a breath when he clamped his mouth over her nipple and tugged. He repeated the same to the other. Glancing up at her, he looked her in the eye and released her nipple. "Don't move and don't make a sound for the next several minutes."

He ran the tip of his tongue around her nipples and Carla stiffened and drew her hands into fists to keep from arching into his mouth or to moan as her pleasure heightened. Slowly, his fingers reached her clit and circled the swollen bud in the same rhythm as he was doing with his mouth.

Dipping his finger inside her channel, he spread her wetness over her folds. Not moving her hips was torture. Carla stared straight out a small window in the back of the shack. Snow had started to fall and moonlight streamed through bare tree branches. Even with his light touch, she was so hot and turned-on right now, she could probably come anyway. Testing the strength of the ropes around her wrists and ankles that held her in an X position, she found she had less than a couple inches to play with. The unyielding, lack of control was what she liked about bondage. As she stared through the dark trees. A shadow moved, or was it her imagination? If someone was out there, could he see inside?

"Relax, you're tensing up."

"I'm okay. I thought I saw someone walking out there." She took a breath and let it out.

"Focus on me, or I'll have to blindfold you. Even if someone was outside, they would have no reason to come here."

"Yes, Sir." She couldn't help but worry that someone might find them. Then he moved his mouth lower and used his tongue to brush over her ultra-sensitive clit. Now, he did have all her attention. *Don't move.* How was she supposed to remain still when every flick of his tongue increased the need to writhe beneath his touch?

With one hand he spread her folds, and with the other he stroked the hood of her clit, barely touching where she needed the stimulation the most. A tad lower and she'd be in ecstasy. She lifted her hips the slightest bit to help him find that perfect spot, and he slapped her ass. "You moved."

"Sorry, Sir."

He stopped the scorching seduction and stood, leaving her dissatisfied and horny. A wave a dread spread through her as he untied her wrists and ankles. "Are we done?"

He smiled. "Not yet." Taking a thick sleeping bag out of his duffle, he spread it onto the floor. "Kneel. Since you can't focus on your pleasure, perhaps you can focus on mine. Suck my cock. Don't use your hands. Keep them behind your back."

The command was meant as a task, a little punishment for her inability to stay focused, but the punishment was a joy. Pleasuring him was something she had been fantasizing about. "Yes, Sir." She got onto her knees, hands behind her back, and leaned forward, taking his cock in her mouth. He was thick and large and she took as much as she could. Gliding up and down, she felt him get even harder.

"You're very good at that." He voice was labored as he thrust his hips and guided his shaft into her mouth. He groaned. "We're going to have to stop."

She leaned back and looked up at him, wondering what she had done wrong this time. Laughing, he scooped her up in his arms and laid her on the sleeping bag. "You did nothing wrong, pet. I don't want to come quite yet."

Relieved, she wrapped her arms around his neck and enjoyed the feel of his body as he lowered his weight onto her. Even though her muscles were sore from the day's workout, every touch was glorious. This program would be so much more tolerable if they dared to share some moments like this.

"Imagine that I have you restrained." He spread her arms and legs apart in an X again.

"Don't move?" she asked a little playfully.

"That's right. And keep your eyes closed. I'm going to fuck you. This time I do have condoms."

"A well-equipped storage shed, Sir."

"Indeed." She heard a wrapper tear, but the delicious torture was not knowing where he would touch her or when he would fuck her. The erotic mystery intoxicated her.

Something brushed over her breasts and she realized it was the thongs of the flogger. Her nipples tightened and elongated. The nerve endings, raw and sensitive, ignited as the first strike nailed her. She arched as heat radiated and pain throbbed from her peaks and across the mounds. "Be still."

This time, a smaller flogger whipped between her legs, the thin suede tassels evoked intense pain followed by a surge of pleasure. Her body shook, but she had to bite her lip to keep from rocking and raising her hips. Yes, she could come if he kept this up, but it wasn't her place to ask him. He had complete control of her pleasure—where, when and how. Part of the excitement was not knowing.

"When we're in here, I take control. Out there is a different story. Although, you must follow orders of the FLC and the Eagle Guard's commander." He put down the flogger and glided his hand over her heated skin.

"Yes, Sir."

"You want me to keep going?" he asked. The lust and desire in his voice made her heart soar.

"Please, Sir. I want you inside me."

"Would you prefer a different place? A nicer room, with a bed?"

"No, this is perfect. Any place you decide." His fingers teased between her legs. She was so wet, so achy. If he stopped now, she'd scream.

"I can't guarantee how often we'll have together." His finger slid inside, only a little ways. Had he given her permission to move yet?

"I understand, Sir." The walls of her cunt tightened

around his finger. "Am I allowed to move now?"

"Yes," His finger slipped out of her and he shifted his position. "Try to keep your voice down." He eased between her legs, and with little warning, he pushed mercilessly deep inside her, lifting her ass off the floor.

Biting her lip was the only thing that kept her from crying out and being heard across the compound. Arms and legs wrapped around his body. And she angled and rocked her body to meet each thrust. The hardness of the floor, allowed him to drive into her deeper.

When she came, she let out a groan louder than expected.

Chapter 9

When his sweet sub offered him her release, he thrust deeper and changed the angle, knowing he'd increase the pressure on her clit and G-spot. Carla's groans intensified and her cunt tightened around his cock. The masterful attention to his dick was enough to set him over the edge. His orgasm slammed into him hard. The release was heady and drained everything out of him. Afterward, he collapsed beside her and pulled her into his arms.

Stroking her hair, he kissed her mouth and the top of her head. She curled into his chest and sighed contently, his sweet, beautiful sub. "Look at me," he ordered softly.

She gazed up into his eyes, her cheeks flushed and glowing, her expression without worry, and only a little dazed. Not too subspacy. "This was very nice," she said. "I enjoyed it."

"Hmmm. I got that impression." His fingers drew lazy circles over her hip and up to her breasts. It was hard not to keep looking at her.

"Feels good." He noticed her expression change as her thoughts drifted far away. Then she frowned.

"What up, sugar?"

"Will there be a problem if the team finds out about us?"

He let out a long breath. "There are men and women in the Eagle Guard team. We work close together in highly stressful situations. Sometimes the friendships become intimate, but we know we have a job to do and sex doesn't get in the way. They may frown on an intimate relationship with a new trainee, so best we keep it quiet."

"That makes sense." Carla got up, grabbed her clothes and started dressing. "How long is this program?"

He didn't answer right away. "Usually six to eight months. It depends."

"Six to eight months?"

Someone knocked at the door. Carla froze and her eyes went wide. Jag quickly slipped on his pants and boots. He didn't answer, but stuffed the ropes, flogger and sleeping bag into his duffle.

The knock sounded again. "Jag? You in there? It's Beth. I thought I saw you and Carla go in a while ago. Hate to interrupt, but Greg's looking for you."

ഇരുബ

Jag left Beth and Carla in the storage shed. He handed the duffle to Carla to bring back to her room. Fortunately, he didn't have to worry about Beth. She hadn't been surprised about the not-so-secret romance going on. She said she picked up on the chemistry the moment he met Carla at the hospital. "Not to worry," Beth said, "Carla needs all the support she can

111

get. Just keep it private."

Greg was waiting in his office in the lodge when Jag got back. He was on the phone to someone official by the formal tone of his voice. When he hung up, he pointed to a chair. "Have a seat."

"Beth said you wanted to see me."

"I just got off the phone with the White House. The FLC is pressuring us to finish Carla's training early."

"Her training was supposed to be six months, minimum."

"We don't have six months. More like six to eight weeks."

"Weeks? That's impossible," Jag said. "She's not close to the physical shape she needs to be in, and she has to learn a few languages."

"We'll have to do what we can in the time frame we have. You'll be in DC as her backup. The FLC has a project planned for her in a few months. After the project, we can continue her training."

"Are they planning a sex scandal in the Red Tape Room?" Jag asked. The idea of her blackmailing some foreign diplomat—his sweet sub—unnerved him.

"No, she won't be doing that. This will be something completely different."

"Dangerous?"

Greg stared at him. "Anything involved with the FLC and the Eagle Guard is. When she's called, you'll be with her, but you won't know the details until they're ready to implement this program."

"I understand." Jag didn't have a guess as to what they wanted Carla to do, but he suspected it wouldn't be an easy job. "What do you want me to do now?"

"Train her hard."

∞⌘

Weeks had gone by during her training with the Eagle Guards. Carla stepped out of the shower and stood in front of the mirror. She liked what she saw. Never had her body been in this shape. She had muscles she didn't know existed, and tight, flat abs. She could swear she had start of a six-pack. Even eating double what she normally ate, she had lost a ton of weight. She was running ten to fifteen miles a day, sometimes twice a day and she didn't feel winded as she had during the first couple weeks.

Besides the muscles and a thinner Carla, she was kicking butt in the martial arts class. Mr. Li wasn't beating her up anymore. She was nailing the kicks and punches without losing her balance. A slight smile or quiet nod from him was like a gold star. He was teaching her to read peoples' expressions, their tone of voice to get an idea as to whether someone was lying, crazy or dangerous. She had acquired a heightened level of awareness, almost a sixth sense.

Jag and the team had kicked her butt into shape. She felt more than ready to deal with any unruly men who hassled the members of the FLC during their presentations in the Red Tape Room. Tonight she was going to ask Greg if she could contact Julia about returning to DC.

She quickly dressed in her fleece-lined running gear and insulated boots. There was still snow on the ground, and depending on Jag's or Greg's mood, they could do a run, cross-country ski or venture out in snowshoes. Several times they'd taken her to the mountains for rappelling lessons. Rappelling was cool. Whatever they had planned, she was going to burn a ton of calories and she wanted to get in plenty of carbs this morning.

Three knocks at the door. Jag. She knew his knock. "Come on in, Jag." He opened the door and had a stern expression with a deep frown. Usually his eyes brightened whenever they were going out for their morning run. Whether or not they were alone or with the team, he loved the outdoor workout despite the freezing temperatures.

"We're skipping the run this morning," he said and didn't seem happy about it. "Dress warm though, we have a long drive."

"Where are we going?"

"You'll see when we get there."

"Do I need any special gear?"

He shook his head. "Supplies will be provided. We'll be back by lunch. Put your coat on, you have a short assignment before breakfast."

As they walked out of the lodge, the blue sky broke through the steel-gray clouds and Carla breathed in the cold air, detecting a hint of spring even though it was still February. He led her toward the rifle range. The door to the shack was open, but she didn't see anyone or hear any shots. "We're going to do some target practice before breakfast?" she asked. One thing the Eagle Guards were known for was a strict, consistent schedule. A run, then martial-arts training in the morning, meditation and weapons training and or target practice in the afternoon with weight training or other exercising, followed by language lessons, computer and other research and field training in the evenings. This was off schedule and she couldn't help but feel out of sorts.

"Not target practice as you're used to," he said in a quiet tone. When they reached the shack, they walked around the back and found Greg, Nick and Todd standing beside a white-tail deer with a four-point antler rack.

"Oh, how cute," Carla exclaimed, smiling. Then she noticed he was tied between two trees. She stopped smiling.

"What's going on?"

"Jag said you used to target shoot with your dad and grandfather. They were hunters," Greg said.

"Yes." Heat spread over her body, an adrenalin rush, she could taste it in her mouth. Whatever this was, it wasn't good, by their posture and attitude. One thing she had learned in her evening lessons on how to read people.

"Did you ever hunt with them?" Todd asked softly. The deer tugged in its binds and Carla resisted the urge to untie him and let him go.

"No." *Don't offer more information unless they ask.*

Greg retrieved a Sig Sauer P229 pistol, pulled back the slide and held out the gun to her. "It's loaded. Shoot him. Double tap will be the quickest."

Carla gasped and took two steps back, not taking the gun.

"Hold this for her, Jag." Greg handed the gun to Jag and strode into the shack. A moment later he came out with a baseball bat.

At first Carla thought he was going to threaten her with it. "We keep this for the snakes in the summer. But if you prefer to watch me beat this creature to death." He raised the bat.

"Stop!" Carla cried out, rushing up to take away the bat.

"Pick your weapon of choice," Greg said. "Either way you're taking this animal down."

"Why?"

"You don't need to know why," he said. "If it's an order, then there's a good reason."

Glancing at Jag, she looked to him for guidance or help. He held the pistol out to her. No way out. At that moment she hated him, hated all of them. Jag was right when he had said trust no one. Why hadn't he warned her?

With a shaky hand, she grasped the gun, then held it in

two hands toward the poor creature and followed orders.

"Is that all?" she asked between clenched teeth, handing the gun back to Jag.

"Yes, for now," Greg said. "Breakfast, then we head out. The cook will be pleased to add venison to the menu."

Carla had no appetite for venison.

Nausea rolled through her stomach. Todd and Nick stayed behind with the deer as Greg and Jag walked her back to the lodge. Greg still had the baseball bat, which unnerved her. Why hadn't he put it back inside the shack? When they got to the lodge, she noticed two SUVs parked in front. Greg walked up to one and tossed the bat inside. Jason placed a large cooler in the other one.

Fortunately, her training had taught her to rein in her emotions. Otherwise, she probably would be crying.

No one at breakfast said more than a handful of words to her, even Zoe. They'd heard the two shots. They knew. At least Carla figured they did. Was this an initiation of sorts? Did they all have to go through this? Beth sat next to her and patted her arm. "We've all been there."

Todd sat across from her and gave a short nod. Oddly, she felt a part of the team now. One of them, an equal. But since she had months to go yet in the program, she suspected these sort of initiations would only get worse.

⊱⊰

After breakfast, she followed Jag outside to the SUV. Greg and Dan, the driver, looked over a map on the hood of the car. She only saw Dan when he brought supplies into the compound in large trucks. She had never seen him participate in the training. Zoe and Jason got into the other SUV, and Nick drove. This car had the cooler, and both vehicles left the Eagle Guard facility. Beth, Todd and Mr. Li stayed behind, for what reasons, Carla didn't ask.

This was the first time in eight weeks that she left the compound. The change in scenery was a welcome break.

They traveled along deserted country roads for several miles. While Greg was busy talking to the driver, she dared to ask Jag. "I guess you can't tell me where we're going. Can you tell me how much longer this program is? I know you said six months, but I feel I can get back to work at the FLC now."

He stared at her without saying anything for a while. "You have more training to do."

"You can tell her about the job if you want, Jag," Greg had overheard her question.

"We'll be leaving the country tomorrow. We have a contract overseas for a client who needs personal protection. We want to bring you along to watch how we do things."

"Sounds interesting. This isn't part of an FLC project?" she asked.

"No," Jag said. "But it'll be good field experience on a number of levels."

"How so?"

"The details will be explained later," Greg said.

"And what about today's lesson?" she sneaked in. "I'm assuming this is a lesson of sorts."

"Of sorts," Jag concurred. "It shouldn't take long."

She didn't like the sound of that. They drove for about two hours and she saw an occasional house or farm, rarely any cars. When Jag told her they were far from anything, he wasn't kidding. The scenery was beautiful. Snow over wooded mountains and pristine farmlands, like a picture on a Christmas card. But Carla sat with her hands clenched, her heartbeat kicked up a few notches with each mile they traveled. The team in the SUV was too quiet.

This wasn't a trip to a farmer's market to buy fresh cider and vegetables. She had no idea what they had in mind and it was driving her mad.

She couldn't help but remember Jag's warning if she failed—they couldn't just let her go. Jag had promised to let her know if she was in danger of failing. She glanced at him with questioning eyes. By the way he returned her gaze, she must have looked terrified. "When we get back, I'll help you pack so you'll know what to bring on an assignment."

"Good idea," Greg added.

Was he saying they weren't taking her someplace to kill her and dispose of her? Why the large cooler. Would they cut her in pieces—God, she had to stop reading those serial killer novels.

Taking a few deep breaths, she used Mr. Li's techniques to calm and center her mind. *Keep thinking, take in information, process it, don't panic.*

Jag reached across the seat and squeezed her hand. She glanced over at him again and he had a slight smile. He rarely smiled. He gave her a small nod and winked at her. How she needed that bit of reassurance. She loved him for that. He must know how nervous she was. That interaction was the burst of confidence she needed for whatever they had planned for her. Maybe it was all a mindfuck and not as bad as she thought.

Did she love Jag? After all they've been through during this ordeal? He had been her bodyguard, the man who had abducted her, her handler and now her lover. Could they ever have a normal relationship? Or was it the intensity of the situation that made the sex hot? What would happen after the training? Would he move on? Was their sex just stress-release in a highly testosterone-riddled atmosphere?

She wanted him again, wanted him to command her sexually and make love to her every spare moment, even if it was only for a brief time.

The SUV slowed and turned into a small farm. Carla's pulse kicked up several paces. They were here. Wherever *here* was. She scanned the small farm that looked like a dairy farm to her by the type of cows in the field. The two SUVs parked behind the large barn. There were several outbuildings and structures with three large silos. Was this a real farm or a private facility made to look like a working farm?

A few chickens scampered around a chicken coop behind the barn. A fenced-in area held a half dozen pigs. She glanced at Jag, hoping to get confirmation.

Greg and the driver got out of the vehicle and met a thin gentleman in his late fifties wearing jeans and a heavy coat. He waved them inside the barn.

"Is this a real farm?" Carla asked.

Jag laughed. "Yes and real animals. I thought you were a country girl."

"I am. Just all this cloak-and-dagger stuff is making me nervous. I thought it might be another facility disguised as a farm."

"No, it's a real farm, but the owner used to be an Eagle Guard. He's retired and lives here with his wife, Meg."

"Jag, tell me honest. Did I fail the program?"

"What? No, you're doing fine. You have a few faults that need to be fine-tuned. "

She turned toward him and glared at him. "Like what?"

"You're doing very well in the training, except you worry too much, which affects your logic. Your emotions are your blind spot. Learn to control them and you'll do much better."

"I can accept that. Now what the hell is going on here?"

119

"Part of the training. It's about to get harder."

Zoe, Jason and Nick were in the SUV behind them and they got out of their car. "Should we get out too?" Carla asked.

"Not until they tell us," Jag answered.

"I'm not going to like this, am I?" She focused on his expression. He wasn't easy to read. Even after the Mr. Li's lessons, she couldn't tell what was going on in Jag's head.

"No. But it's necessary."

She nodded. "Any advice?"

"Follow orders. Don't ask questions."

Greg walked out of the barn and waved them to come inside. "Ready?" Jag asked. "Let's go."

Chapter 10

Inside the barn, the smell of cow manure and hay overpowered her senses. The farmer and Greg didn't seem to notice. Two rows of wooden stalls lined both sides of the barn and black tubing ran down to each stall for milking. The three men from the other vehicle were talking to a woman about the same age as the farmer. She smiled at Jag and Carla then left the barn with Zoe, Jason and Nick.

The wooden stalls were empty, all the cows were out in the fields, having finished the first milking of the day. They'd return early evening for the second milking. The farmer and Greg led Carla and Jag to another room off the large main area. On the wall was a .22 rifle, the farmer took the gun, then walked outside to a private fenced-in pen.

Carla stopped at the door and grabbed Jag? Had he lied to her? Was this farmer going to kill her? "You told me I didn't fail," she whispered.

"You didn't. You're safe. Follow orders, no questions." He nodded for her to go outside with Greg.

In the pen, a cow was tied to a post. "It's loaded and ready to fire." The farmer handed Carla the gun. The man nodded and took a step back. A tremor coursed through her body.

"Kill him." Greg pointed to the cow.

"You want me to kill the cow?" she asked astonished. "Is he sick?"

Greg glared at her, his teeth clenched. "Follow orders! Do I need to get the bat out of the car?"

Would he beat this animal and then her? She glanced at Jag, but he didn't even look at her. She had gotten her orders and she had questioned them. He'd given her advice and she had ignored it. Swallowing, she raised the gun and pointed it between the large brown eyes. Bile rose to the back of her throat. She heard Greg huff in impatience. She swallowed again and took the shot. She hoped she was helping in some way, a sick or old animal that needed to be put to rest quickly.

She walked back into the barn, placed the gun on the wall rack and strode back to the SUV. Zoe, Jason and the farmer's wife were loading up the cooler with packaged meats, milk and eggs. She got into her car and slammed the door. Jag talked to the woman and he went back into the barn with her. Several moments later he came out with a box. He placed it in the back of the SUV.

ဢၢ၃

Greg refused to talk to her on the drive back to the compound. Even though she had completed her task, she'd questioned his authority by hesitating. He was pissed. She got it. They wanted to make sure she wouldn't be afraid to use her

122

gun on an assailant. If a member of the FLC was threatened, she wouldn't hesitate to pull the trigger. Hadn't she proved that? She'd explain it to Jag when they got back. Mr. Li had taught her there were three stress responses. Most people spoke of fight or flight. Well there was the third, freeze.

Many people in highly stressful or dangerous situations would not react at all, they'd freeze. And that could be the deadliest response.

After lunch, Jag walked her out to the main lounge area. A roaring fire blazed in the fireplace. They sat close and absorbed the warmth. Carla checked her watch. "I have a few minutes before Mr. Li's lesson. When I get back will you help me pack what I need for our trip tomorrow?"

"Sure." He lowered his voice. "Do you understand where you went wrong at the farm?"

A wave of anxiety washed over her. "Because I questioned the point of killing an animal that appeared perfectly healthy? I questioned an order because I didn't understand it."

Jag shook his head. "No, that's not right. You questioned the order because you didn't want to do it without a reason, not because you didn't understand it. You were told to kill the cow and you wanted to know why. You understood the order. Why doesn't matter."

"When I worked missions with the FLC, we were given information about the men who we were blackmailing in the Red Tape Room. Some had brutally murdered innocent women like their lovers or wives, or made deals with terrorists that threaten their own country as well at the US, or manipulated policies to increase their own personal wealth at their detriment of their own people. We understood why these men deserved to be destroyed."

"Your new position will be different," Jag answered abruptly. "If you're given an order, you must follow it without argument or question. Do you understand?"

"Yes, I do now."

"Good. You will be working for the FLC, but in a different capacity."

Carla worried she wouldn't fit into this new position that everyone talked about, but gave her so few details. Maybe it was her background as a lawyer and a nurse. She liked to know the details of a situation before taking action. "I get that." Not really, but she hoped she would eventually.

"Come up to your room. I brought back something for you from the farm. I bought it from Meg, Frank's wife."

Carla smiled. "I never had a chance to meet them."

"Next time." Jag stood and took her hand, leading her upstairs. She stepped inside her room and glanced around, not knowing what to look for. "What is it? A jar of pickles?" she teased.

"No, on the windowsill."

She gasped and covered her mouth with her hand. A ceramic pot of African Violets in brilliant-purple blooms sat in the window. The vivid color stood out against the bare winter scenery and their drab fatigues. "They're beautiful. How can Meg grow these in this weather?"

"She has a greenhouse for flowers and vegetables," he said. "I felt bad guarding you all those weeks in the hospital and noticed no one came by with flowers or get-well cards. Every time I made a run for you for ice cream or M&Ms at the gift shop, I was tempted to bring flowers."

"I would've loved that. It was obvious why I didn't get flowers or cards."

He nodded. "Julia could've brought some."

Carla laughed. "Not likely." She pressed a hand to her chest. "Thank you. It's a thoughtful gift." She kissed him.

He checked his watch. "You have your class. After Mr. Li's, head over to the rifle range. Greg wants you to get in more practice before we leave tomorrow." The brief moment of closeness quickly ended as soon as he mentioned their mission. Carla felt the distance between them growing. The ache in her heart struck deep.

As they left her room and walked downstairs, Carla asked, "Can you say where we're going tomorrow and give more details tonight?"

"Iraq. A businessman and his wife hired our team to move them safely out of the country. Besides the military activity making the area unstable, rebels bombed and destroyed their factory. The wife has family in France and they want assistance to leave so they can have safe passage to Baghdad and take a flight to France. There has been a lot of fighting and their airport has been overrun by terrorist control. The sixty-mile trip to Baghdad is dangerous considering the unsettled area and that's the nearest international airport that's still running."

"My Arabic is pretty bad. I've only learned the basics, but I'm excited about being a part of this." Carla was both nervous and thrilled to be working with Jag. If only he didn't seem preoccupied. Just as she thought she had found her strength and courage again, he seemed to be pulling away from her. The idea of helping two people escape a dangerous situation, made her nightmare at the FLC fade.

"Don't worry. You won't be alone. After your language classes, meet me in the storage shack at ten. It may be our last opportunity for an intimate session for a while."

She smiled. "I'm glad you're my handler. I feel safe with

you. And I'd like a session."

He frowned. "Don't depend on me for your safety. Depend on your instincts and your own training. Never let your guard down. And trust no one. After your training, I'll be gone."

Carla felt as if she were kicked in the chest. "And what happens after this training? We go our separate ways?"

His expression softened. "I don't know, Carla. We don't work a regular nine-to-five, and we don't know where we're going to be in a few weeks, or a few months. It'll be difficult."

"You're saying relationships don't happen in this business. And yet I look at Zoe and Jason who started out in the CIA, ended up in the FLC, then here and they're married."

"There are exceptions," he said, smiling. "I do care about you."

She gave a dry laugh. How many men had said they *cared* about her as a cop-out when they only wanted to avoid saying they didn't love her? What the hell had she been thinking all this time? Did she really believe the flirting and the sex games meant anything to him? He was intoxicating and hot, and she had been a fool for pursuing him. She was just a mission to him and the sex was a distraction. The humiliation cut deep. "Apparently we can't make plans beyond what's on Greg's program" Standing now in the main lounge area, she pointed to the whiteboard with the schedule.

"We have a complicated life and dangerous job, Carla."

"Even Todd has a wife and son," she argued. She should've known having a relationship under these circumstances was practically impossible.

"Todd's divorced. He hasn't come to terms with it yet."

"Oh, I didn't know." She checked her watch. "I have to go." She only had five minutes to meet with Mr. Li unless she wanted to get body slammed.

"I'll see you later," Jag said with a somber tone.

"And by the way, Sir, I respectfully decline our meeting this evening at ten. I have a complicated life, and I won't be able to fit that appointment into my schedule." She turned and walked out the door through the kitchen.

If she hurried, she might get to her session on time. Halfway across the yard, Jag came running out. "Carla, your meeting has been canceled. Mr. Li is ill. He has the flu."

She kept walking until Jag's words clicked, then she stopped and turned around. "Mr. Li is sick? Is he okay?"

She saw the flash before she heard the explosion.

Boom!

When she opened her eyes, she was flat on her face in the snow and didn't remember getting knocked down. Wood debris rained down around her. The heat of fire not too far away warmed her back. Stunned, she didn't move at first. Then remembered—fight, flight, freeze. She pushed herself to her knees and glanced over her shoulder at the demolished cabin. Flames leapt from broken windows and through a large hole in the side of Mr. Li's place. Then Jag stood beside her, dragging her to her feet.

"Run!" She and Jag ran toward the lodge, at the same time Beth and Todd raced out.

When Jag brought her inside the kitchen door of the lodge, he made her sit in a dining chair. "Are you all right? Are you injured?"

"I'm fine. Just had the wind knocked out of me. Was anyone inside?"

"What the hell happened?" Greg asked, holding a rifle as he rushed into the kitchen and out the back door. Jag and Carla followed.

Flames and black smoke continued spewing out of a hole in the side of the cabin and broken windows. "Old gas stove," Todd explained. He and Beth had been at the rifle range. "I shut off the gas line." Dan and Nick showed up with large fire extinguishers and entered the cabin.

"You sure it was an accident?" Greg asked. The flames died as the two men put out the fire. Smoke spilled out of the cabin.

"These stoves are fifty or more years old. We should check the other cabins for damaged lines," Beth said. Rifles in hand, she and Todd approached the building and looked inside. After a quick check they returned to the group. "Thank God Mr. Li was in his room and no one was in there."

Greg nodded. "I know these gas stoves are old, but I don't want to assume it was an accident. Jag, Carla and I will check the other cabins, and Beth, Nick and Todd will look around the compound. Zoe and Jason are checking the trails. There's snow on the ground, if anyone has entered the area, you should be able to find tracks. After, I want all the stoves inspected for leaks. We leave tomorrow. I'll have Dan take care of it while we're gone."

The teams gathered equipment and weapons and began their searches within the camp and outside the compound. When Jag and Carla returned, Dan was examining Mr. Li's cabin. The fire was out and there wasn't much remaining. Mr. Li stood there with a blanket wrapped around him, looking awful.

"Mr. Li, you should be in bed," Carla scolded. "Beth says you have a fever."

"I wanted to get a sense of the place."

"It's freezing out here," Carla argued. "You should be inside."

"The sense is, the stove was shot to crap," Dan said. "I mean old. I'll have them all serviced before you get back."

Mr. Li stared out in the distance, as if he was focusing on something. His breathing became slow and deep.

"Mr. Li, are you all right?" Carla eyed him warily.

"Thing are not always as they seem," Mr. Li answered in a soft tone.

"What do you see," Jag asked.

Mr. Li looked at Carla and frowned. "You will need your training in Iraq."

It sounded like a warning. "Martial arts and meditation training?"

"Everything," he corrected. "You have two more near-death challenges to face. The bombing you survived, these other two will occur during this mission."

How was she supposed respond to that? "I'll be careful."

Mr. Li's eyes rolled up and he collapsed on the ground.

Beth rode with Dan when they took Mr. Li to the nearest hospital which was a couple hours away. He had collapsed from dehydration and fever. Beth said he'd be fine in a few days. She'd be back in time to leave with the team by morning. Dan and the farmer would make repairs to the Eagle Guard training facility while the rest of the team was on the mission.

⅌

Carla gazed out the window of her room. Spotlights cast an otherworldly glow as it reflected off the crisp snow. It was after ten p.m. and she hadn't shown up at the shack for Jag's invitation. Beth had told her not to anyway because of the added security. Mixed feelings tugged in her chest. She did love Jag, but why pursue a personal relationship with him if after her training he'd be gone. If they continued, it would be more painful when they had to end it later. Still, she wanted him, even if they only had a little time left. She'd be starting it off with a lie, on who she was, what she did and where she came from. They hadn't told her yet what her new cover background would be, only a new name. Didn't she get a new identity along with the new name?

A guard strolled the compound, rifle in hand. It looked like Nick. After the explosion, Greg had decided to take extra precautions and post a guard. They never had to before. Was he worried about threats because of their mission or had someone discovered she was here?

It would be a long night, and even though she was going to be with a well-trained team, she expected it to get a lot worse.

Carla heard footsteps by her door even before the knock. She crossed the room and opened the door. Zoe and Jason waited in the hallway and peeked into her room.

"We're not interrupting anything?" Jason said, grinning.

"No. I'm packing." Carla suspected that most everyone at the camp had figured out what was going on between her and Jag. She was in no mood to hear a lecture about messing with her handler was a bad idea. She got that already.

"We wanted to say goodbye. We're leaving early tomorrow before you get up."

"Leaving? I thought you were going on the mission." She didn't dare tell them she didn't think she was prepared for this assignment. Having them with her would've made the trip much easier.

Zoe shook her head. "We have to get back to DC. We'll see you when you return." She gave Carla a hug. "Don't worry. You'll do fine. Trust your team."

"Follow the rules and your training, but gut instinct trumps them both," Jason said. "Never ignore your intuition."

"Thanks. I'm sure everything will work out." She smiled and hoped it didn't look forced. How good was her gut instinct? "Have a good trip back."

Jason opened the door and Jag stood there with a sardonic smile and some black cloth folded in his arms. "We're leaving," Jason said to Jag as he and Zoe stepped out into the hall and Jag entered Carla's room. "Good luck. See you when you get back."

"Thanks. Have a good trip back to DC." Jag closed the door after they left.

"I knew you weren't coming to the shack. Greg said for all personnel to remain inside this evening for security reasons. He made a point of saying no extra-curricular activities."

"Beth sent me the message. I guess our events in the shack weren't so secret."

He shrugged his shoulders. "Hard to keep secrets around this crew." He held up the black cloth in his hands. "I have one other item you need to pack."

Carla crossed her arms and sighed. "What is it?"

"Since our mission is secret and we'll be posing as businessmen, not going in wearing fatigues. At least for most of it. The women will need to wear proper clothing too."

"I expected that." She took the abaya and placed it in her duffle.

The next knock on her door startled her. Jag didn't hesitate, he opened it. Beth was standing there. Her eyes widened when she saw Jag.

"I didn't expect to see you. Then again, I'm not surprised." Beth's tone had a sarcastic edge.

"What did you want, Beth?" Carla asked pleasantly, ignoring Beth's attitude toward Jag.

She stepped into the room without being invited. "I know

131

you're doing well on your training, but you're months from completion," she said to Carla. "I thought, considering the dangers of this mission, you should ask Jag and Greg if you could sit this one out." She glared at Jag and raised her chin as if she expected him to argue.

"She's coming on the mission, and she is ready," Jag stated.

"You're taking a rookie into a warzone," Beth argued. "It's a risk to her, the mission and the team's lives."

"It's a simple mission and the team can handle it, so can Carla." Jag didn't raise his voice and somehow that was more threatening than if he had.

Beth huffed. "Well, I offered my opinion. I'll let you two get back to…whatever you were doing." Again the sarcasm. She left and closed the door.

"What's with her?" Carla asked. "Have you two had history or something?"

"Not really. She hit on me over a year ago and I turned her down. She's not into the BDSM lifestyle at all. And she's not my type even if she was. She never seemed upset by that."

"Maybe it's me," Carla said. "Considering we're on the same team, I thought we would've gotten along better."

"Don't sweat it." Jag sat on her bed, not ready to leave. Part of her wanted to wrap her arms around him and beg him to strap her to the bed, and part of her wanted to kick him out. As her handler, she needed him and she needed to maintain a good rapport. "What will my duties be for this mission? No one has told me anything."

"Since this is your first, you won't be responsible for much. You will be informed of the details before we leave and during the flight over. It's not a difficult one. That being said, all missions must expect the unexpected. We plan to arrive in

Dhuluiya, make arrangements at the client's home, escort them to the Baghdad airport so they can fly out by private plane."

"The Iraqi military hasn't taken control of the area?"

"One day the Iraqi forces take control and the next, the terrorists regain command. There's a lot of fighting going on and our clients fear for their lives."

"What do you think Mr. Li meant about me facing two more near-death challenges? That kind of scares me."

"Mr. Li is very intuitive, some think he's precognitive. Whatever it is, we've learned to trust his insights." He took her hand and pulled her down on the bed to sit beside him. "You'll do fine. You may not have completed your training, but you're doing well. I'll be with you all the way."

That did give her some comfort. "Why haven't they given me a new background? They gave me a new name, a new face and new look. No one gave me a new identity to use, like where I was born or grew up. What if people ask or I start dating someone? Or is there a reason why I haven't been given a new identity? Should I be worried?" She smiled a bit to lighten the tone.

He took a long breath and waited before answering. At first she thought he wouldn't give her an answer. "Planning on hitting a single's bar anytime soon?"

"Seriously, Jag."

"I get what you're asking, and I don't know. I'll ask. In the meantime, make something up. You never told your targets in the FLC who you really were, right? From what I heard, you were Mistress M, or if you were submissive, you had made up a name."

"True. But I did have a boyfriend outside of the FLC. He didn't know what I did, only that I worked at the White House as a researcher."

"Are you giving up on us?" he asked, his eyes darkened as he brushed a strand of her hair behind her ear.

"What? You said after my training you would be gone. I took that to mean we would be over."

"I didn't say that. I'll be gone because I have a mission to do after this one. It's difficult to maintain a relationship in our business. I didn't say it was impossible." His thumb caressed her cheek to her lips, down her throat then between her breasts. "Take off your clothes."

She hesitated, although her body heated up at his order. She wanted him, ached terribly for him.

"I won't ask again. I'll leave," he warned. "And I don't want to leave. I want you, Carla."

Common sense fought with her desire. She wasn't convinced they had a chance for something more than casual gratification. At least she could have him on her terms. The thrill of his words won out. She undressed for him. With every bit of clothing she removed, the lust in his eyes increased and her own body throbbed with desire. He stood beside the bed when she got down to her underwear.

"Keep going. When you're completely naked, kneel." He locked the door and removed his clothes. "I can't use a flogger on you or spank you. The sound will travel. I can restrain you though." He took off his belt and tossed it on the bed.

She still had bruises on her butt and thighs from a recent session in the shack that had been especially intense. He'd used a crop on her and a paddle. She shivered remembering the sharpness of the pain, the most she'd ever endured. And she'd cried, pushed beyond her limit and brought back so tenderly. He'd untied her and she'd fallen into his arms. He had made love to her with a passion that was so shockingly intense with desire. That night was the first time he had said he wanted to possess her and collar her. At that moment, she had truly believed he loved her. And her orgasm had been the most powerful of any she had before.

Jag, I love you. She didn't dare say that though. Naked and shaky, she knelt at his feet and gazed up at him, her heart breaking and soaring for this man she loved so much and feared she'd lose soon. "I'm here to please you, Sir."

Standing in front of her, he gently held the sides of her head. "I'll miss hearing those words, Carla. I will miss these moments when we go on our assignment. There will be other times, after we return, if you wish it."

"I do wish it, Sir." She wasn't sure how they would work it out, but she wouldn't think about that now.

"Good girl. Right now, I'd like for you to lick my cock as if it's a rich dessert."

"With pleasure, Sir." With the tip of her tongue, she licked around the rim, then took his full length into her mouth.

"Hmmm. Nice, I think you like this," he teased.

Quickly, she licked from the bottom of his shaft and slowly lapped up to the tip, again and again. He grabbed her shoulders and pulled her up. Then he took the belt from the bed and fastened it around her wrists. "On the bed, on your back, spread your legs and put your arms over your head."

She did as told and Jag wrapped the other end of the belt around a wooden slat on the headboard. He knelt between her legs and she felt exposed and deliciously horny as she anticipated his next move. With the size of his body and his skills as a Dom, he could do anything. For all the years she thought she was a switch, Jag had drawn out the submissive side.

He bent low and whispered in her ear. His fingertips held her nipples captive. "I may not be able to use a flogger, but I can inflict other means of pain and pleasure. But do not cry out or I'll gag you."

She nodded.

The pain in her nipples was so sharp, she arched her body off the bed and moaned. He'd pinched them both. The sensations radiated to her pussy and her clit swelled with pleasure. Then he replaced his fingers with his mouth, sucking and using his teeth. Slowly, he increased the torment followed by caresses. Her head was spinning.

Despite the pain, her cunt was soaked. He even slid a finger inside and groaned. "I thought so, you're wet." He sucked and tugged on the tender nub, the scrape of his stubble in need of a shave rubbed at her skin. Then he returned to her breasts, his hands massaging and his mouth nibbling on their peaks. With all this attention, her nipples were sensitive and swollen. She was in heaven. "You remember your safeword if this becomes too much?"

"Yes, Sir." She didn't want to stop. The pain and pleasure threshold was like a drug and brought her to levels of passion she never experienced before. Even past lovers and Doms at Paradise Underground hadn't been so skilled.

Her body vibrated and warmth radiated through her as he moved slowly down her abdomen, taking tiny nips at her hips until he reached her pussy. Licking at her labia, he made her shiver with joy. When she tried to shift her bottom so he'd touch her clit where she needed to be tended so badly, he pinched her ass.

"Don't move, and don't come. I will take you at my speed. I will determine the time."

This was more torture than the pain he imposed on her tits. He plunged a finger inside her channel and licked all around her clit but kept her on the edge of reaching orgasm.

"And when you do come, don't make a sound."

She groaned. He slipped on a condom, then returned to punishing her nipples. "You can come anytime you choose now," he said as he pressed his lips on hers. The kiss was deep, and slow. Still, it didn't take her mind off the glorious sensations.

Now her level of pain tolerance was at the limit. Just as she thought she couldn't stand anymore, he thrust his cock inside. The orgasm was instant and rolled through her, bucking her body in spasms. Jag's mouths caught her cries and his body held her down on the bed. The restraint increased her pleasure.

He released the belt, freeing her arms, and pulled her onto his lap. The position sent his cock deeper into her. Wrapping her legs around his hips, she rocked and moved to the rhythm of his thrusts. Then he climaxed with a devastating groan. Afterward, still inside her, he tumbled onto the bed beside her and held her close, arms and legs entwined.

He pulled the blanket over them. "I'm staying here tonight."

It wasn't an order, or a request, only a statement.

"Good, can you hit the light?" she asked.

"Sure. In a second." He ran his hands up and down her back, bruised butt and raw nipples. Kissing her forehead and neck, he pressed her head to his chest.

"Do you think I'm ready for this mission?" she asked without looking into his eyes.

"Only you can answer that." He stroked her hair and she closed her eyes.

Even the comfort of Jag holding her close the whole night didn't calm her thoughts. Mr. Li's words kept tossing in her head. Two more death challenges were coming her way. How could she sleep?

Chapter 11

The day they arrived in Dhuluiya, Iraq, the sun was shining, but the air was thick with dust. In the village, a warm breeze blew through the tall palm trees and stirred the scents of cooked onions and exotic spices wafting from the storefronts. Surrounding the beige concrete buildings, were the rubble of several structures indicating the violence this town had recently suffered. Carla took in the sights and observed everything, watching for signs of a threat. An outlier. Someone who looked suspicious, was acting nervous or overly observant, the approach of a vehicle, moving in an erratic manner, or someone sitting along the side of a road who didn't seem to belong. Anything could be a potential danger. Would she become paranoid after a few months or years working this job?

It was difficult to determine what was out of the ordinary when this environment was new to her. Thankfully, she was there to be more of an observer than an active participant.

The first thing she noticed was the minimal number of military police standing at street corners, armed with various types of automatic or semi-automatic rifles.

Street vendors had their wares set up and men and women bought fruits and vegetables, and other items, and rushed from shop to shop. Was this like a regular workday or had a break in the fighting brought residents out to purchase necessities? Vehicle traffic swarmed the streets consisting of paneled trucks, small Japanese cars, motorcycles, bicycles, pedestrians, a few mule carts. Most of the women wore black abayas, a few had on conservative clothing and head scarves, called hijabs. There was still the occasional expat businessman living in town despite the military unrest. The social environment had quickly disintegrating by the looks of the bombed out buildings and boarded-up structures. Concrete walls as high as the roofs surrounded many properties. Not the most welcoming village. Already Carla didn't have a good feeling for this place. It's another universe and anything could go wrong during their mission.

Sitting in the back of the SUV, Carla pressed her hands tightly between her knees. The abaya already felt warm and confining. It was the end of March, how did these women wear this in the summer months? Beneath it, she carried her Beretta M9 and a couple extra magazines. How would she retrieve the damn thing in a hurry?

"Where does the client live?" Carla asked Jag. They were riding in one of two SUVs. A local security group had picked them up at the airport. Jag had said they had worked with them before on other assignments. Nick was in their vehicle, and Beth, Todd and Greg were in the other one.

"The client lives across town," Jag said. "We have a stop

to make first at another agency's facility."

"Who are they?" Carla asked.

"This group works independently providing assistance to civil and military authorities. They're a much larger outfit than ours," Nick said. "They've assisted us before. Although the Iraqi military isn't crazy about their existence, Ahmed's group has helped stop many terrorist raids and provided valuable information to the Iraqi military, the CIA and US military intelligence."

"They're a militia group," Carla added.

"Yes, but most militia groups want to defend and protect people, not overthrow governments," Jamil, their driver, said in his Iraqi accent. Jamil was a young man in his early twenties, clean shaved, short dark hair with a warm smile and innocent dark eyes. Carla thought he looked more like a college kid than a member of a militia group. During their journey from Baghdad, Jamil had pointed out unsettled or very dangerous areas. Mostly everywhere between Baghdad and Dhuluiya was dangerous.

They drove out of the residential area and entered a more battered section of warehouses and factories.

"We're not near Sayef's factory," Jamil assured us. "That's on the east side of town. We're south, far from Faruq and his men."

"I've not heard that name before," Carla said. "What terrorist group does he lead?"

The driver gave a snort. "He runs a band of smalltime rebel forces, but causes enough trouble to draw the more organized groups into the area. That's why Sayef wants to leave. He says he believes they intend to turn all his factories and his home into a central command post."

"It's a volatile situation," Jag added. "We'll get them out."

"Sayef has more than one factory?" Nick asked from the front passenger seat.

"Yes, he has three," Jamil said.

Nick glanced at Jag then turned back to their driver. "All three are in Dhuluiya? And were they all destroyed?"

Jamil frowned. "Yes, they are all in town, but only one of his smaller plants was bombed. Ahmed wishes to talk to you more about Sayef's plans for leaving. Do you know his main plant is still operational?"

"Interesting. Sayef left that point out," Jag told Jamil.

"If Ahmed is suspicious of Sayef, why did he make it sound like Sayef's one and only factory was destroyed and he and his wife needed to flee the country?" Nick's annoyance was evident in his tone. "Does Ahmed know what's going on at the other factories?"

"He'll give you details after we arrive," Jamil said.

Jag shook his head. "Holding back information will only make our job more difficult. I want to find out more before we talk to Sayef."

Jamil twisted his hands on the steering wheel. "I assure you, we are not holding any information back. We will pass it on as we learn more."

"We have to know what's going on before we take them to Baghdad," Greg added.

"I know we can't use the local airport because of the rebels. But isn't there one between here and Baghdad?" Carla asked. It's a long drive to Baghdad. It took us over an hour, and Jamil showed us that most of the area isn't secure."

"It's ninety-nine kilometers," Jamil agreed. "A military base is along the Tigris, but I doubt you could get anywhere near there without being shot."

"Just a thought." Carla sat back and studied the streets.

Not too many people walking around here.

"Is she the one?" Jamil asked. When no one answered, he tried again. "The trainee assigned to the job at the warehouse?"

The young man grinned at her through the rearview mirror. Did she miss a joke or something? She glanced at Jag for clarification. He returned her look with his typical blank, unemotional stare, like a freaking robot. "Did I miss something?"

Jamil laughed.

"She'll be briefed when we get to the warehouse." Jag's tone held an edge and the driver stopped laughing.

Why didn't they give her more details about this mission? Even though she wasn't an official member of the Eagle Guards, she hated being kept in the dark. All she was supposed to do was ride along when they drove their clients out of town. Although the area was unsettled, and fighting was known to breakout frequently, their trip from Baghdad to Dhuluiya had been uneventful. Somehow she didn't see why an armed military escort for the Sayefs was necessary.

The SUVs stopped in front of a tall concrete building on the edge of town in an industrial district. A garage door opened and they drove inside. After the door closed, several armed guards stepped out from around steel crates and gave the okay for the passengers to leave the vehicles.

The Eagle Guard team was led around rows of stacked crates, forklifts and overhead cranes. Down one row, a guard pressed a sequence of numbers on a keypad that appeared to work the crane. A panel in the floor slid open and a set of stairs appeared, leading to several lower levels.

"Welcome back. How long will you be staying?" one of the men asked. He wore a dark-colored shirt and pants, and a work cap. The strap of a rifle was hooked over his shoulder. A heavy black beard covered most of his neck.

"Thank you, Ahmed. If all goes well, we shouldn't be here longer than a day or two," Greg said. "I'd like to hear what you know about Sayef's factories and take a closer look if we can. Uncle Sam would be interested."

"I'll tell you what I know and what we plan to do about it."

Greg checked his watch. "After our business here, we'll head over to Sayef's home to brief them. But I don't want to leave quite yet. I need to make a few phone calls with that info on the factories. I promised the US and Iraqi military I'd keep them informed."

"Yes," Ahmed said, his face straining. He then gave orders in Arabic to his other men. "My men will show you where you can rest and get something to eat and drink."

The guard and Ahmed gave them a brief tour of the facility. Mostly the place consisted of storage rooms for supplies, weapons, electronic and computer equipment, extra food and clothing. In another section were offices, surveillance rooms, bathrooms and several sleeping quarters with cots. "The women can stay in this room." The guard showed them to a small office that had two cots set up. Beth glanced at Carla and gave her a shrug. Now that they were working together, Carla hoped her attitude would change about her.

Carla tried to hear what Ahmed was saying to Jag and Greg while Beth looked over the towels, blankets and other personal supplies left on the cot. "Get used to it," Beth said, sitting on the cot.

"Get used to what?"

"The men here pretty much ignore a woman on the team. It can come in handy when I want to snoop around, but now with two of us, it might be a little difficult."

"Is that why you were giving me a hard time during my training? You didn't want another woman on the team?"

Beth rolled her eyes. "We're not going to get into this now."

"Yes, we are. If we have to work together in a dangerous situation, I need to know if I can trust you."

"It has nothing to do with trust. You haven't been trained long enough."

"You don't think I can handle this?"

Beth stood and crossed her arms. "No. You're a risk to the team."

"If they thought I was a risk, wouldn't they have left me behind?" Carla argued.

Beth laughed. "No, because Jag wants you close by to fuck you when he pleases."

"I doubt Jag would risk a mission for a good fuck." Beth didn't have a response for that. Confusion tangled Carla's thoughts. "I don't get it. Do you have an issue with me because you don't think I have the skills for this mission, or because you want Jag in your bed?"

Even after she said it, Carla wondered if she went too far. Beth strode over to the door and reached for the handle. "Wait!" Carla exclaimed.

"What?"

"Did you take a shot at me in Vermont on purpose when Jag and I were jogging during the beginning of my training?"

Beth rubbed her face. "Greg said you'd be kicked out if you showed signs that you didn't have what it takes to be an Eagle Guard. I was trying to scare you, not kill you. I didn't think you would make it this far. I thought you were wasting our time."

"You still think that?" Carla asked softly.

"No, you have amazing skills with firearms, you're in good shape and have learned a lot. But you haven't learned nearly all you need. And you have an attitude problem."

Carla dropped onto the cot. "I think we both do," she agreed. She'd had an attitude problem before the car bomb. That almost had gotten her killed. She had to work on that. "Did you blow up Mr. Li's cabin?"

Beth shook her head. "No. Mr. Li had told me later he was feeling chills from his fever and kept turning up the gas on the stove then forgot to turn it off when he came to see me in the infirmary. The stove blowing up was an accident."

"Okay. I'll try not to put anyone at risk, and I'll stay out of everyone's way. Now let's go and find out what the guys are discussing."

In the hallway, Greg said something to Jag. He swore and pressed his lips together, then nodded to Greg. Ahmed and Greg then left, walking down the hall and entered another room.

The guards took the rest of them to a small chow hall with food and drink set out. "Help yourself, please," the guard said. He left them alone. A table was set with tea, dates, apricots, lentil soup and pita bread. "Eat something," Jag said. "We may not get a chance later."

Nick, Todd and Beth didn't hesitate to start eating. Carla didn't have an appetite, but thought it best to eat something. She glanced at Jag. "What was that about with Greg? You didn't seem happy."

"Just business," he said sharply. "You'll find out soon. We'll go over details of the mission too." One thing Carla learned through her training was to detect stress in peoples' voices and their expressions. Jag was stressed, and he never got stressed.

They were all working together, he shouldn't keep anything from her. Was this mission more dangerous than they anticipated? "If there are dangers in this mission and you're worried that I can't handle it, don't worry. I won't be a burden."

Beth gave a snort.

He frowned at Beth. "She'll be fine as long as she follows orders."

"I get that," Carla told both Beth and Jag.

"I hope you do. Remember what I said about this being your second chance after the White House scandal."

"If I fail the program, they'll eliminate me."

He nodded. "They can't risk exposure."

Every time she thought they were exaggerating and just trying to scare her, she remembered how another member of the FLC, a woman, had been eliminated by an assassin. These people didn't screw around when it comes to national security.

Greg entered the room. "Ready?"

Jag nodded. The team was escorted to a type of boardroom. Greg showed her and Jag a map on a table and explained their plan. Three vehicles would enter their client's compound then leave at slightly different times. If they drove in a three-car caravan, they would certainly be stopped. "We'll take the highway down and cross the Tigris and use back roads," Greg said. "Ahmed showed me the areas that have yet to be seized by the rebel forces. It's a longer route, but rebels are blocking these areas of Route 1. We can't get through. We can cross either of these two bridges and we'll be fine. Baghdad is still holding up, but not for long. We have radio contact and if we get separated, we have check points at these locations or at the final one in Baghdad."

"Will we have any help?" Jag asked.

"Yes, Ahmed's men will offer some assistance, but only for about forty kilometers out of the city. It's ninety-nine to Baghdad. He can't afford to send his men any farther out of the village with so many rebels around. Any questions?"

"What do you want me to do?" Carla asked.

"Stay with the group, follow orders and keep your head down," Greg said. "You're here mostly as an observer, unless we need your sniper skills."

"Sniper skills?" Carla gasped. The air was sucked out of the room and the temperature seemed to rise ten degrees.

"Yes," Greg said. "Besides your duties for the FLC, we made a deal with the first lady that you would occasionally work for us as a team member. During your training, you proved you're skillful with firearms."

"No one told me this. I was trained to protect the members of the FLC, not to assassinate people."

"Sometimes it's the same thing, darlin'." Greg's flip comment pissed her off.

She glanced at Jag, hoping he would argue. He made a slight shake of his head. A warning?

"No one sends in a resume to become an assassin. It's something they enter into," Greg answered, his tone firm, but with a level of compassion too.

This was not a job she could easily quit and she couldn't just leave, not in the middle of Iraq, possibly not ever. She glared at Jag. He knew, damn him. God, what had she gotten herself into? Her insides knotted into a huge lump and she could barely breathe. Had he known from the beginning that he was training her to be an assassin?

"When do we pick up our passengers?" Todd asked.

"Before we evacuate the Sayefs, we have another mission to accomplish. CIA, ICE and military forces have been investigating Sayef's factories for a while," Greg said. "They've discovered illegal importing and exporting of weapons and bomb materials inside the machine parts crates. Weapons are taken apart and not easily detected in the usual scans. Authorities believe someone in customs is being paid off. They're not sure if Sayef is behind it or if he's a victim. They also believe it could be part of a larger operation. They want us to get the couple safely out where officials can question them."

Carla whispered to Beth, asking what ICE stood for.

"U.S. Immigration and Customs Enforcement."

"We've recently confirmed that shipments of weapons have come from their factory hidden inside their machine crates," Ahmed added.

"If Sayef was organizing the weapons transport, why would he want to leave? It would make sense if the rebels took over his plant, and it's out of his control. He could've been threatened and won't tell anyone because he fears for his life," Jag said.

"Any of that is possible. We have to figure all angles. If he is involved, why would he want to leave? Why would he need a security escort? And what is he planning once he gets out?" Greg asked.

"That's a hell of a lot to consider," Nick offered. "We must deal with the intelligence, not opinion or hunches."

"If they're selling weapons illegally here, why don't we turn them over to the Iraqi military?" Carla asked.

"Good question," Greg said. "My orders are to bring them out and place them in protective custody. They could be innocent, but if they're not, our agencies have the opportunity to learn more. If we turn them over to Iraqi forces, they might just imprison them and we'd lose that chance to uncover a bigger operation."

"No arrests until we get to the airport. The US military will be waiting for them there," Greg said.

Nick and Todd gave a hoot.

"There's another issue here," Greg announced. "Ahmed's men have been planning to blow up this factory for quite some time."

Ahmed nodded, leaning on the table. "Initially, we were going to do it tonight, but if we do, it might compromise your rescue mission. The Eagle Guards will help us in coordinating the bombing so it will occur right after we leave the Sayefs' home. The bombing will be a diversion."

Greg sat in the chair at the head of the table. "We'll set the bombs tonight and take the Sayefs out at dawn."

"When does this start?" Carla asked.

Greg smiled. "We leave right after your final exam. We'll meet with the Sayefs first, then set the bombs at the factories."

Carla's pulse was racing. Maybe Beth was right. Maybe she didn't have enough training to do this. Escorting a couple to the airport was one thing, blowing up factories was quite another.

"What can we do to help Ahmed's men?" Todd asked.

"Come with me," Ahmed said. "My men have been preparing. I will take you to the trucks where they're loading supplies. We'll meet here to go over specifics."

"Jag and Carla will remain with me. I have a few things to discuss with them first."

After the group left, Carla turned to Greg and calmly asked. "You're not leaving me behind are you? I can do this." Honestly, she hoped she could.

"I have no intentions of leaving you behind. You're about to graduate."

Carla glanced at Jag, but he wouldn't make eye contact. "I

don't understand."

Greg stood. "Come this way, and take off your abaya. You won't need it for your final exam."

Chapter 12

Fluorescent lights glared harshly onto the man strapped to a chair in the middle of the bare room. Bruises and cuts covered his face and arms, and blood stained his gray shirt. He glared with defiance at the group as they entered. Jag had seen this before and didn't envy Carla's position.

The prisoner focused his attention on Carla. "Ah, you bring me a whore. How thoughtful."

The guard struck him on the side of the head to silence him. It didn't.

"You think she could get me to talk?" the man taunted them.

Greg pulled out his 9mm and the man quieted. His eyes widened. Greg held out the gun to Carla. "Shoot him. Shoot to kill."

"What?" the man shouted. A stream of swear words in

Arabic followed. "You can't do—" The guard struck him again.

Shaking her head, Carla took a step back. "Don't ask me to do this."

"I gave an order," Greg warned.

Still Carla didn't move. "Who is he? What did he do?" The horrified look on her face sliced a hole his Jag's chest. She wasn't ready for this. She glanced up at him and he saw the pleading and outrage in her eyes but he couldn't help her. Didn't dare for her own good. She had to or she'd fail the program. *Please, Carla, just do it.*

"Doesn't matter. I gave an order." Greg waited a few more seconds and when she didn't move, he lowered the gun and grabbed her by the arm, dragging her out of the room. The man in the chair laughed.

"Greg, give her a minute," Jag pleaded. "Let me talk to her. It was hard for all of us our first time."

"She was given an order." Greg brought her into another room, a small office with a desk and laptop. He turned on the computer and opened a file. "Sit and watch."

Shaking, Carla sat. The video came on. "It's that man in the chair," she said. "He's torturing someone. Oh my God. Who is it?" She covered her face.

"The prisoner on his knees is an American doctor, a volunteer doing charity work. He was accused of being a spy. He was not a spy," Greg hollered, pointing to the computer.

Jag knew how this video ended.

"Don't cover your face." Greg slammed his fist on the desk. "You watch it. Every second. And see why we're executing that man in there. You're lucky I'm giving you an explanation to my order since this is your first time. In the future, if you disobey my order, the bullet might go through your head. Other lives on this team depend on us all following orders." In a way, Jag was relieved because Greg must've known he'd have to show Carla this video. He had this laptop all set up and ready to view.

The video didn't have to reach the most gruesome part, the execution of the doctor. Slowly, Carla stood and held out her hand. "Give me the gun. I don't need to watch any more." Her voice was unusually calm, but Jag noticed she had a slight tremor to her hand.

Greg gave her the 9mm. She walked directly into the next room and passed her exam.

&⊗⋈

Carla left the interrogation room and gave Greg back his gun. She continued walking to the chow hall. She needed water. Footsteps strode up behind her. "Are you all right?" Jag asked.

She had to think about that. Numbness spread throughout her body. Technically, she felt nothing. Even her feet didn't feel as if they touched the floor. "I need something to drink."

"Sure." He grasped her elbow, led her into the break room and poured her some tea.

Her hands shook so badly she had to use both to bring the cup to her mouth. "There are two things that upset me about this."

"And they are…"

"You were right. I can't trust even you. You knew all along they were training me to be an assassin. That was their plan from the beginning, wasn't it?"

He rubbed his forehead and groaned. "Yes, I couldn't have told you. You wouldn't have survived the training with that hanging over your head."

"I don't like people keeping things from me," she scoffed.

"I get that."

"I could have handled it. I can't handle secrets."

He nodded. "That's fair. I'll remember that from now on."

She leaned back in her chair and stared up at the ceiling, feeling trapped like a prisoner. "I guess I've known. I just didn't want to believe it. I was too busy trying to do well."

"What's the other thing that's bothering you?" He patted her arm and she gave him a cold look. He pulled away his hand.

"That terrorist was easier to kill than the cow in Vermont."

"Carla, I know this is tough for you."

"Forget it. I understand you were following orders. What I don't get is how easily you were able to hide things from me. How can I be with you?" She stood up. Did she want to continue a relationship with a man who might keep information behind her back?

"Where are you going?"

"I need to find a bathroom to throw up. Then I'll be ready to go. After we get back to the States, we're done."

೫ဢ

Carla's first impression of the Sayefs' home was luxury villa among a city's devastation. The Eagle Guard team arrived at the entrance of Mr. and Mrs. Sayef's home. Armed guards opened the heavy iron gates and waved them inside. Security cameras and guard dogs ruined the atmosphere of a lush desert oasis. By American standards, it was a huge home, but far from a mansion. The two-story beige stucco structure gave the feel of a Moroccan resort. It was surrounded by palm trees, small plants, flagstone walkways and patios.

Jag hadn't said a word to her since she told him their personal relationship was over. Just as well. They had the mission to focus on, not a troubled love affair. Still she ached inside for what might've been.

A man greeted them at the door and directed them to a sitting room. All the Eagle Guard members were there. The drivers remained with the two SUVs. Beth and Carla wore abayas.

Rasheed Sayef entered the room with smiles and a hand out to shake and welcome the team. "Thank you for coming and taking on this job. My wife and I hate to leave our home, but after the bombings and the continued fighting, we can't stay. Now, I'm afraid we've stayed too long."

The man was in his late thirties or early forties. Handsome, under six feet, dark hair and neatly dressed in business clothes.

"You said your wife has family in France?" Greg asked. "Where in France?"

Rasheed hesitated for a moment. "Her family lives in Calais. We made our flight arrangements for Paris."

"Good. How did you meet?" Greg asked in a friendly, conversational tone.

"We met at university in England," he said.

Greg smiled. "Will you stay in France or return?"

Rasheed shook his head and gazed at the floor. "Sadly, I can't see us returning for a long time. I plan to open a new business in France. It will be safer."

"I'm sure it will be a success. We're glad to help," Greg said. "I'm sorry about your factory. It's difficult to have your business destroyed like that."

Rasheed nodded. "Thank you. It has been difficult. But we will survive this challenge."

A woman appeared at the door. She wore an abaya with a colorful silk headscarf. The woman had a lovely face. Delicate features and large brown eyes.

"Sabine, come in and meet the Eagle Guards." Rasheed waved his wife in, took her hand and introduced her to the team. Something crossed the woman's face when Rasheed grasped her hand. Tension, fear, Carla wasn't sure. The moment the woman made eye contact with her, Carla knew something wasn't right. Rasheed may seem polite and gracious, but there was more to the story.

Greg went over the details of what they were going to do. Rather simple. Pick them up before dawn and drive to Baghdad to catch their plane.

"Your fees have been deposited into your account," Rasheed assured.

"We checked earlier," Greg said. "Thank you."

Carla glanced at Beth and an unspoken acknowledgement passed between them. Beth had noticed Sabine's behavior. "I have gifts for the ladies visiting us." Sabine spoke when there was a lag in the conversation. "May I show them into the next room?"

"Of course." Rasheed waved her on, as if her request was unnecessary.

A guard followed them into the hallway and Sabine stopped him. "I plan to show these women how to properly tie their head scarves. I don't think it would be appropriate for you to be there. You may wait outside."

He nodded and Sabine directed Beth and Carla into a small sunroom next to the kitchen. She closed the door. On a table were two beautiful silk scarves in shades of blue, green and gold.

"These are lovely Mrs. Sayef, but gifts are not necessary,"

Carla said.

"It's my pleasure. And please call me Sabine. Let me show you how to tie a scarf. It will stay even in a strong wind." She took off hers and demonstrated.

Carla and Beth removed theirs and used the silk ones, practicing the way Sabine had showed them.

"Almost," Sabine said. "It's like this." She move closer and her voice changed to a whisper. "I must warn you. My husband is working with the terrorists. Please help me leave him when we escape Iraq."

"What?" Beth spoke softly so the guard outside wouldn't hear.

"He's shipping weapons through his other factory. Please, I'm afraid of him."

There was a knock at the door and the guard announced that Mr. Sayef had requested his wife to return to the sitting room.

When they returned, Sabine's husband gave his wife a stern look and Jag glanced at Carla and Beth. Carla knew not to show any strained expressions. "What do you think?" Carla asked, smiling and holding up the scarf. "A kind gift from Mrs. Sayef."

"Very nice," Greg said. Jag nodded his agreement too.

"Bring only what you can carry in a small bag," Greg continued to Mr. Sayef. "I'd advise no valuables in case we're stopped on the way."

"We have already shipped those to my wife's family. We just want to be safe." He put an arm around Sabine and Carla saw how she stiffened even though she smiled and looked up lovingly at her husband.

"We'll return at three a.m. Be ready." Greg gave the signal for the team to leave.

ॐ

Jag should've known this wouldn't be a simple civilian rescue. Every mission he'd ever been on had become more complicated. How much danger was he putting Carla in? This job was way over the complication level for a newbie. They'd rushed her training and he had assured Greg she was ready. What if he was wrong?

Once they were on the road, Carla told Greg and Jag what Sabine had said about her husband.

"How do we know Mrs. Sayef isn't setting her husband up?" Greg frowned at her. "Maybe she wants a divorce, or she's covering her ass. Maybe she thinks they're in over their heads."

"I hadn't thought of that." Had Carla been fooled by Sabine's words? "She truly seemed frightened."

"People can put on a good act if necessary." Jag had to agree with Greg. They couldn't assume anything.

"Exactly, we'll separate them in the two vehicles, but continue as planned." Greg's tone sounded hard, cold. "We'll let Uncle Sam figure out if Mrs. Sayef is a terrorist or a victim."

"Sayef hadn't mentioned the existence of his other plant, or that it was still operational," Greg added. "That's suspicious."

Was Rasheed working with the rebels? Or were they letting him leave on the condition he didn't mention what was going on? Either way, Greg and Ahmed recommended they go on with the rescue as planned, with one exception. They'd have to help coordinate the bombing as a diversion. Part of their payment to Ahmed's team was to assist them in bombing the factory.

That evening, half of the team parked Ahmed's dusty white trucks behind a deserted building across from Sayef's largest factory. The rest of the group headed to the north end of the plant. Twilight cast long shadows along the streets and buildings. The team wouldn't move on the factory until it was dark enough to give them some cover.

Every nerve, every brain cell in Carla's body was firing. If her heart didn't stop pounding, she swore it would explode. Jag gave her leg a squeeze as they got out of the truck. "Relax. We'll observe from this apartment building and be backup in case something goes wrong."

She nodded, afraid her voice would come out as a squeak. She wasn't wearing the abaya anymore, but the Eagle Guard gear in gray camouflage, boots and a cap. She also had her M16 rifle and a Beretta M9 with a small pack. Their rifles were equipped with night-vision scopes.

Jag spoke into his headset. "Greg, are you guys ready?"

"Roger. Holler when you're set." Ahmed had taken Greg, Beth and Nick and his men to a field across from the factory, hidden beside an empty building, while one of Ahmed's guards brought Jag, Todd and Carla to the third floor of the empty apartment building. One unit was open at the end of the hall. It had been a studio apartment. A torn couch remained and empty kitchen cabinets. On the floor was a broken plate. Had someone, rushing to leave, dropped the plate and just left it? Sad to think someone once had lived here and had been forced to leave because of the fighting. The benefit of this apartment was it being a corner unit and it had windows lining two walls.

"Look through your scope at the north side of the factory," Jag ordered. "Watch for guards as the team approaches. Tell me if you notice anyone walking toward our guys." He took out binoculars and Todd pulled out his rifle and peered through his scope. "Just don't shoot anyone," he teased.

"Funny." She did appreciate him trying to break the tension. Carla opened a window, knelt on the floor and rested the barrel of the gun on the windowsill.

"Well it is heavily guarded and they're armed," Jag said, seriously this time.

"I have the south side covered." Todd settled into position.

"The question is *whose* guards?" Jag asked. "Sayef's hired hands or the rebels?" Jag let Greg know their team was ready.

Jamil, their driver, asked to use the binoculars. "We know they are not ours, and they're not Iraqi military. We're not aware of any other private security agency in this area other than you."

"Would Sayef have hired this many guards?" Todd asked.

Jamil shook his head. "Sayef never had this level of security. Not for shipping mechanical parts. When the extra security and trucks started showing, that's when we started watching. We were suspicious that more than mechanical parts were being shipped. Then the fighting began."

"And one factory blew up," Todd added.

"Not sure who was responsible for that." Jamil lowered the binoculars and gazed down at the streets below the apartment. They had to be vigilant about the safety of their own surroundings as well and those who were heading toward the factory. "We have a man on our team working inside this factory. He's a cousin of one of the electricians, and he said he saw weapons and possibly bomb materials being shipped. He couldn't tell where though."

"Why would they bomb the other factories?" Jag asked. "If they can use it, it doesn't make sense."

"We haven't figured that out either. Maybe an accident, disagreement?"

"Can you see inside, Carla?" Jag spoke to her as a team member, not as a trainee.

She took a deep breath and exhaled before answering. "I'm trying. The windows are dirty, but I do see a few men walking around and I can see a forklift with a large crate. The floodlights are on now. How will our team get close enough?"

"Don't worry," Jag assured her. "They know what to do."

In small groups, Ahmed's men and Greg's team, ran across the field from different directions and slipped around the building. The few guards were stationed at the front entrance and back loading dock. "It's not heavily guarded," Todd said.

"I thought the same," Jag said. "Maybe the bombing of the smaller factory was used to scare people away?"

"Or they finished shipping what they had intended and don't need the added security right now," Todd added.

"Do they have to get inside to set the charges?" Carla asked.

"Ideally, but we're not going. Too many people around twenty-four hours a day," Jamil said. "We'll cause as much damage as possible. The military is planning an air strike later."

"The explosion will give them something to aim at," Jag added.

"How much longer should they be?" she asked.

Jag glanced at Carla to make sure she had her focus on the scope. "Stay cool. A few more minutes. Have you considered the wind speed, distance?"

"Yes, it's dead calm. Look at that flag in front of the factory. It's a four-hundred-yard distance."

"Four fifty," Todd corrected.

"We're done, heading back," Greg cut in on the radio. "See you at the warehouse."

"Copy that," Jag said.

Two of Ahmed's men ran across the field, followed by a couple more and disappeared in the darkness outside the range of the floodlights. Then a side door opened from the factory. A man appeared, carrying an automatic rifle. He lit a cigarette and strolled toward the dumpster Beth and Nick hid behind.

"Jag," Carla whispered, not moving.

"Hold up, Greg. A guard just came out. He's a few feet from Beth and Nick."

Greg didn't answer, but he must've given them a signal because no one was moving. The guard, puffed on the cigarette, the ember glowed in the night. There was enough light from the floodlights to see he had his gun at his hip and could easily raise it.

He walked around the dumpster.

"Carla?" Jag had a commanding edge to his voice.

"Yes?"

"When I give the word, shoot to kill. Do you understand?"

"Yes, he's in my sights. Give me the word."

Abruptly the man stopped, jerked around, raised his gun—

"Now. Shoot."

Carla took the shot. The delay seemed like an eternity. He heard Carla whisper "please", but he couldn't take his eyes off the scene through his binoculars. The guard didn't fully raise his gun to aim. His head jerked forward and he collapsed.

"Score," Todd let out a quiet hoot.

Greg, Nick and Beth leapt out of the shadows. Without hesitation, they grabbed the guard and quickly dragged him across the field. They couldn't chance the other men finding the body. Hopefully, those inside wouldn't miss the guard or would figure he left. When the team was out of sight, he glanced over at Carla.

She peered through the scope, frozen in position. Her knuckles looked white from gripping the stock of the gun so tightly, and her throat kept moving as if she was swallowing, trying to fight the emotions building inside. "You did good, Carla. You can put the gun down."

Still she didn't move. Slowly, he approached and took the gun out of her hands. "You okay?"

She glanced up at him and nodded, but he wasn't so sure. Her eyes had a blank, faraway glaze to them.

"Pack up, we're going back to the warehouse." He reached out his hand to help her up, but she didn't grab it. Was he losing her?

She collected her gear and charged down the stairs.

"She upset with you or something?" Todd asked Jag while they finished packing up the equipment.

"Or something."

∞⋈

Carla marched downstairs without waiting for Jag or Todd. She knew killing that guard had to be done, and she didn't blame Jag for giving her the order, but her head pounded and her teeth ground with the impossible situation she was forced into. One day she was wearing expensive suits and designer shoes, seducing men, having dinners and drinks in fancy restaurants, in total control of her life, and the next day she was hauling a sniper rifle and shooting people.

Right now she wanted far away from these dusty, rundown buildings, to breathe fresh air, not the putrid stench of piss and garbage and who knows what. She missed the smell of pine and snow in Vermont, or the scent of her favorite coffee shop in DC.

At the bottom of the stairs, she kicked open the door, strode out onto the parking area and stuffed the equipment in the back of the truck. She took a walk along the side of the empty building to work off the stress. If she went back to the warehouse, would Jag or Greg give her hell? As she rounded the corner, an arm wrapped around her neck. A stranger—a man's voice—said something in Arabic that she didn't catch. He smelled of body odor as he pressed her against his chest then slammed her up against the wall. A hand grabbed her breast. Anger boiled up inside Carla and she exploded.

She smashed the heel of her boot onto his instep, and at the same time elbowed him hard in his gut, then punched his nose and scratched his eyes. Recoiling from her attack, he eased up on his grip and she shoved away, then turned and continued punching and kicking. The man collapsed and covered his face. As she continued to kick him, someone else grabbed her. She turned with raised fists, ready to strike her new assailant when she realized it was Jag. "You okay?" he asked calmly.

"He jumped me."

Jag mashed his lips together, holding back a smile. "Looks like the other way around," Jag said.

"He grabbed my breast," Carla argued, defending her actions.

Jamil chuckled, then apologized.

Todd yanked the man to his feet. "Get the hell out of here before we let her finish you off," he said in Arabic.

The man held up his hands and limped away.

"Guess you remember Mr. Li's classes." When Carla didn't respond, Jag squeezed her shoulder. "Ready to go back?"

"Yes."

When they returned to Ahmed's facility, Beth gave Carla a hug. "Thanks, you saved us. You did a great job."

Carla didn't have words. Her body was numb and stiff, like a block of ice. Would she ever get those images out of her head of the two men she had killed today?

"We'll bury the rebel in an unmarked grave so he won't be found, as we did with the prisoner earlier," Ahmed said.

Carla cringed. She kept telling herself the man was a terrorist and if she hadn't taken the shot, Greg, Beth and Nick would be dead, or captured and tortured. It still didn't make her feel better. She didn't feel as if she had "scored" as Todd had said.

Nick patted her on the back and Greg gave her a nod and a smile. Had she ever seen the director of the Eagle Guards smile?

"Miss Carla, we have something for you in the boardroom," Ahmed said.

When she entered, the team stood around the table while Ahmed poured her a small glass of clear liquid from a bottle, obviously alcohol of sorts. "I think you need this," Ahmed said, smiling. "You won't be picking up the Sayefs for a few hours so this small taste won't harm you. This is a thank-you for your assistance. For the entire team, Miss Carla's impressive skills, and good luck for the safe completion of your mission."

They raised their glasses and drank. The strong alcohol burned on the way down, made her eyes tear and instantly warmed her on the inside. "What is this?" she asked.

"Raki," Ahmed said. "Turkish brandy."

"It kind of tastes like Greek ouzo," Beth said, making a face.

"Yes, yes, it is a bit like ouzo," Ahmed said, laughing. "It's very strong. I wouldn't drink anymore."

"Thank you, I won't," Carla said, putting down her glass. "That was very kind."

The team left the boardroom to rest and make final preparations. "Hang on," Jag asked Carla. He took her hand in his.

She stopped and held back the emotions building inside. She wanted to lean against his chest and feel his arms wrapped tightly around her. How could they be a couple when their job required them to keep secrets from each other? "We have a mission to complete. This isn't the time to discuss our personal issues."

He pressed his lips together then nodded. "You're right. The personal issues can be addressed when we return home. But as your handler I must have your trust for the mission. Without it we have a bigger problem."

The formal tone of his voice cut through her. Long gone was the sexy teasing she had craved during her training. "I'll listen to instructions and follow orders."

He released her hand and smiled, but it was a sad smile. "Get some rest. Don't worry, everything will work out fine."

Hours later they arrived at the Sayefs' home. The couple was waiting, each with a small bag. Greg explained to them how they would take only two vehicles, and he wanted to have an equal number of his men in each vehicle for security and would then have to split up Rasheed and his wife.

"No, that's not acceptable," Mr. Sayef argued.

Greg checked his watch. They didn't have time to debate this. The bombs would soon be going off at the factory. "You contracted us to get you out safely. If we run into any military or rebel activity, I need my men equally placed. There is no discussion."

Mr. Sayef huffed but conceded. Mrs. Sayef got into the car with Jag, Carla and Nick. And her husband was with Beth, Todd and Greg. The drivers were the same ones they had used throughout the trip. It was before three-thirty and they drove at a steady pace through the empty street of Dhuluiya.

Carla checked her watch a few times. The bombs were set to go at three-forty-five, then a high-altitude plane was supposed to hit the factory shortly after. How long after they weren't sure. This was going to be the longest ride to the airport she'd ever had.

They were almost out of the city when they heard the first explosion, followed by several more. The sounds were at a distance, a few miles off, but it was enough to make everyone jump.

"What was that?" Mrs. Sayef asked, frightened. She looked behind and pointed. Smoke rose in a large black cloud. "The rebels and the military are fighting again." She covered her face.

"We'll be fine," Carla assured her. "We're driving away from that."

"It looks like it's in our area."

"Hard to tell," Jag said. "That's behind us, so don't worry."

It wasn't long until cars and trucks jammed the main road heading out of town. Local residents must have heard the explosions and, suspecting more military action, were trying to evacuate the city. Like the approach of a hurricane, everyone raced away from the danger. Cars cut in between their two SUVs, and it was nearly impossible to stay together.

"Our driver says there will be check points at the bridges," Greg said over the radio Jag held. The other SUV was still directly in front of them. "The traffic is about to get worse. We might get separated."

"No worries," Jamil replied. "We can get through the road blocks as long as the fighting doesn't start."

"Our driver doesn't think we'll have an issue," Jag announced over the radio to Greg. "We know where to go if we get split up."

"It's a mess. People are panicking," Greg added. "Don't stop for any reason. Meet at the check point in Baghdad, if we miss that, then on to the airport."

"Copy that," Jag said. A small car zipped in front of the SUV, cutting them off and clipping their bumper. Jamil honked his horn and swore at the guy. The other driver continued on as if nothing happened.

"Are you going to arrest my husband when we reach Baghdad?" Mrs. Sayef asked.

"We'll worry about that when we get there," Jag said. "Let's just focus on securing your save passage first."

The din of gunfire broke out in the distance, then a large blast and boom shook the ground. Cars and people scattered. Nick glanced at Carla, raising an eyebrow. She got the message. The air strike hit the factory. Mrs. Sayef flinched and covered her face with her hands, whimpering.

Military trucks packed with armed Iraqi soldiers raced past, heading toward town where they had just left.

"Don't stop," Jag ordered. "We need to get over that bridge and away from the fighting. Baghdad is secure." Some of the drivers had the same idea as the road rage heightened, banging and scraping their vehicles into cars to form the single line.

Armed military guards ignored the chaos. Men, women and children were crammed into cars. After the gunfire and explosions began, the guards only made a brief inspection inside cars before waving them across the bridge. They weren't asking questions or checking IDs.

"There goes our first vehicle," Jag announced. "It shouldn't be much longer. Hang in there Mrs. Sayef." Their SUV with Greg, Mr. Sayef and the others had moved several cars ahead and crossed the narrow bridge. The woman nodded, her eyes wide as she glanced side to side. This would be a really bad time to have a panicked passenger.

As they waited in the long line, Carla watched the SUV reach the other side, enter the road and continue south. When they were out of sight, she glanced at Nick. He gave her a wink. Waiting was murder for all of them.

"Make sure your weapons are well hidden under your cloak," Nick said. "We don't need any excuse to be delayed."

Their vehicle inched closer to the entrance of the bridge. The guards stopped a flatbed truck, signaling the driver to pull over. The driver shouted and argued. The guard shook his head and pointed to the stacks of crates strapped on the back. He probably demanded to look inside.

Jag groaned. "This is going to take a while."

Gunfire and explosions erupted behind them. The roar of battle rose. Carla resisted the urge to cover her ears. "Come on." Jamil punched the steering wheel.

The argument ranted on, and Carla tugged at the cloth of her abaya as she watched the last car drive onto the bridge. Only a few more cars and they'd be next. But then the vehicle stopped dead center. The driver got out and ran. "What a place to break down," Carla commented.

"What?" Nick asked. "Oh fuck."

"That car on the bridge. It's stuck," Carla said.

"Fuck!" Jag shouted. "It's not stuck. Get us out of here."

Chapter 13

Jamil jerked the SUV into reverse and smashed into the car behind him, getting a loud blare of a horn. He swung the truck around and headed back toward town. Carla gripped the seat until her fingers went numb.

"Where are we going?" Mrs. Sayef yelled. "We can't go back. That's where all the fighting—"

An explosion shook the truck. Jamil swerved off the road, cut the wheel and managed to get the vehicle under control. Carla swung around and looked through the rear window. The center of the bridge was gone. Pieces of concrete and steel dropped into the river. The wide gap made Carla shudder. If the guy in the flatbed truck hadn't gotten into an argument with the guards, they would've been on the bridge when it blew.

Jamil turned down a side street. "I know a short cut."

"Short cut to where?" Nick asked.

"Out of the city. There's another bridge farther south, about fifteen miles. I'll make a call and see what I can find out. Make sure it's clear."

"Go for it," Jag said. He called Greg and explained their situation. "Meet us at the airport. We'll get there one way or the other."

The driver punched a number into his cell phone and requested an update for their target area. They left most of the traffic and turmoil behind them when they were about ten miles out of town. They hadn't been driving for more than forty-five minutes, but to Carla felt as if they'd been driving several hours. Jamil's cell phone rang with the bad news. The other bridge was closed because of security. If they couldn't get to the other side of the river, what chance would they have to make it to the airport?

A red pickup truck and two white Japanese cars sped around them, nearly running their SUV off the road. Jamil swore under his breath again. *Insanity*, Carla thought. People are panicking and driving like maniacs. Then two motorcycles raced passed doing about eighty. "Oh my God. They're going to get killed driving like that," Carla said.

"This is insane," Jag said. "Luckily, we have a good driver."

Jamil gave a short laugh. "We are not there yet, my friend."

Minutes later the same red pickup and two white Japanese cars returned, racing in the other direction, followed by the motorcycles. "Hold up," Jag ordered. "Something's wrong." They couldn't see anything. But then they heard it. Gunfire and a rumble.

"Turn around," Jag said. "Turn around. Now!"

The driver slammed on his brakes to make a U-turn. The gunfire and explosions grew louder. Then a large military truck raced over a rise in the road. He must've been watching the action behind him because he crashed right into their SUV in the middle of its turn.

The front end of the SUV was smashed and knocked the vehicle off the side of the road.

"Everyone okay?" Jag asked when they came to a stop.

Mrs. Sayef, Nick and Carla all nodded. Carla tried to see the men inside the truck, if any were injured, or if they would pull weapons on them. Both vehicles sat there motionless in a surreal moment, stunned by what had just happened.

A dusty army tank slowly rolled by, totally ignoring the roadside accident. Carla stared at the tank. *This is nuts.* The guy in the back of the pickup hopped out and rubbed his shoulder, but he seemed all right. He stared down the road toward the fighting. Jamil waved to the other men and smiled. He got a nod.

Jamil tried starting the vehicle, but it wouldn't turn over. He and Jag got out and opened the hood. Steam poured out. "We're fucked," Nick said.

Nick, Carla and Sabine joined the others on the street. The front tire was flat and the fender was crushed against it. Even with a crowbar they couldn't pull it off. And if they could, the SUV wasn't going anywhere.

One of the soldiers from the truck walked over, carrying an AR-15 and dressed in combat gear. "Don't show your weapons," Jag said. "Be relaxed and friendly."

"He's Iraqi military," Jamil told the group, keeping his voice low. "It's okay." Jamil raised his hand and said a number of things in Arabic. Carla picked up a few words. *Sorry, accident, leaving city.* The soldier, who looked about sixteen, nodded. He didn't appear angry or upset, but he pointed back to town. There was a pause, no doubt while Jamil tried considering a good response, then stated, "Baghdad." And the soldier shook his head.

Jag swore. "That's not good. We're still at least fifteen miles away," he whispered. "That's a long walk and they're not letting us through."

Explosions shook the ground and everyone hit the dirt. Black smoke rose and gunfire exchanged over the hill and beyond the dried brush and palm trees. Then more explosions several hundred yards toward Dhuluiya. They were caught in the middle.

The soldier glanced around at his comrades. They jumped off the truck and headed south. The young soldier waved his arm for them to move, pointing his gun toward the river.

Jamil pointed back to town but the soldier frantically shook his head. "Not safe," he said in Arabic. "The riverbank."

Sabine draped her bag crosswise over her shoulder as Jag and Nick stood on either side of her. They all raced through scrub brush and down the riverbank. Jamil followed and offered to help Carla. She'd worn a loose abaya to hide her shoulder-rig holster and her Beretta. Nick and Jag already had out their guns. Jag handed Carla her rifle that she'd left in the SUV. At this point they were the least of the soldiers' problems.

Moving swiftly, they headed south toward Baghdad along the river, past the main source of fighting. The shoreline was slippery and the brush caught at their clothing. "This will take forever," Jag said. "I'd say we should swim across, but that's a long way and the river is moving pretty fast. I don't know what type of currents there might be."

"Maybe we should go back toward Dhuluiya," Jamil said.

"I could call Ahmed and he could get a car. In a day or two we could try again."

Jag shook his head. "My contract is to get the Sayefs out today."

Carla knew he didn't want to say they were probably in too much danger to stay after bombing the factory. And she did know that the authorities were expecting the Sayefs at the airport. They were persons of interest with terrorist connections. "Any chance we could get a boat or raft?"

Nick laughed dryly. "Somehow, with all this fighting, I don't think anyone will be out on their boats today to offer us a ride."

"Steal one," Sabine said. "I read in our newspaper where a mother and daughter took a boat to escape the fighting in Dhuluiya and meet family in Baghdad. Their trip was much longer and they made it safely."

"Two women in a boat are less conspicuous than five people," Nick argued.

"I think it's the fastest way to get to where we're going," Carla pleaded. Anything but stand there another minute. She'd start running if they didn't move soon.

"I have to agree we need to change our itinerary—a cruise on the Tigris," Jag said with enough embellishment to sound like a tour director. He smiled at her and her stomach twirled. It was rare for him to smile, and now, in all the madness, he finds humor. It did set her mind at ease though. "We'll walk and look for a boat."

He turned away from her and their group marched silently along the bank, watching and alert for any danger. The river appeared peaceful for the moment. As she watched Jag, anxiety filled her again with a deep ache. The words *don't trust anyone* continued to haunt her. He'd told her that when they had met in the hospital. Was that a warning of things to come? Would there ever come a time when she could trust him? Trust was vital for a team's survival. She desperately wanted someone she could count on. The physical attraction was there, but that wouldn't sustain them forever.

After they walked a couple miles, Sayef begged to stop and rest. Jag agreed, but only for a moment. They'd reached a small village and the sound of traffic and people drifted down. The pops of gunfire was replaced by the rush of water.

Nick and Jamil strolled up river a ways while Sabine rested. "Can you go on, Mrs. Sayef?" Jag asked. "We shouldn't stop very long."

She stood. "Yes, thank you."

Nick rushed back without Jamil.

"What's going on?" Jag asked. "Where's Jamil?"

"We found a boat," Nick said. "But Jamil is arguing with the owner about borrowing it."

Sabine marched passed the group. "I will talk to him."

When they reached the boat—a large john boat with a motor—Jamil was in a heated argument. Sabine cut in. In Arabic, Carla caught most of Sabine's conversation. Essentially, she said these men were taking her sister-in-law and her to her husband in Baghdad. They had weapons and could take it by force, but she would pay him for the loan and his troubles. This other gentleman would bring the boat back.

The man made a face and glanced at the weapons. Realizing he was out-numbered, he nodded. Sabine reached beneath her abaya and retrieved a fistful of money. The man seemed pleased and stood back as they got into the boat. Carla wondered what else Sabine was hiding under her garment.

"Keep an eye out along both shores," Jag said. "Keep your weapons handy."

The closer they got to Baghdad, the more nervous Sabine got. "What will they do to me when we get to Baghdad?"

"What do you mean?" Jag feigned ignorance. "You have tickets to fly to France. We're contracted to take you to the airport."

"But I told you my husband is working with the terrorists. What about him? I don't feel safe with him."

"Authorities may take him into protective custody and question him. If he's smart, he'll cooperate." Nick shrugged. No one said that she too would be detained and questioned.

"So I'll be allowed to leave?" Sabine asked. "I don't want to be alone with my husband. I'm afraid he'll kill me. He will if he finds out what I've told you."

"Don't worry, Mrs. Sayef," Jag said. "Let's just get to the airport first. We won't let your husband harm you."

Whether Mrs. Sayef was satisfied with that or not, she stopped arguing. Throughout their journey, the river had been deserted and silent. Carla searched the riverbanks for signs of danger and kept her rifle close.

"I'm not sure which is worse, the gunfire and explosions or dead quiet," Nick said. The boat skimmed over the choppy water. All the members of the team scanned the shorelines and downriver for armed soldiers or more fighting, but so far all was peaceful.

"I was thinking the same," Carla said. She glanced at Jag and he gave her a reassuring wink. Her heart tugged at the simple gesture. Leaving him after this mission would be the hardest thing she ever did. Would she see him again if she had to do more training? Jag was on the phone and radio, trying to contact Greg without any luck.

While Nick and Jamil talked to Sabine, Jag leaned over to Carla and whispered, "I know this has been hard on you. I hated having to do what I did. You may not believe me, but everything I did was because I knew it was the best way to help you through the program. I wasn't sure if the FLC was serious about their threat to eliminate you if you failed, but I didn't want to take that chance. I hope when we're finished with this mission, you'll find a way to believe in us again."

Carla let his words sink in. She wanted to have a man she could trust and a relationship she could count on, but her mind came back to the lies and half-truths. Right or wrong, she felt betrayed. "I'm not sure how I'll feel after this is over. I understand it was necessary. It doesn't make me feel better about it." She gazed up at him and the intense pain in his eyes broke her heart. She loved him despite all they've been through, but could they make it work?

"Don't give up on us yet, Carla. Please." He squeezed her hand. "When we get back I want to talk more. I can't say what I want to, not here, not now."

"Can you tell me one thing?"

"Sure," he said.

"After all this training, do you know what Julia or the FLC has planned for me?" Carla spoke low enough that the others in the boat couldn't hear them above the sound of the motor and river.

"I believe they plan to use you for an upcoming mission. The specific details, I don't know. I do know Julia said they needed a woman. I have my suspicions in what capacity. I think you can guess too."

Carla studied him suspiciously. "You know a lot about the FLC."

"We were briefed when they decided they would use our assistance."

As they drifted closer to Baghdad, Jag tried to contact

Greg again and got through. "Greg's meeting us," he announced to the group when he turned off the radio. "There's a bridge coming up in a couple miles according to my GPS. It's closed, but he'll be waiting on the east side."

A few more boats and shallow draft barges appeared on the river. "We're getting closer to Bagdad," Jamil said.

At this point, Carla knew not to assume anything. Her muscles were sore from tension and she had to stop clenching her teeth. She was getting a headache.

"Snap to, people. We're approaching Baghdad. The city is supposed to be secure, but the perimeters may still have hostile activity. Watch the banks and shoreline carefully," Jag said. "Use your scope, Carla, check down river."

Carla peered through her scope, scanned the shoreline and focused on the occasional boats. They were moving away from them so didn't appear to be a danger.

"Oh no, oh no, I can't do this," Sabine cried. She shifted around in the boat, rocking it.

"Sit still, Mrs. Sayef," Jag ordered. "We're almost there. He didn't put down his gun, he kept watch. His words didn't calm Sabine. She began to sob.

"I see Greg and the truck," Jag said. "He's waving. Keep watch on the banks and the bridge as we pull ashore."

"Thank God," Carla said. She took a breath and for once her muscles relaxed.

"You're going to have me arrested with my husband, aren't you?" Sabine wailed. "Please, let me go. I don't want to go to the airport." She began shifting in the boat and rocking it.

Carla lowered her rifle, reached around and patted Sabine's knee. If the woman didn't calm down she might flip the boat. "It'll be all right, Sabine. They'll take you into protective custody. Authorities will ask you questions, that's all. Just tell them what you know. We'll let them know you alerted us to your husband's activities. We'll ask them to keep you separated from him."

"Carla, get back to your post," Jag ordered. In trying to console Sabine, Carla had disobeyed orders, again.

In the distance, a shot was fired and Carla swore she heard it speed past her ear before it splashed beside the boat.

"Down. Location!" Jag yelled as he knocked Carla onto the floor of the boat. He used his body as a barrier and raised his rifle.

Jamil shoved Sabine to the bottom of the boat and scanned the shoreline and riverbanks with Jag.

"Let me up." Carla struggled under Jag's weight. "I can help."

"No, stay down."

"The bridge. I got him," Nick said as he fired. Sabine cried out as the rifle shot. A second later the lone man on the bridge dropped. Greg had rushed onto the bridge, but Nick had killed the gunman before Greg had a clear shot.

Jag didn't have to say anything, Carla knew she had been wrong and it could've cost them lives. When he helped her back up to her seat, Carla wasn't sure if she should thank him for protecting her or yell at him for not allowing her to assist. "Don't you think I can handle a crisis?" she asked him.

"Reflex," he argued. "With so many of us upright in the boat, it would be like shooting fish in a barrel. He missed the first round because he hadn't judged the distance right. He wouldn't have missed the second time."

She didn't argue with his logic.

As they pulled up to shore, Nick helped Sabine out of the boat. "Will you be okay on the ride back, Jamil?" Jag asked.

"I will be fine, thank you. I will return the boat. Hope to work with you again."

"Thanks for your help," Jag said as they shook hands.

Carla watched Sabine. The woman glanced up and down the shore, her eyes wide. She had that look Carla had seen with submissives who had gotten in way over their head and were about to panic. Sabine slid her bag off her shoulder and slowly reached beneath her abaya. At first, Carla thought she was going to give Jamil some money for his efforts, but then she saw the gun.

Sabine raised the gun and turned toward Jag, Nick and Carla. "I'm not going to the airport."

"Put the gun down," Jag warned.

"No, I'll find my own way now."

When Sabine turned her attention away from Jamil for a second, he jumped in the water. It was enough to distract her. The woman jerked toward the splash, Carla grabbed the gun and used one of Mr. Li's kicks to knock her off her feet. Sabine released the gun and fell to the ground. Jag retrieved Sabine's gun and stood over her while Nick secured her wrists with wire ties. They weren't taking any chances.

"It wasn't ready to fire," Carla assured them. "She didn't even have her finger on the trigger."

Jag and Nick lifted Sabine. Still stunned, she wasn't fighting them. "Good job, Carla. Smart, Jamil, except you'll have a wet journey home."

Jamil shrugged. "I should head back." He pushed the boat out into the river.

"Be careful," Carla smiled, but inside she considered the turmoil and fighting he had to face.

He nodded and started the small motor. He swiftly maneuvered the vessel up stream.

Greg raced down the bank and helped Nick drag Sabine up to the truck. Armed Iraqi soldiers drove past in military vehicles practically ignoring them, then one pulled up and stopped. Carla glanced at Jag while holding the rifle in her hand. Were they going to question them? They all had weapons clearly visible and they had an Iraqi woman bound.

Greg raised his hand and waved. "We're ready to go," he said in Arabic. The driver nodded and gave him a wave. They got into the SUV and followed the soldiers in the truck.

"Friends of yours?" Jag asked.

Greg smiled. "We're getting an escort to the airport as a favor. Baghdad's secure for the moment, thanks to some recent assistance and air strikes by American military forces. At the airport, we informed the Iraqi and US military stationed there as to our VIP guests. They've agreed to have the American military take the Sayefs in for questioning."

"My husband hired you to get us out safely, not have us arrested," Sabine spat out.

"Not arrested, protective custody, Mrs. Sayef," Greg corrected. "We've met our agreement. You and your husband did get out safely. And if after questioning they decide you did not conspire with the rebels to ship weapons and bombs illegally through your factory, then you will be released and allowed to continue onto France as planned."

Sabine eyed him with loathing. After what Carla witnessed, she doubted either of them were going to France.

৪৩৩

Carla sat on the plane next to Jag, staring out the window as they took off. The pilot had warned them to remain seated with their seatbelts on because of expected turbulence. The restraints did little to tamp down her restlessness. She heard a crack, an odd sound, then felt a burning sensation in her left calf. The plane made a sharp dip and banked to the right. White clouds streamed past and rain splattered the glass. Once the plane got above this bank of clouds, the sky would be clear blue and the flight would be less rough.

The flight attendants got on their speakers and talked privately to the captain. "What's going on?" Carla asked. She rubbed her leg. It was really sore. Why, she didn't know. Probably cut herself and was only now feeling it.

"Not sure," Jag said. "The flight attendants seem nervous and they got up and went into the cockpit before they turned off the *Seatbelt* sign." He glanced back to the others sitting in the private plane. It was the size of a small commercial jet. A few extra military soldiers had hitched a ride back to the states too, considering they were paying for part of this mission. Everyone shrugged their shoulders. Then one male flight attendant strode slowly along the rows of seats, examining each one.

"How is everyone?" he asked.

"Fine," Nick said. "What's up?"

The flight attendant didn't say, but continued on.

Stretching her leg out, Carla tried massaging the muscle. It was really stinging. What had she done to it?

"What's wrong with your leg?" Jag asked.

"I think I injured it during the mission. The soreness is setting in now." She held up her hand and there was blood, fresh blood."

"What the hell?" Jag yelled. He unbuckled his seatbelt and got out of his seat. "Need help over here." He yanked up her pant leg. "She's been shot."

"What?" Carla looked down at the blood oozing from her calf. "How is that possible?"

Jag and the flight attendant examined her. Another of the

crew arrived with a first aid kit. A moment later the captain came out.

"How serious is it?" the captain asked. A middle-aged man with deep frown lines partly covered by his uniform hat.

"Let's get her to stretch out on the floor," the flight attendant said. He was a young guy in his mid-twenties with short, blond hair. He laid down a blanket and Jag cleaned the wound with sterile gauge and peroxide.

"Just grazed," Jag said. "A couple steri-strips and dressing should do it. She doesn't need stitches."

Carla tried looking over her shoulder.

"Sit still," Jag ordered.

"Where did the bullet come from?" she asked. Greg knelt beside her and held her hand. "Greg?"

"They're checking," Jag said. "Almost done."

"How're you feeling?" Greg asked. He had never showed concern like this before. She couldn't help but wait for the other shoe to drop. Would he reprimand her for getting shot, as if it was her fault for sitting in the wrong seat? Then she remembered Mr. Li's predictions, or warnings. He'd told her during the mission that she would have two near death challenges. In the boat she heard that bullet *whiz* by her ear, just missing her head. And now this bullet grazing her leg. Was he psychic?

"I'm fine," Carla said. "Thanks."

"You have more to learn, but you did okay on the mission," Greg said.

"I appreciate that, Greg." From him, that was a huge compliment.

"Here's where it came in," the captain pointed to small bits of plastic where the bullet had pierced the fuselage. "It entered the plane on an angle just after takeoff. As we were taking off, I saw a number of military vehicles rushing to the end of one of the other runways. The report I got was someone broke through the perimeter fence and was shooting at the planes." He looked around the ceiling and wall, then one of the attendants picked up something on the floor.

"Here's the slug." The flight attendant held it up.

"Small caliber." The captain examined the bit of metal. "We'll fly low and land at the next closest airport that's safe and change planes. The instruments aren't showing any mechanical problems or damage to the fuel tanks, but I'd rather play it safe than try for a trans-Atlantic crossing."

After she was patched up and sitting back in her seat, the flight attendants fussed over her with tea and sandwiches. She thanked them and felt the weight of the mission ease. Exhaustion from the trip settled into her bones. Would she ever erase the images of the men she had killed? Although the experience was disturbing, she was numb to it now. Since the car bomb, this was this first time she wasn't afraid anymore. If she had to spend her life looking over her shoulder for Aleid's assassins, she'd be ready for them.

"What's up, Carla?" Jag asked. "You haven't spoken a word in a while. Are you in pain?"

"No, I'm okay. What's going to happen to Mr. and Mrs. Sayef?" She gazed out of the plane. Could he read her eyes and see she wasn't ready for him to recognize all the conflict stirring there.

He gave a grim laugh. "They'll be in custody while Uncle Sam does the investigation. Greg said he talked to the CIA and they've been watching them for a while. Mrs. Sayef had been traveling prior to all the fighting in Iraq. It's not unusual for women wearing abayas not to be searched at airports. They believe she was transporting large amounts of cash and information for the rebels. They also believe the Sayefs had planned to set up a terrorist center in Calais, France using their business as a front. They hope to acquire the information they need about those rebel, the weapons and bomb shipments."

"That's good."

He patted her leg. "Want something more to drink? Tea, coffee, Raki?"

She laughed and leaned back in her seat. "No, thanks I'm good. Raki will knock me out."

"Maybe you could use the rest. Are you going to tell me what's really bothering you?"

She shrugged. "After all the weeks we've spent together, I don't really know anything about you. Where you're from, if you have a family? I hardly know anything about anyone on our team."

He smiled. "Our team. So you consider yourself a part of this team now?"

"I hope so."

"You are a member of the team. You've earned it." He probably enjoyed pointing that out.

"Thanks, I know I have more to learn."

He nodded. "I do have a family. I have a brother and sister, both younger. Parents live in North Carolina and have a summer place on Cape Hatteras. We all meet there over the Fourth of July. Maybe you'd like to go someday."

"It all sounds very nice and so normal." She wondered if she'd find a sense of normal in her life again.

He leaned forward and narrowed his gaze. "Do you regret leaving your old life behind? Do you fear who you've become?"

Carla smiled and touched his cheek. He looked worried. "No, I have no regrets and don't fear who I am. Alana

MacKenna doesn't exist anymore. I wouldn't go back even if I could. I've finished running. I'm no longer afraid."

"Good. You did well on this mission. But I still see the worry in your eyes." He took her hand in both of his.

She stared down out their grasped hands, unable to look at him for the moment. "I'm sorry I put the gun down in the boat to console Sabine. I was disobeying an order."

He raised her chin with his finger. "Yes, you were told to keep watch for any danger and you disobeyed orders, but sometimes that's a call you have to make in certain situations. The woman was panicking and could've capsized the boat. You prevented a worse situation. It's okay."

"Thanks. It will strange going back to DC."

He nodded. "You'll adjust. Get to the point. What are you dancing around? You want to ask me something."

She took a deep breath and let it out slowly. Looking into his eyes nearly broke her in two. The nurse in her wanted to heal the cuts and bruises on his face, hands and arms. The woman in her wanted to wound him deeply because she knew after this plane landed he would leave her. She had to go to Washington, back to work with the FLC, and he would go with the Eagle Guards on another mission.

As much as she expected it would hurt, she had to know what would happen next. "All right. I have a couple concerns."

"Go ahead," he said formally.

"Did I pass this part of my training? What comes next?" She wanted to ask him when he would leave on his next mission?

"For the most part, you've passed. You will continue your martial arts skills for years and also the language classes. And you'll always continue with weapon and knife training and hand-to-hand combat. You'll return to work in DC. These training sessions will be scheduled. What else?"

"What about us?" Like downing a shot of tequila in one swallow without a hint of a cough. It was time to get straight to the point.

"That's up to you. I talked to Greg weeks ago about relocating to DC. I may have to travel for my job, but I can have a home base in DC. The FLC will be utilizing our team anyway." He took her face in his hands and lowered his voice. "I knew you were more than another assignment the first day I became your bodyguard. I knew I wanted you the moment I caught you trying to run away. You possessed my heart. I saw the pain you were suffering and I intended to show you how to transfer that into a heightened level of pleasure."

Carla gasped. She'd never heard Jag talk like this. The intense look he gave her tore her apart inside. How could she say good-bye to him?

"Right now I'm desperate to touch you, but this isn't the time or place."

Lust burned in his gaze and she ached for him. Carla reached out and gripped his arms. "Running away did it for you?" she teased.

"Did I give you permission to speak?" he teased back.

She shook her head. Tears welled in her eyes.

"I love you, Carla. I'm your lover, your Master, your protector for always."

Her throat tightened. "I love you, Jag, but how can we?" she whispered.

"Shhh." He kissed her now possessively. Carla liked being possessed and protected, but also maintaining the strength and control of her own mind. The kiss deepened she melted into him. Jag's arms wrapped around her, crushing her into his chest. And her body screamed for release, but that would come later and she imagined all the luscious things he would do to her to bring her pleasure. The problems would be worked out later, much later. Then an odd thought came to mind. Can two assassins fall in love?

"You're smiling," Jag said. "What's so funny?"

"Just happy."

"It's about fucking time," Nick announced from the isle.

Carla looked up and Jag swung around to look up at Nick, grinning down at them. "What?" Jag asked, feigning annoyance.

"About time the two of you hooked up." Nick grinned. "The chemistry was obvious."

Carla and Jag glanced at each other. Hadn't Nick guessed they already hooked up at the camp several times? "Guess you're right."

"Damn right," Nick held up a can. "Want a beer?"

"Not right now." Jag shook his head. "Want one, Carla?"

"Maybe later, thanks."

"You did great, Carla." Nick leaned against the seat across the aisle and took a swig of his beer. "Good to have you on the team. But I hear you'll be mostly working at the White House."

"I'll go wherever they need me. Thanks for your help."

Todd and Beth walked by with cups of coffee and stopped to ask how she was feeling. "I think you're due for another cut and color." Todd studied her. "Can't allow that old red to show through."

"Right. Someone might recognize me." Carla laughed.

"I doubt that." Beth frowned. "Even without the surgery or hair color, you don't look or act anything like the person you were." Had they taken an oath not to ever mention her old name again? "Do you forgive me for deceiving you at the hospital?" Beth asked. "And for trying to scare you off at the training facility? It was my own insecurity, and I'm sorry. I thought they were looking to replace me."

Todd put an arm around Beth's shoulders and squeezed. "We couldn't do without you, Beth."

"I understand. Don't worry," Carla said. She really wasn't upset with Beth anymore.

Beth let out a breath, relieved. "Good. I'm glad you'll be on our team." She and Todd returned to their seats.

Jag stood and retrieved a blanket and pillow from the overhead compartment. He covered Carla. "Get some rest. We have a long flight, and you've been through hell."

She tucked the pillow under her head. Slowly, her body began to relax. Now that she dared to open her heart to this man, what next? "Jag, if I go to Cape Hatteras, what will I tell them? I don't even know who I am. They gave me a new name, a new face, a new job. But before a few months ago Carla Hillman didn't exist."

He stroked her hair. "Don't worry, we'll make up something."

The weight of the mission finally eased from her shoulders. This time when she closed her eyes, the images that drifted into her mind were of Jag and her making love, not of the violence. The bad would remain in her life, but not rule it.

After a few moments, she felt him tucking the blanket close around her. He laced his fingers within hers and pressed her head onto his shoulder. Peaceful sleep came for the first time in months.

Chapter 14

Weeks after Carla settled into her new condo in Washington,
DC and several months after Alana MacKenna officially died,
she entered Julia Flynn's office. The press secretary had made a
number of changes to the space. The desk had been moved
away from the window and was angled to face diagonally
across the room. A hostess table held a teapot, coffee pot and
new colorful mugs. The collection of New Age crystals Julia
called paper weights were no longer on her desk but were now
located on the bookshelves. Her Zen sand garden and a
Newton's cradle were set up on a small coffee table in front of
a sofa. Maybe Julia thought redecorating would replenish the
energy in the room. A new feng shui makeover? If it helped
the woman calm down a notch or two, Carla was all for it.
There were numerous folding chairs set up in the office for the
meeting. No one else had arrived yet.

"Am I early?" Carla asked.

Julia pointed to a chair for Carla to sit, then took a seat herself at her desk. "I wanted to talk to you first before the others arrive. We'll be working on a new project very soon and the FLC will need added security, especially a female."

Carla made a point not to give away her confusion about why Julia felt a woman security officer was needed over the several men they had on staff. "Can you say who the target is, or what country he's from? Is there more than one?"

Julia leaned her elbows on the desk and clasped her hands together. "This is going to be a difficult case, and it's going to take quite some planning. You and the other members will be informed as soon as we have something more definite. I can tell you our target is an American senator."

"A senator? I see." She didn't really, and she didn't want to sound shocked. But this person had to be extremely dangerous to become an FLC target. The details had to be quite complicated.

"The others will be in shortly to meet with you," Julia said. "Just relax and act as if you've never met them before. Zoe will show you around and take you through orientation. Even though you've been through it before, you'll go through it again. Remember, you're a new employee. It's imperative the others never find out who you are. Only Zoe and Jason know who you were."

"I understand." Carla wished Jag could be with her, but he wasn't officially part of the FLC, so he couldn't be at this meeting. He was waiting for her at her new condo. He hadn't moved into DC yet. He had a few things to tie up in Vermont first, sell his place for one. The FLC had helped her find a condo at The Wyoming on Columbia Road. She loved the historic twentieth-century building Julia had recommended, and thought her condo was haunted, but Jag didn't believe her. She wondered if Mr. Li had a thing for ghosts.

The FLC had also assisted her in recovering her funds from her bank account in the islands. Most of her other assets had been passed on to family members after her fake death, at least the portion the FLC couldn't acquire without looking suspicious. The balance, along with a little buffer, they gave to Carla.

"I'm looking forward to beginning a new project," Carla said. And get back to a normal life again. As normal as this one could get.

"Good, because we'll be starting very soon."

"Will you need me to do any presentations in the Red Tape Room as a submissive or Dominatrix?" Carla asked. She actually enjoyed those presentations as they called performing for their target while other members of the team recorded them on video tape on hidden cameras.

"Not in the Red Tape Room, but possibly outside. Our operation may need to be moved away from the White House. Your training will protect you and the other women. We want to be prepared for anything, and we want to protect our members. Especially after Zoe's abduction and the attempt on your life."

A knock at the door stopped Carla from adding anything more. Her argument was that no matter how much security they had, it couldn't protect all members in all situations.

"Come in and take a seat," Julia called out. The men and women of the FLC entered the room. Carla glanced at Zoe and Jason and instantly regretted it. It would take some control not to show emotion or recognition when Zoe and Jason knew her true identity. Jag had taught her to hide her emotions and expressions. She was learning but still had to be careful not to be caught off guard.

The group took their seats. Jason and Zoe sat together, as husband and wife it wasn't surprising. Melissa and Tyler claimed the chairs beside them. Had they become a couple yet? They always were flirting or arguing or maybe that was one in the same. Then Blake, Clay and Johnny joined the group. They were all secret service, and were occasionally called to participate in the Red Tape Room if needed.

"I'd like to introduce Carla Hillman as our newest member," Julia said. "She has extensive training in security and some in foreign languages. She's undergoing more extensive study for this position, but we feel she's ready."

"I remember what you had said about her *position*," Melissa asked with an odd emphasis. What did they know about her? "Can she work as a sub or a Domme or both? We're short a couple women now and we do need more than two."

"Carla will be mostly in charge of security. On a rare occasion, she may be called to participate as a sub or Domme."

"I have experience in both, and can easily step into the role of a submissive or a Dominatrix if that's what's you're asking, Melissa," Carla answered directly, one Domme to another Domme. Melissa smiled and appeared pleased with the answer.

"Good," Melissa said. "And she has some attitude. As long as it comes with discipline. Our last member had a cocky attitude and it got her killed." Carla sensed the anger and hurt behind the words. They'd never been close friends, but they would always stand up for each other.

"Ms. Hillman is well trained. She recently returned from an unofficial mission in Iraq where a small team bombed a factory suspected of shipping illegal weapons and bomb-making materials for terrorists. She and her teammates brought out the two owners of that factory who turned out to be working with a terrorist group."

Melissa raised her eyebrows. "Impressive. I guess we're in good hands."

"Be nice to her, Melissa," Johnny said in his Bronx accent. "Or she'll kick your butt."

"If she uses a flogger, I'll look forward to it."

"Okay, people," Julia said, raising her voice. "We will be getting another female member shortly. So we'll have two new members we need to train and orient in our procedures. Zoe will start and give Carla a tour after this meeting. Everyone will be briefed on our new project next week. Enjoy the weekend. Dismissed."

‽ʒʘ

A hundred memories flipped through Carla's mind as she walked down the hall of the basement toward the Red Tape Room. In there, she'd helped set up the sex scandals used to manipulate and blackmail several foreign diplomats into the signing of the controversial peace treaty. It was amazing how effective a kinky sex tape was when a government official's reputation was at stake. In some cultures their life could be at risk for such a dishonor. In many instances, sex tapes were more effective than sanctions or threats of violence.

As they approached the end of the hall, she noted the extra keypad lock on the Mason Room, the door adjacent to the Red Tape Room. "That's new," Carla noted.

"After my ordeal with a target, they decided this room needed more security. Let's take a quick look. They installed new equipment." Zoe unlocked the door and inside the smell of incense permeated the room. On top of the old desk, a candle, metal bowl with powdered incense and a skull were arranged on a black silk scarf. The setup looked similar to an altar of a Freemason ritual. The room had been used as a private meeting or meditation room by fourteen past presidents who were Masons. Dark drapes covered the back wall, which would appear to be a decorator choice, perhaps to cover cracked plaster, but it actually hid a narrow, hidden hallway.

"Is anyone home?" Carla asked as she flipped on the light switch, illuminating the passage.

"No, otherwise, we couldn't get back here." She opened the door into the camera room.

"Oh my God," Carla exclaimed. "Have I been gone that long? This is all new. Talk about state of the art equipment."

"Told you we've upgraded." Zoe smiled. "The video recordings go directly to two other locations now as a safety precaution, in case something happens to this room or its occupants."

Peering through the cameras, Carla could see beyond the wall, inside the Red Tape Room. "This is amazing."

"The cameras and video have a much higher resolution. Let's go into the next room. Not much has changed."

When they got into the Red Tape Room, Carla walked around and studied the new floggers, canes, ropes and various BDSM implements. "A few new toys. Otherwise, it's the same, but it feels different." Her thoughts traveled to her D/s moments with Jag in Vermont. They were always rushed and stressful, worrying someone would discover their secret. Apparently, some of the members did know, but only Greg had said something when he warned they were not to go out the night before they left on their mission.

Zoe placed her hand on Carla's shoulder. "I know. I'm glad you'll be here, protecting us. As a woman, you know what we go through."

Carla nodded. "More than anyone will know."

"You don't even sound like Alana did. Your voice is more regimented, confident."

Carla sighed. "Good. That will make it easier if they don't suspect."

"How are you doing with all this? How's Jag?" Zoe asked.

"He said we need time and I agree. We love each other, but after all we've been through, we need time to adjust to a normal routine."

Zoe laughed. "We don't have a normal life or a normal job, what do you expect?"

"But look how we started. He practically abducted me, never told me what they had intended for me. Not very romantic. I understand why, it's just taking me time to grasp that."

Zoe made a face. "You're acting like a brat, like a woman I used to know named Alana. No, you didn't meet on a tropical island or at a friend's romantic wedding. Jag did what he was ordered to do and saved your life. It would've been easier to give you a lethal injection and let you die. If Aleid knew you were still alive and continued his assassination attempts, the media would start asking questions about what this unknown White House researcher had done to bring this wrath down upon her? Questions like this by the media can only risk exposure of the FLC."

"You're right, Zoe. Jag has been awesome. He suggested we don't live together right away, but we plan to spend a lot of time together."

"The guy loves you," Zoe added. "Give him a break."

"I will. I love him too. I know I've been bullheaded. I need time to find out who I am now. He's taught me well, and

I'll do everything in my power to protect the members of the FLC and keep its secrets."

ೲೞ

Carla came home to the smell of food cooking. A glow of candles lit her dining room and flickered across her polished tile floors. Soft piano music played on her stereo in the background. She figured Jag for hardcore industrial or metal. She entered the kitchen and the sight of him in a T-shirt, jeans and socks blew her away. "What's cooking? I didn't think I had much in my fridge." She walked into the kitchen to find him stirring something in a pan on the stove.

"You didn't. I picked up a few things. We're having chicken Marsala, wild rice and glazed carrots."

"Smells wonderful. Thank you for shopping. I didn't know you could cook." She gave him a quick kiss.

"There's a lot you don't know about me. That's going to change. How did the meeting go?"

"Good. It'll take time to adjust, but it went well. I'm glad Zoe and Jason are there and they know."

He took her into his arms. "It'll take time for us too. We've been through hell. I'd like to make up for that."

She smiled. "I was thinking the same, but I understand. You did what you had to do to save my life and protect the FLC."

He stroked her cheek. "We need to create something special outside from all that."

"We do have something special." Glancing around her kitchen, she noticed a bottle of wine next to her sink, then also saw her pot of African violets on the windowsill. There was second pot with pink blooms. "You got another plant." She smiled. Then she remembered why he got her the first one. It was on the day she had killed the deer and the cow. She narrowed her eyes at him and groaned. "Please don't tell me those flowers mean I have to kill someone."

He grinned. "I did hear you'll be assigned to a new target. Whether your new skills will be needed has not been determined yet. And no, I will never use flowers as a sign for an upcoming assassination."

"Good." She opened the oven and peeked inside. "Yum. So has Alistair kept you company while I was gone?"

"Who is Alistair?"

"My ghost."

He groaned and rolled his eyes. "Your ghost again. No, no sign of him. How do you know you have a ghost, and why do you think his name is Alistair?"

"Things get moved. I've heard one of my neighbors talk about a bootlegger called Alistair who was gunned down inside this building in the 1920s. I think he's our resident ghost."

"Maybe an overactive imagination by ghost-hunting neighbors," Jag explained.

"Men," she groaned. "Always so practical. Someday, when you don't expect it, you'll see him or hear him."

"And I may shoot him." Jag laughed. "Now go see what I have for you on the bed. Wear it tonight. We won't be out late. I know you must be tired, but I think this will be a good start for us. Shower, put on your new outfit, then relax while I finish dinner. After we eat, we'll go."

"Where are we going?"

He frowned. "Trust me."

"Okay." And she did.

He followed her into the bedroom. She gasped when she saw the beautiful corset and skirt. The black corset had lace insets and purple satin. The skirt was soft and layered in tulle. He'd also bought a pair of black heels, not too high, and thigh-high stockings. She smiled, thinking about him shopping and the salesperson who had helped him.

"Do you like everything?" Jag placed his hands on her shoulders. "If it doesn't fit, I have a few other garments in the closet."

She turned in his arms and kissed him. "Thank you, they're gorgeous. I'm sure everything will fit. You didn't need to go to so much trouble."

Holding her in his arms, he stroked her back then squeezed her ass. "I also bought you another item to wear. I hope you like this. It's on your dresser." He turned and frowned. "Where is it? I left it there."

Carla looked around the room and noticed a jewelry box sitting on a pillow on the bed. "Is that it?"

"How the hell did it get there?"

"Alistair? Or maybe you forgot where you put it." She picked up the satin box.

"No way. There is no ghost."

"You didn't need to buy me another gift." Carla shook her head.

He laughed. "Open it."

Inside the hinged box was a silver choker necklace. Her heart stopped. She knew what he was asking. To the average person, it was a beautiful piece made up of several strands of silver, and twisted into a knot. To someone in the BDSM community, it was a collar, a token of possession, a promise of love and commitment. "Are you sure?" Her voice cracked and tears filled her eyes.

"I'm sure, Carla. I love you. If you're not ready, it can wait until you are."

"I'm sure too, Jag. I love you." She took the necklace out of the case and held it up to take a closer look at the detail, then clapped a hand over her lips. "Oh my God. It's a Celtic knot."

He nodded. "You were forced to leave your Irish red hair behind and your Irish name MacKenna. Inside, a part of you will always be Alana."

୫つଓ

When they got to Paradise Underground, Carla tightened her grip on Jag's hand as they waited in line to get into the club. It was going to be a busy night and she didn't want to tell Jag why she was nervous.

"I know what you're worried about," Jag said into her ear.

"It's our first time in a club like this in public," she finished for him.

"No, you're worried that he'll be here."

She nodded. "Most Friday nights Liam was there by ten or eleven." Even if Liam didn't have a submissive with him, he usually worked as a dungeon Master on Fridays.

"He is here, I checked."

"How did you do that?" Carla asked.

"I said I was a new member of the group with Liam, and wanted to know if he would be working as a dungeon Master tonight. The person who answered said he wasn't working but should be there."

"We can come another night," Carla said, hoping he didn't hear the dread in her voice.

"We'll be coming here, you may run into people you've known, especially Liam. You need to get through that. And I need to know you won't try to run to him again if you get into trouble."

Before Carla could protest, their IDs were checked and they were ushered inside. The deep sensual beat of music filled the darkened main room. Several people were at various stations—St. Andrew's Crosses, benches, chairs or tables and busy binding with ropes or shackles, flogging or using paddles and canes. Others were socializing or watching as voyeurs. Jag directed her down a hallway where a group of people were practicing with a violet wand, and another group, elaborate shibari rope tying.

"All the rooms seem pretty packed with people," Carla said. She was disappointed and relieved. Her body heated up and ached to take part in a scene herself. But she was worried she'd run into Liam. What if he recognized her?

"I did reserve a private room," Jag said. "Since it's your first time back."

She nodded. As much as she enjoyed being a voyeur, she wanted to see what Jag had in mind. Wondering what he had brought in his duffle bag was half the excitement.

"Let's take a walk through the back rooms and then we'll go to our VIP room." He pulled her close and kissed her forehead. "Have you seen him?"

"No, I'll tell you when I do."

They turned down another hallway into an open room and Jag pulled her back. For a moment she didn't know what he was doing, then she saw the flogger come around again from behind a support post in the middle of the room. The Dom had almost hit her. The area wasn't the ideal place for a scene since it was a heavy-traffic space. The support post hid the Dom and his submissive. As she came around, she held her breath and stopped walking. It was Liam. The submissive was a tiny thing she had never seen before. The girl looked frail and sweet and Carla felt sorry for her. Liam knew what he was doing, but he could be harsh at times. Not meant for the lighthearted sub.

Liam glared at her because she was in his personal space. Anyone who walked into this area of the club would be walking into his space. Liam should know better being a dungeon Master. The Dom could be stubborn, probably didn't want to wait for a free station. Jag urged her on.

When they were far enough away, he whispered. "That's him?"

"Yes. He looked directly at me and didn't recognize me. I'm also glad I'm not with him anymore. Never a good vibe between us."

Jag looked in the direction of their scene and winced. "I don't see a good vibe between them either."

Carla had to agree. Liam and his sub seemed as if they were walking through the motions, doing everything right. He'd check on her, but it was mechanical, no joy, no connection. Another couple walked into the space and Liam hit the guy on his leg. Liam apologized and shifted position. A few minutes later, a dungeon Master approached and talked to him. Liam collected his things and put an arm around his sub and the dungeon Master led them to another area.

"Seen enough?" Jag asked.

"More than enough. What did you say about a VIP room?"

She was glad *that* life was behind her. She liked the strength of who she was and the abilities to protect those of the FLC. What she might have to do in the future, she may not like but she understood it was necessary for the higher good.

"Ready to get started?" He kissed her long and sensual. Her body tingled from the roots of her hair to her toes. She wanted him with an urgency she'd never felt with Liam.

She nodded. "Yes, Sir."

He used the key card to unlock the door. Inside, chains

and a spreader bar hung from eyehooks in the ceiling. Several strands of rope, floggers and vibrators sat on a nearby table in new packages. There was also a bed with restraints attached. They had the private room reserved for an hour.

"As your captive again?" she asked, teasing.

"Except this time it's by choice. Do you want to give me your safewords?" he asked.

"We can use the same ones that we used in Vermont. Red and yellow."

His cell phone rang and he swore. "Sorry, I thought I turned it off." He pulled it out of his back pocket and checked the screen. He frowned then scrolled through something, pressed his lips together, then stuffed the phone in his pocket.

"Who is it?" she asked.

"It'll wait." His fingers stroked her cheek and slid down between her breasts where he hooked the top of her corset and tugged. He brushed his lips over her ear and gave her chills. Then looked deeply into her eyes and whispered, "Love me?"

"Always."

"Trust me?" His voice was deep and sensual and such a turn-on.

"No. You told me, trust no one, remember?" She smiled when she said it.

"Then I shouldn't tie you up." He picked up a length of rope and slid it over her arm. Her heart did a somersault.

"Hmmm. I might make an exception with you then. You know I'd trust you with my life." Her playful tone turned serious. "Then tell me what that phone call was about."

He sighed. "It was Julia. We're to meet her with the FLC members tomorrow morning."

"We're starting the new project?" Carla's stomach dipped. The idea of getting back to work excited her, but working with the members of the team as if she didn't know them would take some getting used to.

He nodded. The worried look on his face scared her. "This is the project you've been specifically trained for."

"It's not going to be an easy mission is it?" she asked.

"No, it won't. You can handle it. We'll worry about the details tomorrow." He tossed the rope on the floor and scooped her up in his arms, then carried her over to the restraining bed.

She grinned. "You're going to tie me up here?"

He shook his head as he removed his clothes. "Strip," he commanded. "On the bed."

She wiggled out of her skirt and blouse, then her bra and panties. She pointed to her thigh-high stockings. "These too?"

"Yes, everything."

She kicked off her heels and slid down each stocking. Her pulse jumped several paces as she saw lust fill his eyes. This wasn't his usual sexual routine and she wasn't sure what to expect. Stretching her arms over her head, she anticipated his next move. He'd now tie her up.

Instead, he climbed on the bed, his knees spreading her thighs apart. His cock was hard and she ached to feel him deep inside her. His hands roughly massaged her breasts, the way she liked. "We have an hour in this room and I'm going to fuck you the entire time."

She giggled. "But we could've done that at my place or yours."

"This time we do it in a dungeon. We'll continue at home later." Without warning he nudged his cock at the entrance of her sex. She'd been wet before they even arrived at the club, so she was more than ready for him.

He teased at first, or perhaps testing, then thrust all the

way into her channel. Her body arched in pleasure.

Wild and desperate, she wrapped her arms and legs around him, and cursed the hour that would be over much too soon. He fucked her mercilessly. The bed shook and the restraint straps and chains hung freely, slapping the wooden sides. The sounds matched his rhythm and drove her closer to her release. "Jag, please don't stop."

"Mmmm. Never," he answered.

This time her climax was more than physical, it was an emotional release. Tears streamed down her cheeks. As her body pulsed with glorious sensations of pleasure, Jag groaned with satisfaction and collapsed beside her.

Pulling her into his arms, he brushed her tears away. "Crying? Yet you're smiling. Is that a good thing?"

She nodded. "Very good." God, she loved this man. *Love?* And she thought she'd never find it.

"I love you, Carla." He kissed her slow and deep.

"I love you too." Reality came flooding back though, spoiling the moment. She had to begin her a new mission tomorrow. She had an idea what she would be expected to do, and it wasn't pleasant.

He stroked her hair. "Stop worrying. I see it in your eyes."

"I haven't learned how to hide my feelings." She didn't want to admit all the fears she still had. "What if I get into a situation and I'm by myself?"

"You're trained and I will help you with what you need to learn yet." He tapped the back of her head. "You have a chip here. I can always find you if something goes wrong."

"Okay." She did trust him now.

"Do you miss your old life?"

She shook her head. "It will take time to adjust, but I like my new life better." Carla rested her head on his shoulder.

"You will. If you need me, I'll always be close by to protect you."

~The End~

Watch for: Red Tape

FLC Case Files, Book 1

By Kathy Kulig.
Available now in eBook and print. Read on for a
sneak peek excerpt.

Prologue

Cimi stood at the base of a pyramid next to two stone monuments that were at least six feet tall and two feet wide. Four vertical rows of carved symbols—ancient Mayan glyphs—decorated the surface, including a carving depicting a maize god. On top of the pyramid a large fire burned, casting flickering orange shadows on the stones.

The sight frightened her. Another sacrifice would come.

Where was he? Kayab was late. The sky was turning a deep bluish gray, streaked with the crimson rays of the setting sun. They needed to leave now. Her heart pounded as panic seeped into her veins. As she bowed her head and closed her eyes, her black hair fell over her face. She prayed to the gods to bring Kayab safely to her.

Her hands formed tight fists and she realized that she still held Kayab's gift—the jade owl. Fear seized her soul. She felt she didn't have much time. If Kayab didn't come soon, she would have to go back to the village. She couldn't leave without him. She couldn't survive alone.

Tears dripped down her cheeks as she gripped the tiny jade owl. If she took the owl back with her, the shamans would surely take it away.

Dropping to her knees between the two monuments, she placed the carving on the ground and frantically dug a hole several inches deep. She placed the owl inside then covered it with dirt. Now they couldn't take away her treasured talisman. It would be safe. But would the stone still protect her while it was buried?

Tears dripped onto the ground, christening the earth above her buried gift.

Her vision blurred for a moment and when she blinked the tears away, she found herself standing at the base of Devil's Pyramid. Two warriors stood on either side of her.

One of them gripped her upper arm so tightly that she thought her arm would snap. The other warrior smacked a club as thick as his arm against his palm. Veins bulged in his neck and temples. A third warrior pointed a spear at her throat as he gazed up at the top of the pyramid. Cimi's blood turned to ice. She refused to look up there.

Where was Kayab? The panicked thought pierced her heart. Did he get away? She hoped he did, but was afraid that he would not leave without her.

The warrior dragged her toward the long steps and held the tip of his spear against her back. Slowly, she raised her gaze to the peak of the temple. Flames spewed from a bonfire at the top and black smoke coiled like an evil serpent into the sky.

Then Lauren saw the silhouette of Chac standing next to the fire and icy fingers crept up her spine. She knew it was him by his huge headdress. It radiated around his head like the sun's deadly rays. Chac slowly descended the stone steps. Fear made her lungs turn to stone. She couldn't breathe. Burying the owl was a mistake. When he reached the bottom, he stood over her with a wild, menacing glare in his eyes.

"Cimi, the gods demand more sacrifices. The rain god cannot shed his blood to bring the rains without an offering of fresh blood. You should be honored to be a chosen one. Your sacrifice will secure you a place in the Otherworld."

As Cimi tried to stand, the warriors shoved her down to her knees. She avoided looking into Chac's manic eyes, fearing he would trap her soul and she would be forever lost, searching for the Otherworld.

Behind the cover of the jungle, she heard shouts and people thrashing through the bushes. Kayab suddenly appeared at the clearing. His hands were bound and two warriors brandishing spears flanked him on either side.

"Kayab!" she screamed.

"Cimi, no!" Kayab cried out. "I am sorry, so sorry. I love you, Cimi. I will find you in the Otherworld. I promise."

She felt the sick realization deep in her breast—they had waited too long and now it was too late. The warriors holding Kayab were distracted by Cimi's screams. Kayab slipped out of his bindings and ran toward her. Just as his hands grasped her arm, one warrior bludgeoned Kayab on the back of the head. He collapsed at her feet, his blood soaking into the dried dirt.

Cimi shrieked.

શ્ળ

Lauren opened her eyes as Margaret and Deven ran around the mound and stood over her.

"Lauren, what happened? Are you all right?" Margaret asked.

Lauren's gaze darted around the jungle, expecting to see the warriors with spears for a moment, then realized she'd had another vision. "I'm...fine." Her words didn't sound convincing even to her.

"Why did you scream?" Deven reach for her hand. "You're shaking."

No way was she was going to tell him about this experience. She wouldn't tell anyone, not even Margaret. As she searched for another excuse, several coatimundis scurried out of the jungle and passed within a couple feet of Margaret.

Lauren jumped back and stifled another scream. "I must have dozed off." Watching the coatimundis disappear into the jungle gave her an idea. "A coatimundis ran over my foot and scared the daylights out of me. Sorry I screamed." She forced a chuckle.

Deven's voice gentled. "I thought you were being attacked. Are you sure you're all right?"

"You look a little flushed, dear. Maybe too much sun?" Margaret smiled warmly, a knowing glint in her eyes.

Was she offering Lauren an excuse?

Deven brushed her hair away from her face. "It is really hot out today." He picked up her backpack. "Is your water bottle in here?"

Lauren nodded. "I can get it. Really, I'm fine. I dozed off. I'm probably a little dehydrated. I got distracted during our walk and forgot to drink water."

"Are you sure you're all right?" Deven asked.

"I'm fine." Pulling her hand away, she retrieved her backpack and dug out a bandana and wrapped it around her hair, making a ponytail to lift her hair off her neck.

Deven's grin quickly turned serious. "If you're ready, we'll head back to camp."

"But it's still early, I want to dig more today," Lauren said.

"This would be a good day to quit early and take a swim by the waterfall," Deven said. "We can work a couple hours, then we're calling it a day. What do you think, Margaret?"

"I think we could all use a break from these ancient stones."

∞⊙∞

Deven didn't need his machete for the fifteen-minute walk to the tropical waterfall and pond. The trail was well worn by previous field crews. After a day of hot and dirty work at the dig, the pond offered the only relief.

White water spilled over a stone ledge and dropped about twelve feet into a natural pool about fifty feet across. Mist from the splashing water swirled across the emerald surface and formed small rainbows.

Surrounding the pond were palmettos, giant ferns, banana plants, towering trees and flowers of more varieties than Deven could begin to name. Opposite the waterfall, the pond narrowed and the gurgling stream continued into the jungle. The trail ended at a large flat rock that was raised a couple feet above the water level.

"It's like a paradise or a tropical oasis," Lauren said as she dropped her backpack and yanked out her towel. When she slipped off her T-shirt and shorts, revealing a skimpy bikini, Deven felt his knees buckle.

He hadn't seen how beautiful she was the night before when they had sex, so seeing her here in this jungle setting took his breath away. He felt a quick throb in his groin and tried to take his mind off it. He didn't need to show off a hard-on now in mixed company.

Justin and Kyle let out a whoop and charged to the water's edge. They dropped their towels, pulled off their T-shirts and stood at the edge of the rock.

"Dive or jump?" Justin asked Kyle, his hands on his hips.

"Gentlemen, if you're diving, go in from that side. It's the deepest." Deven pointed to the far end of the flat rock.

The large rock at the edge of the water made a nice sunbathing area and a good access point into the water. The dense vegetation around the pond made it difficult to enter any other way. Justin and Kyle gave each other a quick glance, let out a hoot and jumped into the water.

When they came up, Lauren leaned over the edge and asked, "How is it?"

"Great. Come on in," Kyle answered.

Deven watched Lauren climb down the rock to the narrow sandy shoreline and walk in up to her ankles. "Oh it's cold. It feels great."

"Hurry up, Lauren," Kyle shouted. "We're going to check out the waterfall. Dr. Chandler said we can walk behind it."

She glanced back at Deven, but she didn't say anything. He felt a tug in his chest. What was going through her mind? Their disagreement had certainly put a strain on their new relationship. She'd barely had said a word since the ghost and jade owl discussion. He doubted things would be the same between them. The thought knotted his gut. It was his fault for getting involved with a student. He should've known better. His project was too important to take the kind of risks Lauren was asking of him.

He really blew it with her. When she began to tell him about her dreams or visions, he was quick to discredit her experience, offer her a scientific explanation instead of showing his concern and support. No wonder she pulled away from him. He saw the disappointed look after he told her she couldn't dig for that owl. It was like an iron door had slammed closed, shutting him out.

He'd heard of archaeologists who had some kind of sense or intuition about the location of ancient sites and artifacts. He would rather go by solid scientific evidence.

Ghosts, reincarnation, a sacred talisman was too bizarre to be true. Margaret believed in a supernatural world. His sister Sarita did too, but Deven was the analytical, seeing-is-believing scientist and not one to accept the esoteric theories.

As he watched Lauren's lithe body run into the deeper water and finally dive under, his heart skipped a beat. When she came to the surface, her blonde hair was slicked back away from her face and down to the middle of her back. She swam with Kyle and Justin toward the waterfall.

Deven unbuttoned his shirt, slipped it off and jumped in.

When he reached the waterfall, the students had already disappeared behind the curtain of white water. He heard their echoing voices from the cave-like formation behind the falls. They had to shout to be heard over the rush of cascading water. Deven carefully climbed the slippery moss-covered stones and stepped behind the wall of water.

Lauren stood at the edge of the stone ledge, her arm outstretched, letting the water rush over her fingertips.

"This is so neat back here. Great way to cool off," Lauren said over her shoulder to Deven.

"I guess diving off the top of the waterfall is out of the question, Dr. Chandler?" Kyle asked.

"What are you, a daredevil?" Deven asked.

"Only when he's surfing," Justin answered. "Go ahead, dude. I'll pay to watch you dive off the waterfall."

"Don't you dare. Don't even think about it." Lauren

glared at him.

Kyle smiled. "Why would you be worried if I got hurt?" His tone sounded a bit flirtatious.

"You'd kill yourself. Stick to surfing," she said.

"Okay. But it would've been a wicked dive," Kyle said.

Lauren rolled her eyes.

Deven noticed Kyle eyeing her through his wet blond hair that hung in his eyes. Kyle acted like he had a high school crush on her and hovered over her at the camp and the excavation site. Another reason he should avoid a romantic attachment with her. He didn't need to initiate a soap opera on his dig by competing for the love of a woman with one of his students.

Could Lauren become interested in Kyle? He was a good-looking kid—young man. Women seemed to like the surfer bad boy type. He was younger than Lauren by at least five years. The difference in age wasn't much, but Lauren was more mature than Kyle. Anyone would be attracted to her. He couldn't deny he felt a pang of jealousy. Could he be falling in love with her?

Damn. She'd had several opportunities to talk to him, instead she had confided in Margaret about her dreams long before she told him. The thought stung him—she didn't trust him enough. And no wonder.

Lauren walked past Deven and barely glanced at him. "I'm going back down to swim some more," she said to Kyle and Justin.

"We'll be right behind you," Kyle said.

Lauren left the waterfall cave, using her hands to help support her as she started back down.

"Go on, Kyle, aren't you going after her?" Justin teased.

"Quit, dude. She ain't interested."

"We could leave you two alone and find out. Right, Dr. Chandler?" Justin asked.

Deven didn't answer and tried to give him a blank look. He hoped the guys didn't pick up on his feelings for Lauren.

"Deven!" Lauren shouted from below, her voice cracked and Deven knew something was wrong. He rushed out from behind the waterfall with Kyle and Justin following. Lauren stood waist deep in the water and was walking backward toward the waterfall. She acted like she was backing away from a bear.

At the far end of the pool a man in a camouflage uniform approached carrying an AK-47 rifle.

When Lauren reached the rocky steps leading up to the waterfall cave, she started climbing.

"It's okay, Lauren. He's one of the new guards." Deven raised his hand to the guard in acknowledgement. The man waved back as he slung the rifle over his shoulder.

Deven noticed Lauren twisting her ring around her finger. "You're going to wear your finger to the bone if you keep that up," he teased her.

She quickly dropped her hand. "You'd think I'd be used to these guys lugging military guns around by now."

"It does take a bit getting used to. Think of them as police officers." He rested his hand on her shoulder.

She nodded and gently stepped away from his touch. "I know but it's still unnerving."

"Come on, I'll introduce you." Deven walked Lauren over to the shore where the guard stood. She grabbed her towel and wrapped it around her shoulders.

"Miguel. How are you?" he asked in Spanish.

"*Ola*, Dr. Chandler," Miguel said with a thick Spanish accent. "I making my rounds and hear voices. I come to check it out."

"Miguel, this is Lauren Halpern, one of my students."

Miguel nodded. "*Senorita* Lauren."

"Kyle and Justin are the other students." Deven pointed to the two men swimming in the water near the bottom of the falls.

"We're glad to have you, Miguel," Deven said. "Sorry to see Diego go."

"He was a nice man. Why did he leave?" Lauren asked.

Miguel hesitated, his gaze darted around the jungle. "*Senorita*, his family not want him to stay here."

"Why not?" She asked.

Miguel rocked on his heels. "They don't like him out here. Too far from home."

"Everything all right? I heard Diego's wife was sick," Deven asked.

"Diego's wife? No, she fine, she not sick."

Deven didn't argue. Diego had told him he couldn't stay at the camp because his wife was ill.

Miguel studied the pool and surrounding area. "Nice here. You stay long? Not good to stay when dark comes."

Deven glanced up to the sky. The blue sky had turned indigo. Through the trees, he saw streaks of red and orange. The last rays of sunlight cast long shadows in the jungle. "You're right, Miguel. It's time to head back to camp."

Chapter 1

Jason Merritt swung his racket hard, but missed another easy shot off the back wall. The racquetball bounced past him. *Fuck.* Two points down, with an audience, and he was losing to a man twenty years older.

"Have you talked to Zoe yet?" his opponent asked.

"Not yet, and when she finds out I recommended her, she better not have a loaded gun." Jason's gut clenched as he considered that conversation. He'd tried calling her two nights ago, right after she started her new job, but had gotten her voice mail. His opponent hit a driving serve. Jason swung again and missed. "Fuck."

"If I didn't know you better, I'd say you were letting me win." The older man glanced sideways at Jason.

"Sorry, Mr. President."

President Douglas Bryson laughed. "Not to worry. When do you plan to call her?"

Three Secret Service agents peered through the Plexiglas partition like frozen automatons. They couldn't hear their conversation, and no one else was in the swanky health club. Once a week, the president reserved the entire club for his private use. The silence descended into a surreal Stephen King novel.

"I haven't talked to her since our last mission more than six months ago. I thought I'd let her get settled into her new position first."

The president nodded. "Make it soon. We need her brought up to speed."

He failed miserably in his attempt to smile. On the other side of the partition, the Secret Service guards held their robot expressions.

The president patted Jason's shoulder. "We already had her in mind. Zoe's the perfect type. Blond, attractive, physically fit, top-level clearance and trained for undercover work. We used you as a reference since you worked with her at Langley. Tell her that."

Jason nodded. "Yes, sir."

"Your past relationship won't interfere with this project." It was a statement, not a question.

"No, sir, Mr. President. We've worked on missions together before. She was trained for intelligence gathering, not this."

"I'm aware of your other missions. It's a role like any other undercover work," President Bryson added, locking eyes with Jason. "Get her briefed. Celia was one fuck-up too many. This operation needs Zoe."

If Bryson knew everything about their last mission, would he have selected her? Or was the organization that desperate?

The president checked his watch. "One o'clock and I have an early meeting. Our games may have to be postponed until after the peace talks. You have a busy day, too."

"I'll get on it." He couldn't afford another screw-up.

ଚେଠ

Zoe Summers retied her scarf for the third time, then checked in the hand mirror she kept in her desk to make sure it covered the scar. She had another hour of work to do and desperately needed coffee. As late as it was, there might be a few White House staff left. She hated when people stared at her neck, hated it even more when she had to make up some lie instead of explaining that a mission went horribly wrong. Pity she didn't need. What she needed was to forget and end the nightmares.

She dug an armful of manila folders out of the old, metal file cabinet and tossed them onto her desk. The last batch before she'd head home. This was an honor, not Langley's way to avoid outright firing her. Secret documents, archiving, filing. This was *not* the drudgery that would crush the living soul out of her body and damn her to file-clerk hell.

She leaned back in the desk chair, gazing around at the dusty, basement office surrounded by a dozen filing cabinets. There were always rumors and conspiracy theories by people who had too much time on their hands. She'd escaped one lead-lined dungeon for another, but White House or not, suspicious activity or not, this felt like a demotion. She should have been out in the field, interacting with terrorists, transporting sensitive documents, carrying a gun, not moving papers.

Rubbing her temples, Zoe glanced at the clock on her desk. Ten p.m. Coffee. The door to the hall was open a crack to ensure the guard would check in on her during his rounds. It was best he get to know her since she planned on working a lot of late nights. Maybe if she exceeded expectations and did a really good filing job, they'd move her on to bigger projects.

Even for a basement, she was surprised by the amount of after-hours activity. A group of people came downstairs, entered one of the rooms, then left after an hour or two. It had happened the night before, too. She was never able to see who they were, but couldn't help feeling paranoid after what the Big D had told her. He'd heard rumors and suspected something was terribly wrong at the White House but gave no specifics. The lack of security cameras on her level seemed odd when there were plenty on the upper levels.

Taking her cell phone out, she listened to Jason's message again. The message was three days old. After several playbacks, she still hadn't decided whether to call him back.

She yanked open the drawer of her desk to lock the files away while she went upstairs. The drawer slipped off its track and jammed.

Crap. Banging it with the heel of her hand, she pulled the drawer free and placed it on the floor. She checked inside for papers that had fallen behind. Lying on the floor inside the desk was an employee ID badge with two keys attached and another key ring with a set of five keys.

Turning the badge over in her hand, she examined a red piece of tape dangling off one of the keys like a one-inch flag. Nothing was written on it. The photo on the badge was of a young blond woman in her late twenties with a pretty smile. The woman could've been Zoe's sister if she had one. *Celia Aldridge, Researcher.*

Had the previous worker lost the badge and keys or had they been left behind? She turned the badge over and studied it closely. A six-digit number was scribbled in faded marker. Zoe pursed her lips and rolled her eyes. People who couldn't remember PINs or key codes sometimes wrote them in inappropriate places. Even intelligence agents, men mostly, were known to use 36-24-36 as a pass code.

Did this woman get promoted? Transferred? Did she quit or get fired? Normally when an employee left, security destroyed the ID badge. Who was she, and why had she left? Maybe she worked in another department and Zoe could return the badge. Sitting at her computer, she typed in Celia Aldridge's name to do a search, her finger hovering over the ENTER key. She wasn't at Langley. Anything she typed in on the White House computer could be traced by the IT guys. Frank Phillips in security had warned her about unofficial use of the computers. She could be violating a confidentiality rule. She deleted her entry.

"Zoe, you still here?"

Zoe cried out, palming the woman's badge and slipping it into her blouse. As she rose, she tugged on her scarf. "God, Melissa, I didn't hear you come down."

Melissa Tadeshi, assistant to the press secretary, stood in her doorway. "I was going to leave this under your door. It's tomorrow's schedule." Melissa held up an interoffice envelope. "You're leaving now, aren't you?"

"I had a little more work to do. I was going for coffee." Zoe took the envelope, dropped it on her desk and gestured Melissa inside. "I thought you left hours ago. Is Julia still here?"

Melissa rolled her eyes. "Long gone. What work? We finished our training today. Want to go for a drink?"

"No, thanks. I'm trying to make a dent and make this office livable. I guess housekeeping doesn't clean this room. It doesn't look like it's been dusted since the Kennedy administration." Considering the late hour, Melissa still looked gorgeous and professional, like an Asian Victoria's Secret model in her early thirties. Although Zoe thought Melissa pushed her professional attire to the limit for the White House. She'd wear heels a bit too high, skirts a little too short and blouses cut way too low, but no one seemed to mind. Her long, black hair was fastened neatly with a simple clip, and even her makeup looked fresh. Other than making sure her scarf covered her scar, Zoe hadn't checked her appearance in six hours. She hated to think what she looked like. "Besides delivering tomorrow's schedule, why are you here late?"

"We finished up a few meetings over an hour ago. I was doing some prep work. The president's meeting with a number of foreign reps, so expect another crazy early morning."

Zoe inched toward the door, expecting Melissa to

follow.

Melissa looked inside the office and noticed the drawer on the floor. "Do you need help with that?"

Zoe hesitated for a second. "No, just cleaning out the desk."

"How's everything going?"

"Good. It's not hard work. I'm surprised they just didn't hire a college intern for this. My old boss said someone at the White House recommended me for the position. Did you know about that?"

Melissa glanced at the stack of files on Zoe's desk. "Probably because you had top-secret clearance working in the CIA."

"Any clerk can get a security clearance." Zoe didn't mean to sound so cynical.

"Security threats are always a concern. You of all people should know that," Melissa said, very serious now.

The hairs went up on the back of Zoe's neck. "You're right."

"Don't ever let your guard down."

"Don't get me wrong, I'm grateful to be here. But when I was hired, I expected it was for something more exciting than filing."

Melissa smiled, back to her pleasant mood. "Give it time. Trust me, working here is never dull. The White House wouldn't have hired you unless they had a reason and needed your expertise. They need people they can trust above all."

"I can be trusted," Zoe said, more to herself than Melissa. She stuffed the folders back into the file cabinet, got the drawer back on its track, and then closed and locked it.

Melissa gave a small laugh. "Go home, girl. It's late."

Home. Where silence and four walls only reminded her how long it'd been since she was on a mission? If she hung around, she could do an unsupervised tour. She held up her dust-smudged hands. "I need to wash up first."

Melissa groaned. "Hurry it up. The guards get twitchy when we stay too late."

"I won't be long." Zoe locked her office, but Melissa hadn't moved to leave. "By the way, do you know who worked in here before me?" Zoe watched Melissa's expression.

Melissa's mouth quirked slightly, a nervous gesture the average person wouldn't notice. "I don't know. She must've left before I got here."

"She?"

Melissa huffed. "She...he...whatever. I don't know. This office has been empty for a while."

"Does anyone else work down here? Meeting rooms?"

Melissa frowned and narrowed her eyes. "It's a basement. Nothing more than storage rooms, space for electrical, boiler, and mechanical equipment. Why?"

"Just asking." Zoe wasn't going to mention the late-night visitors until she gathered more information. She didn't want to sound like a paranoid idiot.

The atmosphere chilled between them. "Look, I'm sorry," Zoe said. "It's too quiet down here. See you at lunch tomorrow?"

Melissa smiled. "Sure." She checked her phone, punched a few keys with her thumbs, then headed for the stairs. "See you tomorrow."

Zoe used the restroom and scrubbed her hands. When she strode out of the ladies' room, she stopped in the hallway and contemplated the door at the end of the hall, holding Celia's badge in her hand. The door had a key-swipe lock and keypad. Could it be this easy?

෨෬

"Anything you need me to do before the presentation?" Jason asked Julia. He wanted out of there, wanted to get to Zoe and tell her to resign before she learned anything about the program. At Langley, they may have parted on a sour note, but she would trust him this time. By not trusting her partner, she'd compromised their last mission and much worse. If he told her to leave, she would. Once she was briefed about Red Tape, it'd be too late.

"No, we're ready." Julia's nails clicked on the computer keyboard with enough force he expected to hear them snap. He shifted in the stiff Victorian chair in front of her desk. Waiting was torture. His cell buzzed at the exact moment Julia's buzzed. The target had just left the hotel. *Fuck.* Julia glanced at him with an anxious look. He hated when a mission was starting off on the wrong foot. Already, this one was behind schedule, and everyone was on edge. Not good.

Julia swore. "Where the hell is Melissa?" The petite woman got up and paced the carpeted room. The razor-cut ends of her red hair brushed the collar of her crisp business suit.

"I'm sure she'll be here shortly." That wasn't happening. The text he got said Zoe hadn't left yet but would soon. *Come on, Zoe. Just this once, leave something half-finished.* Melissa couldn't drag her out

225

of there unless she hogtied her.

His schedule as one of the first lady's Secret Service agents was hectic, and he suspected it was about to get insane. Julia gave an impatient huff and checked her watch again for the hundredth time. "If she doesn't come up soon…"

"She will." Jason stood and walked to the window, watching for the black cars that would arrive at the back entrance. If he had been in charge, it would never be going down like this.

"After this presentation, we'll schedule Zoe's training." Julia sighed. "We're pressed for time."

"Zoe's a professional. I won't have a problem training her."

Julia's smile wasn't a friendly one. Her green eyes flashed rage and worry. "What makes you think you'll be training her?" Her tone had a slight edge of condescension.

He stuck his hands in his pockets to keep from clenching them. "For this program to work, wouldn't she feel most comfortable with someone she knows well?" He took a breath, attempting to keep the conversation from breaking down into a shouting match.

She smiled again, and this time, Julia placed a gentle hand on his arm. "You mean someone she knew intimately, Jason. Training doesn't work that way."

"How then?" Before he finished the sentence, reality slammed into him. "Who'll be training her?" Heat rose in his face, and he took a step closer to her. The idea of Zoe thrown into the most dangerous part of the mission, unprepared, grabbed him by the throat.

"Now is not the time." She checked her watch, standing a little straighter, which didn't help her height but made a point. "You know what's involved." She walked over to her desk and leaned on it.

He didn't answer.

Three sharp raps on the door and Melissa barged into the office, giving both Jason and Julia a grim look. "Sorry I'm late. She's still here but should be on her way out." Melissa crossed her arms over her chest. The tight business suit she wore and low-cut blouse pressed the curves of her breasts higher. No wonder the first lady chose her for this particular position.

Julia groaned, hands clasped together and held under her chin. "We need to make this count, people. There's no room for errors."

"Zoe's been working during the setup and practices this week. She wasn't a problem then," Melissa offered.

"No, I don't want the chance of her running into our guest." Julia's voice rose to a level bordering on hysteria.

Jason checked his watch, then looked at Julia, who tapped her tiny, pointy shoe while glaring at Melissa. Four men in business suits walked into the office, the first lady's private security guards.

"The first lady is on her way down," one of the men announced. "And the target will be here in ten."

"We're out of time," Julia said to Jason. "Get her out of there."

Chapter 2

Did she dare? Zoe hadn't even tried her own badge and code on the door at the end of the hall yet. She padded to the men's room door to make sure no one was around, then knocked. "Hello? Housekeeping." No answer. She entered, and it was much larger than the ladies' room with two more showers and a condom dispenser. Zoe frowned at that. *Are you kidding me? In the basement of the White House?*

She left the men's room, and tiptoed down the hall, trying each door she passed. All locked. Not surprising, but her curiosity was focused on the door at the end. Why would a room for storage or mechanical equipment need a keypad access?

She swiped Celia's badge and punched in the PIN, but the light remained red. She tried again, slower, and still got red. Then she tried the PIN in reverse.

The light turned green. She turned the doorknob, walked inside a small vestibule and was blocked by another door, locked, of course. Like Alice in Wonderland, the mystery begins with doors and keys. She flipped on the light in this small antechamber. The key on Celia's badge with the piece of tape opened the next door.

Illuminated only by the light from the vestibule, this room appeared spacious. A few objects or furniture stood in shadows. The scent of leather and disinfectant mingled in the warm air. She felt along the wall for a light switch then decided against it. Using the backlight from her cell phone, she crept around the room, examining each object. One large chair stood in the center. It was elaborately carved with straps attached to the arms and legs.

Zoe stiffened and took a step back. An interrogation room. Not a meeting room. Her mind flashed to Turkey. They'd tied her down when the deal went bad. Her hand reached for her neck, and her body shook, remembering the pain when the knife blade broke her skin. Sweat soaked through her underwear.

She shoved the memories out of her head. The White House was the last place she expected to find an interrogation room. In one corner was a bed with pulleys and more straps. On the other side of the room was a table with several small objects she suspected were torture devices, instruments for pain and truth serum drugs. Her stomach rolled, and the taste of bile rose onto the back of her tongue. At the far wall in the shadows was a tall, wooden cross. That looked familiar, but she couldn't place it. What kind of torture did they do in the White House?

As she moved around the room, she thought she heard voices in the walls. She shook her head. It wasn't real, only memories. The voices continued.

She dropped her phone and covered her ears with her hands. *Go away, you're not real.*

"Zoe. What the hell are you doing in here?" Jason's voice. She *was* hearing things.

Zoe spun around and saw a figure silhouetted in the doorway. "Jason?"

"Yes, you have to get out of here. They're coming." He picked up her phone and handed it to her. It started buzzing, and her thoughts sharpened.

Jaw clenched, she marched up to him and clamped her hand around his throat. The weight of her body continued the momentum until she slammed him against the wall. Her knee pressed into his groin, and her nails dug into his neck. "What the hell happened to you? You dump me after Turkey, then left Langley without a word. Or were you looking for an excuse?"

He winced from the pain in his throat or groin, she wasn't sure. "I didn't dump you at all. I was reassigned and sent out of the country while you were visiting your dad. I couldn't contact you."

"Six months ago," she argued, not releasing her grip. "You could've left a message that you were heading out. When did you get back?" Why didn't he just say the fuck-up in Turkey was her fault? Maybe then they could move on.

"Couple weeks." He groaned. "I work here. Secret Service."

She fought the urge to rush into his arms. Every muscle in her body ached for him. God, she missed him. As reality quickly registered, her body chilled on the inside. Their last job hadn't accommodated relationships and emotions. Why would it be different now? She grabbed her phone and turned her back on him. "If you didn't trust me as your partner, you should've told me. Instead, you disappear."

"I can't explain it now. They're coming. We have to go now."

"Who's coming? What's going on? Is there a security problem?" She blinked several times and adjusted her scarf, but it wasn't necessary. Jason was the only person who didn't gape at the ugly scar.

He grabbed her arm, turned her to face him. "I'll give you details later."

Her body stiffened. "Are they bringing someone down for interrogation?"

"What?"

"Isn't this an interrogation room?"

"Interrogation room?" He chuckled. "It's a bit more complicated." Again, the voices emanated from behind the walls. He looked toward the sounds and held up a hand to be quiet. At least she wasn't crazy. He'd heard them, too. Then silence.

Footsteps approached down the hall. "Shit, too late," he said as he closed the inside door. The room swallowed them in utter blackness. Zoe held up her cell phone for light. Jason flicked on a penlight.

"Which way?"

"In here," he ordered. He grabbed her arm and shoved her into a small storage closet, then closed the door. Her cell buzzed. "Phone off."

Zoe glanced at her phone and let out a sigh as she turned it off. "Thank God."

"What?" Jason asked.

"It's Damien." Zoe let out a breath. She hated when her brother was late, even when he was beating the crap out of her in the Words With Friends game.

Jason's expression softened. "Iran?"

She nodded, her eyes adjusting to the dim lighting.

"Turn it off. Now."

"Okay. What's happening?" As much as she wanted to be angry at him, her stomach fluttered with excitement and her sex throbbed. He always managed to turn her on, especially when they were in danger. He smelled so good, too. A new shampoo, body wash? Whatever it was, it made her remember so many scorching-hot nights, breathless from hours of fucking. She wanted him again, wanted him now.

He took the phone, made sure it was off and stuffed it in his pocket. His penlight was still on. "Now listen to me. We cannot leave this closet or make a sound until it's over, under any circumstances. Do you understand?" His frown grew fierce and his eyes wild.

"Yes."

He cupped her chin with his hand. His mouth was close to hers as he whispered, "I'm sorry, Zoe. I should've called, should've explained." He squeezed his eyes closed then looked at her again. "Please, trust me."

"Trust you? But I don't know what the hell is going on."

"Zoe, please."

She knew that tone, knew him well enough not to argue. Trust wasn't always easy for her.

"No sound." He turned off the penlight.

She leaned against the wall, listening. A rush of

adrenaline surged through her. The sound of her heartbeat pounded in her ears. *Like old times on a mission together*. The doorknob to the room rattled. Then the door squeaked open, and a sharp click of the light switch sent a shudder of excitement through her. The sound of people entered the room. Zoe tried to estimate the number. At least three, maybe more. Women and men by the voices and heeled shoes. She gasped but only a whisper. He placed a hand over her mouth, and she nodded. She held her breath.

"Anything you need before the room is sealed?" a male's voice asked.

"No, we're good. Seal it." Was that the first lady? Slowly, Zoe's eyes adjusted to the darkness, and a sliver of light appeared beneath the door. Another sliver of light cut through the doorframe where the old wood had warped. Angling her head just so, she squinted through the crack, trying to get a fix on the outside room. As they moved around, four people came into view, two men and two women.

Good God, one woman wore leather fetish wear—a corset, thigh-high boots and stockings. And the other with blond hair wore a black scholar robe. Beneath the robe she wore five-inch heels. Their faces were covered with elaborately decorated Mardi Gras masks. Two men were also present. One young guy with a muscular build was dressed in a black T-shirt, tight pants and wore a leather face mask. Between the robes and the guy all in black, the scene had a Gothic, macabre feel. What kind of rendezvous was this?

The older man wore business clothes. He was the only one without a mask. When he turned, Zoe thought he looked familiar. He was a small man, middle-aged and not very attractive. By his smile, he appeared to be enjoying the encounter. Zoe studied the furnishings now that the room was lit. *Shit.* This wasn't an interrogation room. It was a kinky-sex dungeon. Under normal circumstances she'd have been laughing. This wasn't funny. This was the White House.

The blonde had to be the first lady. The voice, the mannerisms. *Oh my God.* Shock and panic ripped into Zoe. She didn't want to be here to see this. Zoe tugged Jason's arm to take a look. He tapped her hand once, their signal for "no." Then he paused and did a series of two taps. She took that to mean, yes, yes, he knew. So quickly they fell back into their old patterns where they could communicate without speaking during a mission. Why couldn't they talk about their love life? Why had he left months ago without a word?

The woman with dark hair must be Melissa. She had the same build and hair. The first lady was into kinky sex? Who knew? Did the president know? No wonder Jason had looked terrified.

Oh God, oh God. Jason must've heard her ragged breathing. If this hadn't been the White House, or if this had been a torture scene, she could've handled it, but she hadn't been prepared to observe a scandal at this level. He squeezed her shoulders and rubbed them gently. She took a slow breath in and let it out easy. What the hell?

Quiet. She must be quiet. Peering through the crack, Zoe watched the woman with the long, dark hair strut up to the older man and whisper something to him. Yes, it was Melissa. She'd shown Zoe those boots the other day when she noticed the box by her desk. Melissa had called them her party boots. Zoe hadn't thought anything of it.

"Let's get started," the first lady announced as she untied the robe, revealing her outfit. Her breasts thrust high over a red corset, thigh-high stockings and spike heels. Matching satin gloves came to her elbows. She strode to the table, picked up a crop and smacked it in her hand, then came around to stand beside Melissa. Both women kept their bodies angled in a particular way so their backs always faced the one wall with an intricate mural of American national parks.

"I'm Mistress D," Melissa said to the man as she stroked his back, speaking in a soothing tone. "Remove your clothes, please. Place them on the chair, then present yourself to me. When I ask you to present yourself, I want you to stand with your legs slightly apart, hands behind your back, right hand over your left and eyes looking down at the floor. Understand?"

"Yes, Mistress." He lowered his head and began to undress. *Shit.* If only she could figure out who the man was.

"Mistress R is here to observe only," Melissa said, referring to the first lady. "If she feels the scene is getting out of hand, she'll signal by smacking her crop or stopping the scene."

The first lady stepped to an area out of Zoe's view.

Jason placed a hand on Zoe's shoulder to pull her back. She responded with a one-finger tap to his hand.

The man was standing as Melissa had requested. She made a few adjustments. "Very good. This is how I want you to stand when I ask you to present yourself. It's a small task and a way for me to break up our time together. I can also see how well you're handling my session."

Melissa picked up a leather flogger, smacking the knotted thongs on the nearby table. The man jerked, but he didn't look up. Naked, he stood sideways, fully aroused. His cock jutted straight out. Melissa approached the man and brushed the thongs across the tip of his cock.

"Kneel," she ordered, pointing to the bench. He complied. She hit him on the back and buttocks gently with the flogger in caressing strokes, a warm-up. Then harder and harder. Zoe cringed with each strike, her fingers digging into the doorframe.

The encounter was like watching a burning building in slow motion, mesmerizing and scary. Zoe knew people got into this bondage stuff. It didn't do much for her, although her body heated up with each strike. His moans were of pleasure mixed with pain. He was enjoying this. After a time, Melissa stopped, bent down. "Are you okay?"

"Yes, Mistress," he answered with enthusiasm. There was an accent, Middle Eastern, Zoe thought. She knew six languages fluently as well as basic words in a few others.

"Do you like this?" Melissa asked the man.

"Yes, Mistress."

"Good. We'll see how well you obey."

"Yes, Mistress." He rocked on his hands and knees and shifted side to side.

"Relax. Stop fidgeting. You'll enjoy this more."

He took a deep breath and stopped moving, except for his toes and fingers.

"You know the rules and have your safe word."

"Yes, Mistress."

Melissa then picked up a cane from the table. She

touched his buttocks with it, not hitting, just touching as if teasing. She did that several times. After the fourth or fifth time, she smacked him hard, and he swore in Arabic. The moans and strikes were loud. Zoe wanted to cover her ears. She cringed and squeezed her eyes closed.

When she opened her eyes again, the man followed Melissa over to the wooden cross shaped like a giant letter X. "Present yourself to me," Melissa ordered.

The man stood in front of the structure, arms at his sides, head bowed. Melissa walked around him and studied his position. "No, this is not correct," she scolded. "Right hand over the left." He made the correction.

When Melissa was satisfied, she directed him to lean against the cross, facedown. She strapped him down in a spread-eagle fashion.

The implications of what was going on in this room were beyond imagining. If the public found out about this, what would happen to this administration? The peace talks? This was more damaging than a stained blue dress. This was a nightmare.

Jason touched her shoulder. His fingers slowly skimmed down to her upper arm, where he grasped her and tugged her closer. Outside, the bondage ordeal continued. Red marks crisscrossed the man's back and buttocks. She'd seen enough. Jason's other hand slipped to her waist. He leaned into her. Warmth, hardness, and the scent of male. She shouldn't be so turned on. The hairs on her arms stood up. Her breasts felt heavy, and her nipples grew tight. What was Jason thinking? After all this time, he wanted to get busy with her in a closet? Really?

She pulled away and tapped a "no" on his arm.

He tapped "yes" on her hand and slowly turned her around, pulling her against his body. God, he felt good. So many nights she'd imagined Jason in her arms like this. She had to control her breathing to keep from making any noise. The real torment was being trapped inside the closet. Sex with Jason had always been the hottest when they were on a mission. Why couldn't they have sex and a relationship like normal people?

They didn't know how to do day-to-day. Everything they once had came tumbling back. She wanted him again, wanted to give in with complete and utter abandon. Her body was on fire, throbbing, needing him now at the wrong place, the wrong—

Craaack!

In the next room, a flogger or cane smacked what sounded like bare, taut skin in quick repetition. The man cried out.

"Do you want me to stop?"

"No, Mistress, more, please." Another sharp crack sent shivers up Zoe's spine. How could he stand the pain, let alone enjoy it?

Jason's warm, moist mouth pressed on her ear, her neck, and she sucked in a little breath. His tongue drew a line to the hollow of her throat.

Yes, she ached to say, yes. Jason's touch was torture, sweet, sweet torture. She gave in a little, pressing her sex against his hard shaft bulging beneath his pants. She did want him but not here, not now.

On his arm, she tapped "no."

He hesitated long enough for her to wish she had said "yes." After all these months, they'd barely had enough time to say hello and already they couldn't keep their hands off each other. Nothing had changed. He rested his forehead against hers, and she heard his intake of breath and a long sigh. Outside, Melissa shouted orders, and the man groaned. Jason pressed his lips to Zoe's ear and barely mouthed, "I want you."

Then why did you leave me?

Outside their closet, in the dungeon, voices and the smacking got louder. Inside, Jason pulled her against his chest and stroked her hair. She breathed in his scent, and time slipped away to the many heated nights he'd held her close. He knew how to draw out every exquisite sensation with his touch. Before she got too worked up, she backed away, slowly because she didn't want to knock into anything in the tiny closet. The sex party going on was so loud, Zoe doubted they would have heard anything.

His hands slid around her waist, holding her captive. "Sorry. Missed you." His words tore through her, ripping her heart in half. If he wanted to continue where they left off, she couldn't.

She leaned toward his ear. "Missed me? You'll have to do better than that."

His mouth came down on hers, and she sensed his hunger, felt her own heating up her body. His tongue slid across hers, drawing the passion from deep in her core. Her hands reached up along his hard chest, moved up and around his head, where she tangled her fingers in his hair. She resisted the urge to spread her legs. To encourage him would only make their situation more difficult.

Clinging to him, she gave in this time and melted deeper into the kiss. She couldn't fight him here. His hand reached under her skirt and slipped inside her pantyhose. Her sex was so wet, he easily parted her folds and thrust a finger inside her channel. With a silent gasp, Zoe broke away from the kiss and lifted up on her toes. He steadied her against his body. Matching his thrusts to the rhythm of groans and strikes outside the closet, she rode his hand closer to orgasm.

On impulse, she reached for his cock. The hard ridge bulged against his pants, and she pressed the heel of her palm along his length until she heard his intake of breath. The roughness of his hand rubbed her clit. Heat and throbbing intensified, coiling deep, bringing her to the edge of release. *Yes!* She wanted to scream and tell him not to stop, but it was sweet torture having to remain silent. Almost there.

"Did you enjoy yourself?" Zoe heard the first lady say. She pulled her hand away from Jason's cock at the same time he slipped out of her pantyhose. Her body continued to throb, her vagina clenching at empty space and aching. When she peeked out through the crack in the door, the first lady had already slipped on her robe.

"Very much," the male guest answered. "I must say this type of American hospitality was unexpected."

"Our pleasure." She handed him his clothing, and the man finished dressing. "Secret Service will escort you to your car."

"Thank you."

The group left. The man in black was the last to leave, switching the lights off and closing the door. Again, Jason and Zoe were surrounded in blackness.

"Now what?" Zoe whispered.

"We wait a few minutes."

The walls of the closet closed in. "You want to tell me now or later?"

"About what went on out there, or about us in here?"

"Either, both." She leaned against the door and crossed her arms. "You leave Langley without a word months ago, and then you end up here, like me. Funny coincidence. You act like nothing ever happened."

"Not a coincidence. You were handpicked for a project, like I was."

"What project?"

He hesitated. "You'll be briefed soon, but I suggest you don't take this job."

She groaned. "Why would I be briefed about someone's sexual activities?"

He cleared his throat and took a breath. "Zoe." His voice softened. "You should leave before you learn any more."

"Learn about what?" She laughed. "I don't know anything except the first lady might be a sex addict. Oh God. Does the president know?"

He groaned. "Zoe, quit your job, resign. Go back to Langley."

She shoved at his chest. "I can't go back. I think the Big D arranged this job to avoid firing me."

"Firing you?"

She nodded, although he couldn't see her. "Turkey was my fault. He probably doesn't want a repeat."

"It was my fault, too." He swore.

Silence rose between them. "Is that why you left? You didn't want to be my partner anymore and they wouldn't reassign you?" Now that he was stuck with her again, he wanted her to leave. Her throat tightened.

"No. That's not why I left. It was a mission ordered by the White House. I can't tell you more yet."

She laughed. "Whatever it is, it looks pretty entertaining."

"Trust me, you don't want to be involved with this."

"Well, I'm not quitting. Can I have my phone back?" She heard him moving around, then the phone was pressed into her hand. "Thank you." She checked Damien's message. He'd made a play. "Forty-three points? The bastard." She'd check the game later. She had three E tiles among her seven and didn't know what word she could make with that. Sometimes the small, insignificant words had better scores. It was all in the placement. At least Damien was back at the base instead of on a mission somewhere in Iran or Afghanistan, where much of the fighting was.

"How's Damien?" His words had softened a bit.

"Conditions aren't great over there. Deteriorating, from what I hear. Damien's been out on a number of missions. I'm worried. And the peace talks aren't helping. He should be coming home on leave in a couple months." She couldn't wait. At least she could count on him.

"That's good."

Three hard thuds hit the closet door. Zoe launched herself into Jason's arms. It sounded like Goliath outside pounding with a club. "Jason? We're all done here," a man's voice said. He chuckled. "Need a hand in there?"

"Funny, smart ass. No, I'll lock up."

She swallowed and pressed her hand to her breast, feeling her heart slamming against her chest. She never heard the guy come in or turn on the light. Light streamed in beneath the door and through the crack.

"Who was that?"

"Don't worry about it. We can go now." He opened the closet door. The man had gone, and the door to the room was closed. When they stepped into the room, Jason gave her a long look.

"How did he know we were in the closet?"

"He's Secret Service." He grimaced, as if that explained it all.

She strode over to the table and examined the implements of fetish toys and bondage equipment. Floggers, dildos, vibrators, cuffs, canes, gel lubricant, clamps, rope and a few things Zoe couldn't identify.

"What you saw obviously can't be taken out of this room."

"I'm not sure what I saw. Why don't you explain it to me?"

"Not tonight. You'll get a full explanation if you stay, but I recommend you don't." The man was a master at hiding his emotions. She wasn't sure if he hated the idea of working with her again or if there was something about the job she should be concerned about.

She stuck her hands on her hips and glared at him. "And do what? Get a job as a detective in the suburbs? You need to give me more than just telling me to quit my job. If you don't want to work with me again, just say it."

He rubbed his face and looked around the room. "It's not that, Zoe. It was a mistake. They shouldn't have hired you."

She raised her arms up in the air and dropped them by her sides. "Why? Julia and Melissa seem to think an ex-CIA agent is perfectly qualified for filing or whatever they want me to do. All I want is a chance to do something that matters, something important."

He smiled sympathetically and stroked her cheek with gentle fingers. "I wouldn't tell you to leave unless there was good reason." He was dead serious. The pained look in his eyes twisted at her heart.

"Maybe. But I don't walk away from anything unless I have a good reason." The silence stretched between them. Sadness and regret crept into her soul.

"I know." He took her in his arms and hugged her close. Months of anger, bitterness, and pain dissolved. At least some of it. She stepped back and gave him an up-and-down look. Damn, he looked better than she remembered.

She forced a smile. "The suit's a good look for you." They never dressed so formal while gathering intel overseas. His trim dark hair had a more professional look, less military than the last time she'd seen him. The suit couldn't hide the well-toned body-building frame. Even at five-ten, Zoe felt short and small next to his six feet, four inches.

His mouth quirked in a slight grin. With the mix of emotions running through her head, she didn't want to address their relationship right now. The churning in her stomach she attributed to the Chinese food she had for dinner. "I need to go home and walk Dexter."

"Dexter?" He frowned.

"My black Lab. He's still a puppy. My neighbor lets him out and feeds him when I'm home late."

"He's probably eaten your couch by now." His eyes glittered when he smiled this time. "You bought a house, a dog, really settled down. Not the Zoe I remember."

She shrugged. "I guess I'm all grown up." The

teasing look in his eyes changed to sadness. She was sure he knew she was failing miserably in her attempt to live a nine-to-five life.

"I'll walk you to your car." He put an arm around her shoulders.

The door to the room opened, and a man dressed in black walked in. He glanced at Zoe and gave a small nod. He could be the one who wore the black leather face mask. "You're wanted upstairs, Jason."

Jason murmured a few words to himself. He didn't sound pleased. "Great. How'd it go?"

The man shrugged. "Okay, I guess. We're about to find out." He narrowed his eyes at her. "Why is she here?"

"Long story. It's not a concern."

"She shouldn't be in here until she's briefed." The man continued to stare at her, and Zoe knew he was considering whether there had been a breach in security. Not knowing what was going on, she kept her mouth shut and let Jason talk his way out. If there was a way out.

"Julia instructed me to explain the program to Zoe," Jason said. "I haven't gotten to all the details yet."

The man nodded, seeming to accept that explanation. "You'll have to save the rest of your tour for another time. Julia wants us in her office now."

"I'll be right there," Jason said as the guard walked out, leaving the door open. Jason turned to Zoe. "Can you wait for me? I'd like to walk you to your car. It's late."

She laughed. "I can take care of myself."

He frowned. "I know that, but it's a hike to the parking lot."

She knew what he was thinking. "Turkey was different," she snapped. "Stop trying to protect me. I could take down a linebacker with a .357 pointed at my back."

He held up his hand. "Okay. Sorry. See you tomorrow." He pulled out his phone and punched in a quick text.

"You're supposed to tell me what was going on down here."

"Not now."

"Why?"

"Plausible deniability. I'm hoping you'll quit."

"Don't count on it. Should I be worried?"

"Very."

Where to find Kathy Kulig

Website: www.kathykulig.com
Facebook: www.facebook.com/kathykuligauthor
Twitter: www.twitter.com/kathykulig
Goodreads:
www.goodreads.com/author/show/1221829.Kathy_Kulig
Blog: www.TheLustyView.com
Google+:
https://plus.google.com/u/0/108524696126773274250/posts
Join Kathy's mailing list: http://eepurl.com/FC

Also by Kathy Kulig

FLC Case Files series (romantic suspense, erotic, BDSM)

Red Tape, Book 1
Red Tape Protector, Book 2
Red Tape Betrayal, Book 3

Demons in Exile Series (paranormal erotic romance/shapeshifter)

Risky Pleasures, Prequel
Desert of the Damned, Book 1
Damned and Desired, Book 2
Damned and Defiant, Book 3

Single titles: (BDSM, contemporary, or paranormal erotic romance)

Burned Deep
His Lost Mate
Nightlord Lover
Emerald Dungeon
Summer Sins

About Kathy Kulig

New York Times & *USA Today* bestselling author Kathy Kulig writes a variety of sexy romances, including paranormal, contemporary, BDSM and suspense. Her books lean toward the spicy and edgy side, but these passionate and erotically-charged stories always contain a steamy romance and a happy ending. In her past lives she's been a dive master, bartender, cytotechnologist, research scientist, cat sitter, and stringer for a newspaper. When she has a little spare time, she can be found working out, traveling, lounging with a good book or having dinner out with her husband. Kathy resides in eastern Pennsylvania. Find out more at her website www.kathykulig.com and sign up for her newsletter for the latest news on releases, contests and more http://eepurl.com/FC_nP